The Dark Side of Light

Collected Stories

Tony Billinghurst

Grosvenor House
Publishing Limited

This book is published by
Grosvenor House Publishing Ltd
Link House
140 The Broadway, Tolworth, Surrey, KT6 7HT.
www.grosvenorhousepublishing.co.uk

This book is a work of fiction. Any resemblance to
people or events, past or present, is purely coincidental.

A CIP record for this book
is available from the British Library

Paperback ISBN 978-1-80381-597-8
Hardback ISBN 978-1-80381-598-5

Tony Billinghurst explores what happens when crooks and criminal activity overlap with the lives of ordinary people. The stories he weaves – ranging from moody noir to brash thriller – are thought-provoking, surprising, and full of captivatingly idiosyncratic characters.

– Charlie Fish

Dedication

This book is dedicated to my family;
past, present, and future.

Acknowledgement

The stories in this collection were previously published by:

Two Running Men	*London Journal of Fiction (Anthology)*	2016
The Dark Side of Light	*Fiction on the Web*	2018
Lunch with Hilda	*Ham Free Press*	2018
The Occupant of Bench 24	*The Fiction Pool*	2018
Bye Combe Vale	*Commuter Lit (Canada)*	2018
Closure by Proxy	*Fiction on the Web*	2019
The Rose of Tewkesbury	*Fantasia Divinity (Anthology) (USA)*	2019
10 Strinburg Place	*Scarlet Leaf Review (Canada)*	2019

Soft Brown Eyes	*Ariel Chart (Australia)*	2019
Cocktails at Sunset	*Ariel Chart (Australia)*	2020
Just Let Go	*Literally Stories*	2021
Over Cheese Hill	*East of the Web*	2021
A Circle of Seagulls	*Freedom Fiction Magazine (India)*	2021
No Doubt About It	*Freedom Fiction Magazine (India)*	2021
The Bridge at Drochaisling	*Literally Stories*	2021
No Trespassing	*Fiction on the Web*	2021
Barnaby Vole, Hero of the Resistance	*East of the Web*	2021
Dying for a Drink	*East of the Web*	2021
Who Knows?	*Fiction on the Web*	2021
Is That You, Dear?	*East of the Web*	2022
Inheritance	*East of the Web*	2022
A Man of his Word	*Fiction on the Web*	2023

Contents

The Eric Miller stories

Preface

I have been asked why I write. The short answer is I don't know, I just do; it seems second nature to me. Some stories seem to write themselves, but most don't and need a degree of coaxing into existence. Regardless of the theme or genre and whether they are easy to write or not, I always start with the final sentence; I hate surprises. The Eric Miller stories will be more readily understood if read in their order, but it makes no difference in which order you read the other 18. In whatever order you choose to read these stories, I very much hope you enjoy them.

T.B. July 2023

About the Author

Tony Billinghurst published his first story in Ireland in the mid-1960s whilst reading many of the early 20th century greats, Hemingway in particular which was a mistake; for years, everything he wrote was a bad pastiche of Hemingway; he'd got into the habit of using few words. He likes to write in a variety of styles, themes and locations which is reflected in the eclectic nature of this collection.

When young, he tried the usual social activities, like sport, but didn't enjoy them but soon found writing uniquely satisfying. He said he guessed he's hooked on writing and gets withdrawal symptoms when he stops. He thinks he needs to find the literary equivalent of methadone.

Tony Billinghurst has long been interested in English social history and several of the stories he's written are based on historic facts, **The Dark Side of Light** being one.

Bible References (ESV)

Proverbs	13 v 20	Whoever walks with the wise becomes wise, but the companion of fools will suffer harm.
Exodus	20 v 14	You shall not commit adultery.
Psalm	46 v 10	Be still and know that I am God.
Ephesians	4 v 26–27	Do not let the sun go down on your anger and give no opportunity to the devil.
Ecclesiastes	5 v 10	He who loves money will not be satisfied with money, nor he who loves wealth with his income…

THE DARK SIDE OF LIGHT
Tony Billinghurst

THE DARK SIDE OF LIGHT

I sat at my desk, poured a gin and was reaching for the tonic when he came into the room without knocking, as usual.

'How'd it go?'

'Sweet,' he replied, sitting without being invited. The chair creaked as he lent back. 'You were right, the alarms were no problem. Some house, antiques all over the place.' He took his gloves off. 'Nice stuff.'

'Good haul?' He smiled.

'Yea, the van's stacked to the roof, we won't need to do another job for a while. Here, I got a pressy for you, found it in a bedroom.' He took a small notebook from his pocket and handed it to me. 'You like history, thought you'd be interested,' and before I could speak, he added, 'and before you ask, none of the others kept any souviners — I was watching them; besides, they know what you'd do.'

'Ok, you know what to do with the stuff, see you all Tuesday.' He nodded and left, leaving the door open.

The book was old; it had a leather spine and smelled musty. The pages were discolored and some were loose. There was a newspaper cutting in the back and throughout, the pages were covered in small, copperplate handwriting. The ink was faded and some parts were crossed through and re written. There was an urgency about the writing as though the writer was taking dictation. On the first page, dated October 2nd 1847 and in neater writing than the rest, as if it had been added later, was a prologue:

Dear Reader,

I, Rev. Charles de Winter MA, incumbent of the parish of St. George, Fordington, do declare that the following narrative is a faithful account as dictated by Mrs Mary Light, who knowing that her mortal days are drawing to a close; is desirous of setting the facts on record of those dreadful events of long ago:

Tom Light and me were born of good families in Corfe Castle in Dorset. I was 4 and 20 when we were wed. Tom earned an honest living as a labourer and like most in Corfe, he toiled from dawn to dusk for a pittance, but I had a burning ambition that neither me nor any child of mine would go to our beds hungry. The day we were wed, I pledged to Tom I'd have more from life than that. Tom's work wasn't regular; farmers hired by the day, so I sweet talked him into taking work in the clay pits in Norden. The work was steady especially when that

Josiah Wedgewood purchased the clay to manufacture pottery, but the work was hard; in summer Tom was cloaked in dust and in winter, in slurry. The gang bosses drove the men hard and earned themselves large bonuses, but for their part, the men earned rheumatics and bent backs.

I was soon with child. The weather was dire and we suffered several year of ruined harvests and then militias were raised in case Napoleon should take a notion to invade. Everything became more expensive and the cost of bread rose such we thought it a luxury and all the while the farmers made fortunes. I grew more bitter by the day, life was so unjust for the likes of us, so I persuaded Tom to take a larger cottage and we took in lodgers. Firstly, there was John Walsh then Henry Glover and George Longfield. Longfield came from Wiltshire and was the only one who was wed. Tom inquired of him why he'd come to Dorset.

"The work's here and my missus ain't," came his reply.

Clay diggers were known as hard drinkers and Tom and the lodgers spent many an hour in the tavern and soon became a close crew. We then took that devil Richard Hill under our roof. He was hardly 3 and 20 but acted older than his years. I didn't take to him, he was headstrong, shifty, and oft tardy in paying his keep and to my regret, he taught the lads to play Faro. They'd play it in the Greyhound Inn with an acquaintance of Hill's, Henry Oldman. Tom started winning and shortly, was hooked. The stakes started to rise and then at a stroke, Tom began to lose and he built up a large debt with Oldman. At first, Oldman didn't show concern. He told Tom that his luck would soon turn and then he could repay him, but the debt rose further, and then suddenly Oldman changed; he became surly and demanded his money. I'll never forget what Tom told me; they were in the Greyhound when Oldman entered.

'So, Mr Light, Sir, where's my money?'

'Oldman—I've explained, I'll pay in full but it'll take a while.'

Oldman beckoned Tom to a quiet corner. 'I fear that time's run out. You see, I owe a sum and my capital's tied up at present. Now, I must speak plain, my associates are impatient fellows an' are pressing me hard, but I assured them their money's secured by your debt alone an' being an honourable fellow, you'd pay your dues shortly. They offered to collect it from you in person, but I assured them that wasn't necessary, but I could arrange it should you prefer.'

Tom was horror struck. 'In Heaven's name can't you request a few weeks' grace of them?'

Oldman shook his head. 'In the normal turn of events, I'd be happy to oblige, but the matter's too pressing now. It truly is troublesome, aint it? but don't fret yourself, I have a notion how we might resolve the situation, so if you pardon us, I wish to converse with Mr Hill here in private before I explain.'

Tom left them in deep conversation. Later Hill returned to the cottage.

'Oldman desires to meet us in The Greyhound tomorrow night; he has a proposition to put to you.' He looked around to make sure no one overheard them. 'There's a hard side to him and the associates he speaks of are dangerous fellows, you'd do well to pay him heed.'

As they were bid, the following evening, Tom and Hill went to the small, low, oak paneled room at the back of the Greyhound Inn. Oldman was sitting alone on a settle by the fire. He rose without uttering a sound and indicated with a nod to join him in the gloom at a table in the corner away from the lamp, then spoke in a hushed tone.

'Well, Mr Light, I've given the problem close consideration and this is the lay. As you know, of late farmers have been making tidy fortunes for themselves, all at our expense I might add. I've had dealings with one such a farmer who's reneged on the transaction which has left me sorely out of pocket. I have discussed the situation with the gentleman in question on more than one occasion, but he steadfastly refuses to settle the matter which is a situation that I can ill afford to leave unresolved, so what I propose is that you visit his residence on my behalf an' claim goods to the value of his debt to me. At the same time, you could retrieve suffice to settle matters between us as well.'

'What — you mean I go housebreaking?'

Oldman feigned shock. 'Oh, that's such a disagreeable word, no, consider it a settling of debt and a redressing of justice.'

'But I haven't done such a thing before.'

'I don't doubt it, I don't doubt it at all; indeed, that's all to the good, who'll ever suspect you?'

'But I wouldn't know what to do.'

'Now don't fret yourself on that score, as good fortune would have it, Mr Hill here has the expertise that's required; you do as he bids and all will be well.'

Tom was highly agitated. 'But I can't be absent at night without reason, my Mary would demand to know where I'd been, and what about my lodgers, they might talk.'

Oldman's demeanour changed. 'Gracious Heavens Mr Light, you must take me for a fool. I've considered these trifling problems. You'll be in need of extra hands, take your lodgers with you. The farmer's a rich man; there'll be suffice to set you all up pleasantly, very pleasantly and if they're with you, they won't talk, of that you may be sure. I'll dispose of any artefacts that you collect. I know a pawnbroker in London who'll pay a handsome price.' He took a draught of ale, then continued. 'As for your good lady, tell her what you will, but I suggest you inform her that on the night in question, a Lugger is due in Warbarrow Bay with a cargo of brandy and you all have secured employment as flaskers to carry the kegs to the headland. Tell her the goods are legally bought in the Channel Islands, the crew well reimbursed and the merchandise is sold to willing buyers. Now, where's the harm in that? 'Tis only the King who'll be in lack of his excise duty, which is no ill thing, he only squanders it. No reasonable person could object to that, now, could they?' He sat back in his chair and looked well pleased with himself.

'When's the deed to be done?'

'Shortly.'

'Who's the farmer?'

'Richard Tenman, he's in his dotage, so'll be no trouble. He has Grange Farm at Hurpston; it's hardly 4 miles hence, so you'll be back in no time, out of debt an' rich men.'

'But we'll hang if we get caught.'

'So, don't get caught.'

Oldman took a clay pipe from his pocket and proceeded to fill it with tobacco. 'I'm a reasonable man,' he added, 'I'll not press you for a decision.' He stood and lit his pipe from the lamp. 'I'm away to refresh my pot.' He stepped towards the door and then added almost as if to himself, 'you'll have made your decision by the time I return; I shouldn't wonder.'

Tom turned to Hill when he'd quit the room. He made no attempt to conceal his look of desperation. 'What in Heaven's name am I to do?'

Hill lent over the table and spoke without looking up. 'It's a desperate scrape, that's for sure. Oldman's associates are dark coves, dark indeed, if you don't pay up shortly, I'll wager you'll soon have broken legs.' He hesitated, then continued. 'If you see me right, I'll handle the crack. Come some morn soon you'll be free of Oldman and we'll be set up pleasantly. If Oldman says that Tenman's rich, rest assured, Tenman's rich as a king, he'll hardly miss any.'

Tom looked around, then demanded in desperation. 'Are you certain of what's to be done?'

'Don't fret on that score, you just get the others on board and talk sweet to your Mary. I'll arrange all else.'

Neither spoke further, Tom sank into deep deliberation until Oldman returned some ten minutes later. Tom told him that he accepted, albeit with considerable reluctance.

'Capital,' he said with a smirk, 'stout fellow, oh, by the by, take heed there's no tittle tattle about our little enterprise, not before, nor afterwards neither, that'd be most vexing.'

Somehow Tom persuaded the others to accompany him and he told me they were all hired to carry smuggled brandy from the bay to the headland. He added that he had a small debt to settle for a wager he'd made when he'd taken too much cider. It wasn't until later that I discovered how much he owed. The robbery transpired on a Saturday night. The five were most agitated that night when they gathered in the parlour, blackened their faces with soot, wrapped their mufflers about their necks and drew on their greatcoats. Tom took me in his arms and kissed me; he told me later what followed. When I'd left the parlour, Hill produced a bundle wrapped in cloth. It contained a flagon of brandy, a pistol, tools, a dark lantern and some bludgeons.

'I'll mind the barker. Walsh, you bring the lantern. Each take a bludgeon.' He put the tools in his immense pockets, pulled the cork from the flagon, took a drain, and handed it around. 'Here's to a successful caper, boys. Now, mark me well, everyone is to do exactly as I bid. The farmhouse is near the coast, we'll cross the fields, do the job an' return through Church Knowle. We'll meet Oldman behind the New Inn at 2. There's only Tenman, his son and the maid at the farm. Walsh, when we arrive, light the lantern, give it to me and tend to the maid.' He turned to Tom, 'you attend to Tenman and you two,' nodding to Glover and Longfield, 'his son. Are we ready? oh, and don't address each other by name. Any questions? Good, then let's be on our way.'

It was a chill night when they quit Corfe and not a living soul was abroad except a dog, barking in the distance. The fields were bare, the paths were thick with mud and the ground seeped water as it trickled to the ditches whilst a relentless wind moaned in the bare hedgerows. A bright moon slipped in and out of the clouds casting brief spells of frigid light over the valley. For the most part, they walked in single file as they descended the righthand slope of the valley. Shortly, the path joined a sunken lane. An owl screeched as they passed a clump of trees and a distant church clock struck midnight.

'What'll you do with your cut, Glover?' Longfield enquired.

Glover sounded excited. 'I'm for the Americas, 'tis the land of the free; there's no groveling to the gentry there.'

'Sea journeys aren't for me,' Walsh added, but before he could continue, Hill interjected.

'Now, understand this well, lads,' he said firmly, 'no one's to go anywhere after the caper. Let the dust settle first and don't be free with your money, and don't utter a word to anyone. Mark me well, loose tongues cause tight ropes. Now, no more gabbling and by the by, if we happen upon any excise men, don't put up a fight, split up and run for your lives; they'll have a brace of pistols and a cutlass apiece; they'd as soon cut you down as blink.'

Their breath swirled around them in the bleak, damp air as they strode on and joined a path that ran along the bottom of the valley. It was sheltered from the wind and was strangely silent. Walsh glanced up, stopped, and pointed to the sky. 'Look — three seagulls, that's a bad omen that is, three seagulls at night.' They all looked up.

'That's twaddle!' Glover exclaimed. 'They're crows.' But they weren't. The three seagulls flew silently on by and the sea gently breathed in and out in the distance. A cold shiver ran down Tom's back.

'Come on lads, put some heart in it,' Hill ordered. 'we're running a trifle late,' so they quickened their pace and crossed a style and a small bridge over the stream and turned down yet more damp lanes. The moon slid from behind a cloud and bathed the valley in a cold eerie light and a thin mist crept over the hill from the sea. Hill beckoned them to him and addressed them in a whisper. 'The farm's at the end of this lane. If the gate's closed, I'll take it off the latch. If anything goes amiss, don't get over the wall to the right of the house, there's a steep bank with a deep ditch filled with water at the bottom.'

A nervous Walsh turned and addressed Hill in a terrified but hushed tone of voice. 'It's a farm; they'll have a dog; it'll bark before we get anywhere close.'

Hill turned and beckoned Walsh to him. He slowly caught hold of a handful of Walsh's coat and lifted him near off the ground. 'Hold your peace, you buffoon,' he declared through clenched teeth, 'the dog died suddenly these two days past, that's what befalls things that are a nuisance.' Walsh didn't utter another word.

They walked on in uneasy silence and arrived before the squat, two storey farm house. The moonlight made the high grey slate roof glint like silver which gave the building a ghostly appearance. There was no light visible and the gate was open. They slipped through and worked their way around the low wall and behind some trees till they came to the rear. Hill whispered to them. 'I'll enter first. We'll go to the hall; wait there 'till I've opened the door, then we'll go upstairs. You,' turning to Tom, 'find the fowling piece and bring it, it'll be in the scullery like as not. When you get to their chambers, keep 'em in their beds, they're easier to control there. The maid's certain to have the house keys in her closet. Walsh — if you can't find 'em, loosen her tongue.'

Hill led them to a small scullery window which was protected by iron bars. He took the tools from his coat and with no little exertion, prised the rusty bars from the wall, forced the window catch, slipped it open, then opened the shutters, all with the deftness clearly acquired from experience. Then in a twinkling, he wriggled through the small opening. It was as dark as pitch inside.

'Hand me the tools — quick now!' He demanded, then helped the others through. They crept through the scullery. There were bunches of herbs hanging from hooks in the ceiling. They passed a table, still damp from being scrubbed. A row of copper pans glistened on the wall. The dying fire in the range cast a flickering shadow of bars on the flagstones. Tom spied the fowling piece by the bellows and picked it up. They filed past a laundry room full of clutter and a larder with shelves containing a sugar cone and a dry remnant of roast beef. The room smelled strongly of cheese. Something ran across the floor and disappeared behind a barrel.

They entered the hall and stopped as instructed. Hill creped past the long case clock at the bottom of the stairs when it suddenly struck one on a harsh, jangling bell with an ear splitting clang. He froze in his tracks and drew and cocked the pistol in an instant thinking the whole world must have been awoken, but not a person stirred. There wasn't a sound except from the clock which settled noisily before it returned to its, loud, monotonous tick. Tom's heart jumped against his ribcage while Hill turned ashen with beads of sweat on his face. He released the hammer of the pistol with great care and gave Tom an unconvincing smile, then crept to the stout front door, opened it and secured it with a boot scraper. He took several deep breaths of chill air before returning to the others. Hill raised his finger to his lips and pulled his muffler high over his face, motioned the others to do likewise, then led them upstairs. They'd almost reached the top when a step made a loud creak. At a signal from Hill, they charged onto the landing. Hill pointed Walsh to a door at the end of the landing and the rest of them rushed to the other two. Seconds later, there was a blood curdling scream from the maid as Walsh barged into her chamber. Tom opened the door of the master bedroom. The room was shabby and meanly furnished and although it was cold, the small fire wasn't lit. The faded brown curtains were closely drawn but despite the gloom, he could make out a large old man attempting to get out of bed. Tom crossed the room in a trice and pushed him back.

'Where's your money, old man?' he demanded. Tenman wasn't cowered by the fowling piece that Tom was pointing at him, nor by Tom's demand.

'I'll not tell 'e, you thieving scoundrel.' Tom grabbed Tenman's night shirt, pulled him closer and shoved the fowling piece into his throat.

'Damn your eyes,' he grated through his clenched teeth with a level of venom which surprised him. The venom didn't come alone, Tom experienced a new sensation; a strangely addictive, illicit excitement which seemed to flow through his whole being. Tenman was made of stern stuff.

'Go to the devil, you'll not get a farthing from me you idle loafer.' Still holding Tenman's night shirt, he quickly scanned the room again. 'If you don't tell me, I'll blow your brains out, strike me blind if I don't.' Tenman didn't reply. Tom spied a silver pocket watch on the washstand. He lent towards it.

'Leave that be, my missus gave 'n to I.'

'Where is she?' Tom demanded looking around.

'Dead these three year.'

"I'll leave it be if you tell me where you keep your gold.'

'I'll tell 'e nothin', do your worse and go to the devil.' Tom grabbed the watch and shoved it in his pocket.

There were sounds of a fierce scuffle and lots of shouting coming from the adjoining room. Glover and Longfield struggled to keep Tenman's son down, but eventually, they overcame him.

'Where's your money?' Glover demanded.

'I'll see 'e in hell afore I tell 'e.'

Hill came to the doorway. 'Anything?' he asked. Longfield shook his head. He rushed to Tom's room and repeated the question, then left and ran down the hall to the maid's room. The maid was sitting up in bed. 'Where's the keys?' Hill demanded of Walsh.

'She won't say.'

Hill pushed him aside, grabbed the maid by the throat, shoved her down on the bed and jammed the pistol into her cheek.

'If you don't tell me where the keys are, you're going to die this very minute – now, where are they?' He gripped the maid's throat so tight she could scarce breathe, let alone speak so she pointed to the pine dresser in front of the window. Walsh opened the drawers and found a large bunch of keys. Hill released his grip and snatched them from him. 'Keep her here,' he commanded and ran downstairs taking the lantern with him. Walsh didn't have trouble restraining the young girl. She was gasping for breath, then slowly sat up, pulled the sheet to her reddened throat, and whimpered quietly as tears trickled down her face. A few minutes later, Hill called from downstairs. As Walsh left the maid's chamber, he glanced back at the terrified young woman who was cowering and shaking like an injured animal.

Tom and Walsh raced downstairs to a scene of devastation. Hill was in a room which served as both dining room and office. In his haste, he'd failed to find the correct keys, so had ripped open cupboards and cabinets with his jemmy and thrown the contents into the air leaving the floor strewn with papers and account books. Finally, he'd found a metal box in a bureau, located the right key, and opened it.

'Look, boys!' He exclaimed in an excited manner. Inside were some banknotes and a large number of gold guineas. He slammed the lid closed, locked it, and pushed it into one of his huge pockets. 'There must be more, get back to Tenman and his son, search their cabinets again, search everything.'

All three of them raced back upstairs and ransacked the bedrooms, but found nothing. They charged back down again to the scullery and did the same and even inspected a sack of flour in the larder but found nothing more. Hill uttered a terrible curse, then ordered Tom to get Glover and Longfield. They warned Tenman and his son to stay in their beds for half an hour as one of them was to stand watch outside with the pistol until the others were clear, then all quit the building and started off at their fullest speed. A few short minutes later, the farmhouse bell rang with great violence. They ran as never before until they reached the bridge then headed up the valley to Church Knoll.

'Wait a while,' Glover gasped, 'let me catch my breath.'

'How'd we do?' Longfield enquired.

'I've yet to count it,' Hill replied looking ill at ease.

'I'm not in the mood for jesting, you must have an idea, it didn't look a fortune to me.'

'Hundred guineas, maybe a hundred and fifty. I couldn't see the value of the banknotes.'

'Is that all? we've risked our necks for that? Oldman said he was rich — he didn't look rich to me; everything was worn out.'

Hill was highly agitated and replied in a most defensive tone of voice. 'Oldman said he was rich and on my honour, Oldman's seldom wrong.' Oaths flew like hailstones as the lads grew to comprehend the situation.

'Then we missed it somewhere.'

Hill uttered another curse. 'No, I turned the crib over carefully, it's not there, of that I'll wager.'

As they were talking an ashen Walsh had been nervously looking behind them. 'My eyes. Look — over there — I think we're being followed!' They all listened intently but could neither hear nor see a living soul.

Hill addressed Walsh with no little exasperation. 'That is the last thing I desire to hear from you this night, we are not being followed,' he said through clenched teeth, 'so keep your peace.' But Walsh was right, they were being followed. Tenman's son followed them to Church Knoll and then onto Corfe. They set off for Church Knoll at a great pace. The footpath passed close behind The New Inn where they stopped and waited impatiently.

Shortly, a quiet voice greeted them from a gap in the hedge. 'Good evening gentlemen, good pickings I trust?'

Tom squared up to Oldman. 'No there wasn't, you evil dog. You told us we'd be rich men; we've risked the rope for a handful of guineas a piece.'

'Dear me, that's most unfortunate, you must have missed some, he has more than that for certain.'

Hill passed Oldman the pistol and housebreaking tools. 'We turned the crib over right proper; we got all there was. Look — strike up the lantern and keep it low.' He then opened the box and counted the contents. The haul amounted to 100 guineas, a £10 note, a £5 note, the silver pocket watch, and the fowling piece. Oldman counted a large handful of guineas and put them in his pocket.

'That settles Tenman's debt and our little account, Mr Light, the rest is yours.'

'And there's the banknotes, the watch, and the gun. How much for them?' Tom demanded as Oldman extinguished the lantern.

'Oh, I don't think I desire them, Mr Light, you keep them.'

'But you said you'd pass them to your pawnbroker in London.'

'Well, upon my word, I don't recall saying anything of the sort, do you Hill?' Hill looked uncomfortable but made no answer. 'Those notes are drawn on local banks; they'd be difficult to sell; questions could be asked and we might all be grabbed. If you wish, I could make some enquiries on your behalf and should any of my contacts manifest interest, I'll let you know.'

Tom grabbed Oldman's lapel. 'You cheap dog ...' but before he could add more, Oldman cocked the pistol and pointed it at Tom.

'I'll remind you, Mr Light, that I have the pistol,' he said in a sneering manner.

Tom swung the fowling piece around, cocked it and pointed it at Oldman. 'And I'll remind you, Oldman, that I have the fowling piece.'

Hill stepped forward and gently pushed them apart. 'Gentlemen, for mercy's sake keep your voices down! This is not the time or place for a debate, let's away to our homes before we're all pinched.' So, they left Oldman who skulked back into the shadows and they went back to Corfe with all expedition.

I hadn't slept the night long wondering how the lads had fared, but as soon as they returned, I sensed something was terribly wrong. 'Did it go well? did you have any trouble with the excise men?'

Longfield gave Tom a cold look, then addressed me. 'You'd better ask him, I've had my fill of this night, I'm away to my bed,' he said, slamming the door; the others followed. Then Tom, looking tired and most agitated, recounted the whole affair and my heart sank as he spoke and I had a dread fear that from then on wouldn't quit me.

From that moment, no one had a civil word to say. They argued and oft came close to blows. Their friendship was dead and I spent much time keeping the peace between them, but it wasn't to last. At daybreak on the Tuesday, there was a ferocious hammering on the door which woke the whole household. No sooner had Tom unlatched the door than a gang armed with swords and bludgeons burst in. They were led by Tenman's son who waived a warrant in Tom's face.

'Seize them all, don't let any of the rats escape. Search the whole place — tear it apart if you have to. I'll have what's rightly mine, so help me I shall!'

Tom shielded me as I was holding one of the babies, all of whom were crying, and then a battle ensued as the gang fought with the lads. Several pieces of furniture were smashed and thrown around. Someone found the fowling piece and Glover was felled by a crashing blow to his head with the butt. After what seemed an eternity, the gang subdued the lads and tore the house apart till they'd recovered the stolen goods. Tenman's son turned to me with glee. 'Prepare to be a widow, you slut. This lot have a date with the hangman and I'm going to enjoy watching him choke the life out of their miserable necks.'

'Where are you taking them?'

'To the lock up. If you don't desire 'em to starve, you'd better bring vittles as I'll not feed 'em.'

They were all dragged to the lock up, only to find that Henry Oldman was already there. They were manacled, some to the walls. The following morning, very early, I took them food and had just bought a large jug of ale from The Fox Inn when a detachment of Militia arrived with fixed bayonets, chained them together then marched them to Dorchester goal to await trial. From then on, I could neither eat nor sleep I was so tormented. Two weeks later, the Parish Constable came to tell me that the trial was set for the Lent Assizes in Dorchester on the 16th of March at 8 a.m. before Judge Sir T. N. Thornton. Tom, Henry Glover, George Longfield, Richard Hill, and John Walsh were charged with breaking and entering and stealing one hundred guineas, a £10 and £5 banknote, a silver pocket watch, and a gun. Henry Oldman with charged with receiving money knowing it to be stolen, but the charge was dropped when he turned King's evidence and testified against the other five. Oldman swore an affidavit that the money found on him was a gambling debt and that the gang had urged him to take part in the robbery telling him that it would make him a rich man, but in all conscience, he could take no part in such an enterprise. It was reported in the Salisbury & Winchester Journal that Oldman was acquitted and had fled the county. His evidence was all that the court required to get a conviction. May his soul rot in hell.

I resolved to attend the trial, so I put the children in my parent's care and went to Corfe square and took the coach to Dorchester. I had oft seen the stage come and go but had never travelled on one. The cheapest ticket was for a seat outside. The coachman was a kindly man.

'My word lady, you'll need to wear more 'n that, you'll freeze to death, use this,' and he handed me a grubby horse blanket then helped me to my seat. 'Now don't you fall asleep and drop off, now will you? we'll change teams at Bere Regis. Hold tight everyone.' He threw his cape around his shoulders, jammed his greasy hat on his head, climbed to his seat, thrust his feet into some hay in the footwell, took a draft from his flask, gave a blast on his horn, took hold of the reins, let the brake off, gave the horses a crack of the whip and we were off. We swayed, rocked, and lurched in a most alarming manner as we charged along the narrow, rutted roads. I soon started to feel most sick at the incessant swaying and it came as a great relief when we made an unscheduled stop at a wayside Inn for the driver to deliver a small package. 'Fifteen minute ladies an' gen'lmen; fifteen minute please,' the coachman called as he helped me down. 'You look a trifle pale my dear; it takes a while to get used to the motion. You look in need of a brandy and hot water, but don't be long. As soon as I've delivered this 'ere parcel, we're off.' No one alighted from inside the coach and the driver noticed my observation. He leant towards me and said in a whisper: 'We've got a Toff on board, 'E's had them blinds down since we quit Swanage. Thinks the country air's tainted an' bad for 'is constitution. Well, I've bin breathin' it for the last seven and thirty year and it's not harmed me none, but then, I'm only an 'umble coach driver, so what do I know?'

We were soon off again and I was feeling a trifle better for the brandy. We rattled on until we swept into the Royal Oak's courtyard at Bere Regis. The ostlers started to change the horses and everyone rushed into the Inn to take lunch and thaw out by the blazing inglenook. Despite feeling unwell, I took some of the Oak's excellent boiled ham.

We were soon off again, arriving at the White Hart in Dorchester in the early evening. On the driver's advice that it would be more desirable to take a room there rather than walking the town at night seeking somewhere more modest, I was grateful for his advice and took the cheapest room they had to offer. Feeling shaken and exhausted, I gave instructions that I was to be awoken early the following morn and retired to the small, cosy room only to be constantly awoken by the clattering mail coaches arriving and departing the night long.

I awoke at dawn and despite not feeling hungry, I took a light, hurried breakfast then walked the short distance to the courtroom in High West Street. To my surprise, I found a substantial crowd had already gathered to witness the judge and barristers process from their lodgings to the court. There was much deference manifest by the local officials as they passed. The boisterous crowd was restrained until the party had entered the building. I was ill prepared for the uncouth manner in which it dashed up the stairs to the gallery. Realising that the gallery would soon fill, I joined in the pushing and elbowed my way until I secured a good seat overlooking the court below.

The courtroom was much like one of Mr Wesley's chapels. It was rectangular in form with the judge's seat on a raised platform between two large windows below a small canopy and the King's crest. Although it was the first trial of the day, the room already smelt close and unwholesome. A black robed clerk sprinkled lavender on the floor and then the twelve jurors entered through their own door and sat in two rows. They all looked well to do; not our class of people, but not a person challenged them. Little respect was manifest for the proceedings by the unruly crowd who were clearly only in attendance for a little sport. At the stroke of 8, the clerk called the court to order and then called "all rise." Everyone stood and Judge Thornton made an impressive entrance from yet another door and with great dignity, slowly processed across the room and ascended the steps to his chair. He gave a nod of his head and everyone sat down. He spoke a few words to the barristers, then the jury was sworn in and the first case was called.

The lads were brought up from the cells one by one; they appeared pale, confused and in low spirits.

Each trial took the same form. They were asked their names and abode and the charges were read and they pleaded not guilty. Oldman's affidavit was read to each of them. It was the only time any of them put up anything like a defense as they contested it, they were questioned further and were instructed to shout, "Stay in your bed or it'll be instant death." Tenman and his son gave evidence and identified the stolen goods. As the maid was still much troubled by the robbery and since she had left Tenman's employ, it was agreed not to call her as a witness. The judge questioned the barristers, oft in Latin which I could not comprehend. Directly after the questioning, the judge made some remarks to the jury who drew together in a corner and when they'd deliberated, one of their number nodded to the clerk and the prisoner was returned to the cells and the next brought up. Tom's was the third trial. He looked around the room, I waved to him, but he didn't see me. By late morning, all five had been tried and the judge addressed the jury and summed up. It was clear what he thought and he directed them accordingly. They drew together for a few more minutes then returned to their benches. One of them remained standing. The judge addressed him.

'Mr Foreman, has the jury reached a verdict in each of the five cases?'

'We have M'Lud.'

'And is your verdict in each case unanimous?'

'Beg your pardon M'Lud?'

'Do you agree in each case?'

'We do M'Lud.' The judge instructed the clerk to bring all five prisoners back and they stood side by side in the dock. He addressed each by name, read the charges, then asked the foreman for the jury's verdict. In each case, the reply was the same:

'Guilty.'

The judge then addressed all five together and went to some lengths to point out the great enormity of their crime and the violent methods they had used. He added that in the interests of public justice and security of private property, he could not give them the least hope of mercy. He inquired if they had anything to say why sentence of death should not be pronounced on them. Some said no, others shook their heads. The clerk then placed a small square of black silk on the judge's head, who named each man in turn and then pronounced:

'You will be taken hence to the prison in which you were last confined and from there to a place of execution where you will be hanged by the neck until you are dead and thereafter your body will be buried within the precincts of the prison and may the Lord have mercy on your soul.' Sentence was set for March 28th 1807 at 1p.m. I sat in shock, the court was in pandemonium, then the clock struck one. The judge nodded to the clerk who called 'all rise' and everyone left for lunch.

I soon found myself back in the busy street with a dense crowd around me. I wandered aimlessly in a daze, my heart pounding. After a considerable time, I returned toward The White Hart and as I turned aside into Cornhill and as good fortune would have it, I happened upon William Trent, a carter from Corfe. Trent was an old friend of Tom's; he caught sight of me and approached.

'My dear Mrs Light, I can guess why you're here; all Corfe's talking of little else. How's the trial proceeding?'

I just blurted out, 'Guilty, all of them except Oldman who's been acquitted. They're to hang next Saturday. What am I to do? I don't know which way to turn. I can't think straight.'

Trent placed his hand on my arm. 'Where are you lodging?' he enquired. I pointed to the White Hart.

'But I lack the means to stay longer, nor to go to Corfe and return. I couldn't bear that loathsome journey again anyway.'

Trent smiled kindly to me. 'Now here's a suggestion. Firstly, now the five of 'em are convicted, they'll be fed bread and water. Here,' and he reached into his pocket and gave me two shilling pieces, 'I've known your husband for many a year, take that with my compliments and purchase some vittles. Now, my sister has a house close by in High Street and she takes in the occasional lodger. You're welcome to settle your affairs with the White Hart then I'll take you to her and we'll see what we can do.'

In a few minutes, I'd paid for my room and returned to the street. Trent returned and walked with me down two side roads to a house in a terrace. He left me on the street, went up the steps and rang the bell and was greeted by a lady of whom I had a dim recognition. He whispered to her and pointed to me. She nodded and beckoned me in.

'Mrs Light, this is my sister, you're most welcome to stay here the week. She'll feed and provide for you and when you're ready, I'll take you home. Now, I'm going to Corfe shortly and I'll return on Tuesday, is there anything you desire me to bring back?'

I was overwhelmed. 'But we haven't spoken of terms. I have little to spare and my children...'

He smiled and interjected. 'The fee 'll be modest and the ride back is with my compliments.' Before I could even attempt to express my gratitude, he stopped me again. 'Where are your children?' I told him. 'Would you like me to advise your parents of the verdict?' I nodded, but more I could not say. I was exhausted by the day's events and overcome by the unexpected generosity. I slumped into a nearby chair, my heart broke and I sobbed. Trent's sister was kindness itself. They left me for a while, then Trent returned and handed me a small glass of brandy.

'Take heart, Mrs Light, I hear that half of the hanging sentences are commuted. All's not lost, not by a long mile yet. Tell me, what possessed your husband to associate with Oldman; he's a bad lot that one and much disliked. I've heard many a tale about that scoundrel and never a good word — he's the one who should be for the gallows and many'd be glad of it, I can tell you.'

Trent left to go about his business and I told his sister about the two shillings and told her that somehow, I'd repay him. 'Don't fret yourself about that,' she said, 'if brother gave it to you, he'll not expect it back. He sets a high price on friendship, he does.' The following day, I visited Tom. It was heart wrenching to see him so low, but I endeavoured to keep his spirits up. It was then that I told him I was with child. I have never heard a man sob so, the sound of it haunts me yet.

Mr Trent didn't return to Dorchester on Tuesday but arrived on Wednesday. He brought news of my children and told me that my parents would care for them till I returned. I enquired how my parents were and he told me that my mother had taken the news very ill. He also told me that Longfield's wife, Ruth, had arrived in Corfe and was making arrangements to travel to Dorchester. Trent said that if I should desire it, he could bring her to Dorchester on Friday and she too could lodge with his sister, but at the regular terms, he quickly added. I agreed, any company would be most welcome.

It was the following day that Tom told me John Walsh's conviction had been commuted to transportation to Australia and that Richard Hill had broken prison and escaped. The whole prison was in an uproar. Tom was in a better spirit, thinking that he too might be granted a reprieve as well. The chaplain visited him regularly, imploring him to make peace with his maker before it was too late. The days passed in a twinkling and then on Friday, Trent arrived accompanied by Ruth Longfield. It took a while to become accustomed to her direct manner, but as time passed, I warmed to her and when she'd settled, I chose an opportune moment and enquired why she desired to attend the hanging. She closed the parlour door, sat beside me, and spoke in a confidential manner.

'I met George in Amesbury and was smitten at first sight. He was tall and had twinkling hazel eyes; my mother didn't like him, she said I'd have trouble with him, she said he had a roving eye and nothing good would come of him. She was right, soon after we were wed, I started to hear rumours that he'd been seen in the company of other women. I paid no heed, but at length, I discovered that it was true. It was the start of several affairs, rows, new starts, and fresh betrayals, each worse than the one before, then finally, he had an affair with a married neighbour. I'd reached breaking point and told him that it was over between us. We had our worse row ever and he hit me. I told him that if I ever saw him again, I hoped it would be when he was hanging at the end of a rope. That was these three years gone. Whilst he still draws breath, I'm not free to proceed with my life. I loved him dearly once; I hate him now.'

'Have you found someone else?' I enquired. She smiled.

'Perhaps.'

I had my final, tearful visit with Tom in the Castle cells. He still held out hope of a pardon and we spoke of what we'd do if he was transported. The hanging was set for the following day. On advice from Trent's sister, we had an early night, but I slept badly. We rose before dawn. I couldn't contemplate food but Ruth had an ample breakfast and we rushed out of the house. A breeze blew the whole of that cheerless morning. Ruth wrapped her shawl about her and linking arms with me marched us to the hanging fair which was already underway when we arrived. We pushed and shoved our way through the growing crowd and took a place beside a puppet show from whence the prospect was uninterrupted.

Dorchester castle stood on the hill above us. Over its entrance was a large stone ledge on which a gallows had been constructed. A black flag flew from the flagpole. Every conceivable rogue and low life had arrived and were busying themselves, drinking, hustling, gambling, selling, begging, bartering, picking pockets and propositioning. An organ grinder played Lillybullero endlessly and a fiddle player, not ten paces hence endlessly scraped and scratched his way through his one tune repertoire. Shortly a fight between a juggler and a fire eater attracted a large crowd and a gang of unwashed ragamuffins followed by two dogs ran wildly amongst the crowd playing touch. One of them barged into Ruth who gave the young wretch a resounding slap which sent him reeling. Later, a thin man sidled up to us, clutching a bundle of papers and kept looking over his shoulder, as if by habit.

"Ere ladies, 'ere's somethin' to remember the day by, I have a confession made by the three blaggards who'll soon be launched to eternity. They're usually thruppence, but to you 'andsome ladies, tuppence, now 'ow's that for a bargain?' Ruth enquired if they were genuine confessions as she wouldn't wish for less. The thin man pushed his hat back on his head and looked to the heavens as if for Divine confirmation. 'Now, would I offer you anything less?'

he enquired, much hurt. Ruth lent over and said something in his ear. He recoiled and looked shocked. 'That's not a very ladylike thing to say, now, is it?' he said as he turned and oozed back into the crowd. A drunken rabble who'd been in the tavern since dawn started singing vulgar songs.

"Ark at 'e,' a woman behind said, 'they's goin' to 'ave a sore 'ed cum the mornin', ain't 'um?'

A clock struck 12 and a detachment of militia with fixed bayonets marched out of the castle and stood guard. The discordant din from the crowd grew to a deafening pitch. Dogs barked, vendors shouted, barrel organs and musicians played, children screamed, drunks sang, people argued, laughed, and fought and then the castle bell started a slow, mournful toll. Several officials emerged from the castle and climbed the steps to the ledge and after what seemed an eternity, the lads were brought out, each with a warden either side of them. They were followed by the hangman who was wearing a mask. When they were all assembled, someone shouted 'hats off' to the crowd.

'Thank 'eavens for that missus,' the woman behind said. 'I can't see noffin' with you wearin' that. 'Ere, I do like a good toppin', don't you?'

Then the crowd turned and faced the gallows and fell silent. The only sound was of the echoing, tolling bell, it went on and on and on and in my mind is tolling yet. An official stood before each prisoner and read from a piece of paper, then he stood back and the chaplain holding a Bible stepped forward and addressed each in turn with great urgency, and finally, he stepped aside and bent his head in prayer. On a signal, the warders grabbed each man's arms as the hangman removed their shackles, tied their hands in front of them and quickly passed the cord around them twice, pinning their arms to their sides. He moved them to their positions, pulled a hood over their heads and looped the noose around their necks. Heaven knows I had no desire to watch, but I felt powerless to take my eyes from the dreadful scene in front of me. Everyone on the platform stood back and turned towards the most senior official, who appeared to wait forever. Eventually, as the clock struck 1, he nodded to the hangman who pulled a lever and all three hurtled down to their deaths. The crowd erupted. Ruth gave a little whoop of joy at being set free and I wept.

After a few horrific, never ending minutes, all three stopped kicking and twitching and then slowly swayed and turned in the breeze as if in some silent, macabre dance. They were left to hang for an hour. The drunks started singing and the organ grinder played Lillybullero again.

Ruth and I took our leave of Trent's sister. She charged me the most modest of fees and after thanking her for her exceeding kindness, Trent took us on a bone jarring journey back to Corfe. Ruth stayed with me overnight and then left. I haven't seen her since.

As a widow, I was able to claim Parish relief for a while, such as it was, but was unable to find much work as I was heavily pregnant with Hester. I managed to scrape a living doing what I could; in summer I picked crops, but I near starved in winter. The children oft went to their beds crying with hunger.

Hester died directly after her ninth birthday and one by one, the children left me. My mother died shortly after, the family said from shame. I sought help from Tom's family but got none. Both families were of the same mind; I must have known what the lads were up to and should have stopped them. Oh, how I wish I could turn the clock back. The bitter memory of those events haunts me since. I have lost everything, my dear Tom, my reputation, and my home. My children despise me and my family disowned me and I'm alone with a broken heart and shunned by many in Corfe. Eventually, my health declined such that I could no longer earn suffice to stay alive and faced starvation. I had no option but to come to this accursed workhouse. How I endure this mean, verminous place, I know not. Life here is an endless round of hunger, drudgery, and funerals. Every night this draughty tomb echoes to the sound of some poor soul sobbing themselves to sleep. I sleep in a dormitory filled with children sick in mind and old folk sick in body. My fingers bleed from picking oakum and sowing shrouds, nor can I gain solace from sleep either, as I close my eyes, the same nightly horror haunts me. I see the three lads endlessly mouth the same silent plea for mercy whilst their unseeing eyes bore into my soul and I scream at them: 'Let me be!' but I cannot utter a single word and the silence makes my ears ring. Before I draw my last breath, I implore all who read this account to remember that every choice has consequences; choose wisely or prepare to weep.'

And here, the Reverend had added a postscript: "Amen to that."

I closed the book, put it down on my desk, finished my gin and reached for my tablet to message the lads.

Proverbs 13:20

JUST LET GO

The 11th of November was a Wednesday. We were patrolling in dense fog near Mons when at 11 am, Lieutenant Harrison ordered us to halt then glanced at his watch.

'Well, that's it,' he said, 'it's all over lads, the war's over.' I was told that civilians in towns and cities the world over erupted in wild celebration but we just stood and looked at each other and listened in disbelief as the monstrous pandemonium of war faded to an unnatural silence. There was no cheering, no singing, just an unbelievable anticlimax. We'd started the war with optimism and ended it emotionally bankrupt. Eventually, a corporal addressed the Lieutenant.

'Don't know about anyone else Sir, but I could do with a bloody good drink right now.'

'Corporal, as soon as we get back, there'll be a tot of rum for all who want it; and I'll be pleased to drink your health.'

We were all for going home right away, but it was shortly after my father's death in 1919 when I was demobbed. Far from leaving suffering behind, I returned accompanied by men with patched up, shredded bodies and others hearing in their shattered minds never ending screams, the din of explosions; smelling the stench of rotting flesh; feeling they were being sucked into pits of stinking mud whilst watching rats gorge on the dead and dying and on bad days, experiencing worse. The lucky ones of those would be dead before they reached home. As I watched the endless line of wounded and disabled being brought down the gangplanks, I didn't feel pride in a job well done, I felt bitterness towards those who'd sent us and now it was over, it seemed we were little more than a hindrance; there weren't even jobs for us, just chaos and rationing. It wasn't long before I realised that England wasn't the place I'd left four years earlier. Those who'd been demobbed first were greeted as conquering heroes, but we were looked upon more akin to discharged felons. My family had been gunsmiths for four generations. The expectation was that my brother and I would continue the family tradition, but I'd had my fill of guns. My brother wanted to be an architect so, we sold the stock and let the shop as a tobacconist, and as if the battlefields hadn't killed enough people, the towns were rife with Spanish 'flu; folks were well in the morning and dead by night. We'd left one sort of danger in France, only to meet another at home.

The war had changed a lot of things and now it was over, even the lasses had problems. So many men had been killed and injured that dance halls were filled with numerous women desperate to find any man as a husband. As soon as I returned, my childhood sweetheart, Elsie, pursued me with relentless determination; every time I turned, she was there. I tried to explain that I wasn't the person I used to be, nor could I explain to her or anyone else what I'd been through and most didn't want to know anyway.

Although it was them or us, my conscience was uneasy about the Jerrys I'd shot at and no doubt killed but I was more seriously troubled by the Jerrys we'd shot who we could have taken as prisoners. Added to that, I was still grieving for my countless friends who didn't return. Losing them was so distressing I stopped making friends at all; it made the inevitable parting less painful. No, the incident that was eating me alive happened when I came across one of our Sergeants lying in a shell hole with his leg severed and part of his rib cage blown away. He was still alive but clearly would soon die; I could do nothing for him nor stay and comfort him. He could barely speak and had an awful look in his eyes as he mouthed: 'please?' so, I took a deep breath, pointed my rifle at him, screwed my eyes shut and put him out of his misery. Ever since I daren't be alone with myself; on the occasions I am, I see those dreadful eyes pleading with me.

I longed to escape and seek solace; somewhere that was untouched by war and death; somewhere bucolic that was in harmony with nature and where there was peace. I studied my map, put some essentials in my backpack and wrapping my greatcoat around me, left without saying where I was going. I travelled by train and foot to the remote village of Abbots Langford. Although I'd seldom worn my coat in the trenches, it still reeked of rancid mud and cordite fumes and every whiff of it took me back. Although it had cost me £1, I decided to part with it as soon as possible — I didn't need anything else to remind me of the past. But having made the decision to try to put the past behind me, I still couldn't get "It's a long way to Tipperary" out of my mind as I walked; we'd sung it so many times as we marched to our trenches. Not so many marched back singing it, that was for sure.

It was late afternoon when I approached Abbots Langford. It was so remote that if you came upon it by chance, you were probably lost. Following my map, I located the small stream and found where it entered a copse. As I turned towards the village, I spotted an old man, deep in thought, leaning on a five bar gate, gazing towards the horizon; there was something about him that drew me to him. I approached him from behind and not wishing to alarm him, greeted him in a loud voice.

'Good day — fine view, isn't it?' It seemed an eternity for the question to sink in.

Eventually, he replied, without turning around. 'It is that — a fine view.'

'Do you live in the village?' I asked, stepping closer to him.

'Aye.' We both gazed at the view without speaking. I started to feel uncomfortable so attempted to rekindle the conversation.

'Have you lived here long?'

Again, a long silence. Eventually, he replied, again without turning around again. '40 year cum June.'

'What brought you to such a remote place, if you don't mind my asking?'

This time he glanced at me. 'No, I don't mind you asking, young man.' He took his time in answering this question as if he was debating whether to speak or not. 'I was indentured to Josia Buckingham over Sunbury way as a wheelwright. Fine teacher he was and when I became a master wheelwright, I came here with my wife. She wanted to be with her family; they live hereabouts and I set up my own workshop.'

'Do you still practice your trade?'

'Aye, on and off, not much call for it these days. The days of craftsmanship are near gone. Cabinet makers think themselves top craftsmen, but they aren't, it's us wheelwrights. We'll be the ones who'll be the missed the most when we're gone; you mark my word.' I lent my elbow on the end of the gate so I could see him the better.

'So, your wife has spent most of her life here?'

He ran his gnarled hand over his face as if by habit. 'Aye, a good part.'

'How long have you been married, may I ask?'

As soon as I'd asked the question, I thought I detected a tightening of his jaw muscles as if he was having to apply considerable will power to reply. 'Neigh on 50 year.'

'A long time.'

He nodded. 'Aye, a long time,' then without looking at me, he continued, 'you a married man, Sir?'

'No, not as yet.'

'It'll happen. The Good Book says there's a time for everything under the sun; time'll come soon enough.' He turned, glanced at my greatcoat, then turned back to the horizon. 'Been soldiering?'

'Yes.'

'Bad, was it?'

'It was.'

He nodded as if he understood. 'Thought so,' then blinked and rubbed his eye with the back of his hand and clamped his teeth together.

I was about to ask what ailed him, but thought better of it and asked instead, 'Does rationing trouble you much here?'

'The rationing? No, we eat what's local and little else, always have. Rationing's for city folks, not the likes of us.'

'Could you tell me if there's an Inn near where I can get a bed and a meal?'

When it seemed he'd regained his composure, he pointed down the lane. 'Aye, "The Feathers," down there. They'll fix you some vitals I dare say.'

'I expect you'll be away to your supper shortly as well. Is your wife at home waiting for you?' He didn't reply immediately, but just nodded, then eventually said;

'Aye, she's up home,' and as if without thinking, he turned towards me and I noted that his eyes were red. Immediately I felt as if I'd been intruding so stepped back.

'Well, I mustn't keep you, she'll be expecting you home in good time, no doubt,' and I turned to go.

And then I saw such a depth of suffering in his face I felt guilty for disturbing him.

'I've been of a mind to go back these last three hour,' he said quietly, then swallowed hard; 'but I can't.'

As I watched the old man, for the first time in several years, I felt deep compassion again. I spoke softly. 'Why can't you?' Now tears were unashamedly trickling down his face.

'My wife died the day before yesterday; she's lying in the house.' Neither of us spoke. He turned, leant on the gate, and faced the horizon again.

I took another pace backwards. 'I'm sorry — so sorry to intrude — I didn't realise.' Muscles in his jaw tightened again. 'No matter, Sir. The Good Lord spared her long enough for us to say our goodbyes, but parting after 50 year is a terrible hard thing. Maybe by the time the sun sets, I'll have got up courage to let the past go and think of her funeral.' He swallowed hard then continued. 'My old farther used to say, "Forgive others, then forgive yourself and just let the past go, my boy," 'e could be right, 'e often was.' I muttered a few clumsy words of condolence, took my leave then walked down the lane to the Inn.

When I reached the bend, I turned and looked back; he was still there, leaning on the gate. I arrived at the Inn, took a room for the night, and ordered a meal. It was an age before it arrived and when it did, try as I might, I couldn't eat it, I no longer felt hungry; I couldn't get the old man out of my mind. Although I was tired, I donned my greatcoat and returned to the gate. The old man had gone. Maybe at last he'd found the courage to part with his wife. I turned my collar up, took up his position and as nature settled for the night around me and with the old man's words going around in my head, like him, I gazed at the horizon till the sun set behind the hills.

LUNCH WITH HILDA

Audrey Carter was looking forward to lunch with Hilda. At last, Audrey was going to take revenge for the endless times that Hilda had made her look small.

Hilda Frobisher held court at The Copper Kettle restaurant every Tuesday at 1.00 pm. Those attending her lunches were a small but select group of Hilda's acquaintances. Although they were all elderly, none were as old as Hilda who had reached the age when most women stop using makeup and start using embalming fluid. Every Tuesday, one of those attending took it in turn to choose the same meal for everyone. This Tuesday, it was Audrey's turn, but that wasn't why she was looking forward to the lunch. It was 5 minutes to 1.00 when Audrey arrived. Hilda was sitting alone at a table by the kitchen. Audrey joined her and placed a brown paper parcel on the table.

'Come along dear, it's getting late,' Hilda said, handing Audrey the menu, 'it's your turn to order.'

'Is everyone else coming today?'

'No, Mildred has a touch of "her trouble" and Agatha has to attend a Christening.'

That was a shame, but not important. The waitress came and stood by the table, tapping her pen on her pad. Audrey studied the menu with care and eventually made a decision. 'Umm, I think we'll have soup of the day and I'm torn between the Cabbage Surprise and the Crockpot Special; think we'll go for the Crockpot Special and two glasses of dry white wine please.'

The waitress went to the kitchen, pushed the door open with her foot and yelled. 'Two soups 'n stew, table 6.'

Hilda winced. Good form and style were all important to her. She glanced around the restaurant with a look of disdain. Most of the other diners were getting their mid day internet fix from their tablets. The man at the next table appeared to be about to enthral his friends with a photo of his lunch but on further consideration, Audrey wondered if perhaps he might be seeking advice about the meat on his plate; was it animal or alien?

Not only did Hilda disapprove of the other diners, she also disapproved of most things in life as well. She was known in her circle for her self appointed mission to have everything done properly. In reality, all she achieved was to leave officials in her wake with shattered nerves and an aroma of expensive perfume. Audrey, on the other hand, left an air of peace and an aroma of mothballs. Hilda inspected her soup spoon and summoned the waitress. Holding the offending utensil at arm's length, she announced loudly, 'This spoon has a watermark, kindly replace it.' She turned back to Audrey and spoke in a honeyed voice.

'How are you dear?' but before Audrey could draw breath, she continued. 'I've had a dreadful week and to cap it all, I've lost my bridge partner. Dear Reggie lost his driving license. I ask you — Reggie — done for driving under the influence, it's disgraceful!' She rolled her eyes to the heavens as though expecting immediate Divine intervention in the matter. 'As he told the magistrate, he'd only had four Scotches before he went to the club and it was hardly his fault someone bought him a bottle of wine for lunch. Can you believe it? He only went through one red light and the blasted Police chased him all the way home and up his drive. He lost control of the car and crashed into the herbaceous border.'

'I had a bad week too; my drains were blocked.'

'Really dear, did you call the Council?'

'No, it was on my property; I called Dinoblock, they sorted it out. That little devil next door had flushed his sister's party balloons down the toilet — caused chaos.'

Hilda took a notebook and a small pencil from her crocodile skin handbag. 'I must make a note of that in case I ever get blocked; Dime-o-bog you say; what are they, American?' Audrey ignored the question, but grinning, unwrapped her parcel and revealed a book.

'You once told me that you were a FANY during the war.'

'Yes dear, I was in the First Aid Nursing Yeomanry, that's why we were called FANYs.'

'You didn't tell me that you worked with agents.'

'Didn't I dear? well, it was all very hush-hush and it was only for a short time, I did other things as well.' The waitress brought their wine and soup.

'So, it would seem. This book's just been published. It says your Corps worked with the Special Operations Executive. That was Churchill's SOE, training spies, wasn't it?'

Audrey thought Hilda looked apprehensive, but as this was payback time, she pressed on.

'Really dear?' The question was asked with slight trepidation.

'Yes, you're mentioned in it.'

Hilda dropped her spoon and snatched the book from Audrey's hands. Where — where am I mentioned?

'Page 282. It says you were a right Marta Hari.'

Hilda frantically flicked through the pages till she found 282. 'Where?' she demanded.

'Halfway down.'

Hilda found the place and read aloud. 'Could use her charms … she … oh, good grief!' She went bright red but continued reading. 'Left Marta Hari standing … anything in trousers …' Audrey started to feel guilty, she wasn't expecting quite this reaction. Hilda read on and became more apoplectic by the word. 'What?' she demanded with such force that her top denture slipped sending a fine spray of soup of the day into the air, 'this is scandalous! It's outrageous! I'll …' but she didn't say any more. She went a strange colour, gasped and gurgled and with a commendably straight back, died and slowly tipping forward, fell face long into her soup. Audrey recoiled, then froze. Not knowing what to do next, she raised a finger for the waitress who approached the table with considerable trepidation. She looked from Audrey to Hilda lying face down in her soup, then slowly back again.

'Is everything, all right?' she asked.

Audrey was in anguish. 'I feel terrible. It was her lifelong ambition to go in style, I knew I should have ordered the consommé.'

THE BRIDGE AT DROCHAISLING

Georgia was being difficult before we landed in Dublin, which was nothing new. She'd changed and became assertive the second she was promoted to Deputy Head at her primary school; she even adopted a power walk. It's true the flame of our marriage no longer burns like a log fire, but it does glow like anthracite when fanned enough. My friends who noticed told me I'm hen pecked but as Georgia said, I needn't wonder if I'm hen pecked, she'll tell me when I am. We collected our hire car, a Mercedes and headed south on the N11. The car was something else, it was smoother than the plane. Georgia adjusted the air con and relaxed for the first time on the journey. She doesn't like flying. I love touring, I get to hire cars I could never afford to buy. This one was no disappointment and in no time, we'd passed Bray when Georgia broke the silence.

'Neil; we've been married for over three years and you've never told me about your father.' The timing of her question caught me off balance, she's never shown any interest in my family although she told me about hers in forensic detail. I haven't met many of her people, but that doesn't stop her getting annoyed if I get her relatives like cousin Cathy and her school friend Catherine mixed up.

'Not much to tell. My parents got divorced when I was 8. Glad when Dad left, it was like living with a volcano.' I adjusted the near side wing mirror. 'We never knew when he would erupt next. He had OCD, everything had to be symmetrical.' I glanced over to Georgia. 'You won't believe it; Mum had to vacuum stripes in the carpet to match the lawn. He even made random inspections of our bedroom. If clothes weren't folded and stacked in perfect squares in the drawers, he'd throw the drawer across the room and we'd feel the back of his hand. He was worse when he'd been drinking. Mark you, he could switch on his Irish charm when he wanted something.'

'Have you thought of finding him and making your peace? after all, he is your father?' I knew where this was going; Georgia was close to her parents. I shook my head.

'No ... some relationships are best left in the past; anyway, I doubt if I'd recognise him, or him me. I was a skinny kid when he left. He was tall and thin, I'm neither and heaven knows what time's done to him.'

'Have you any photos of him?'

'Mum burned them.'

'Where'd he go?'

'Probably here; he was always talking about Ireland.'

'That's sad.' Georgia took a worn, clothbound book from the glove compartment, read for some minutes, then brought up the subject I'd been waiting for.

'When we've been to Droch... whatever it's called; that's it; no more bird twitching — I'm not wasting my holiday hanging about while you get over overexcited about some ball of feathers; we're sightseeing — right?'

'For the umpteenth time, I'm not a twitcher, I'm a bird watcher. Besides, Drochaisling's close to where we're going. I don't want to miss it; it attracts birds we don't often see in our part of the country.'

'A bird's a bird. I want to go to Kilkenny Castle today.'

'I know — you said. We'll go there straight from Drochaisling. Anyhow, you've got the itinerary, you programme the Satnav the way you want it.' Georgia punched the information into the Satnav, making as much noise as she could.

'Be glad when this pathetic feud with that Keith Hadley is over,' she muttered, 'you're like children; it's pathetic; grown men wasting time and money to be the one who spots the most birds in a year. You're obsessed and I never see you since you joined that club.'

'Be worse if I played golf. It's not pathetic; we don't spot birds, we spot species.' I overtook a caravan. 'I'm right on the edge of beating "Know it all Keith." I'm sick of him; thinks he has a right to be club champion.' I changed lanes to let a lorry pull in. 'I can't wait to see his face when I take the Club Trophy off him.' Georgia didn't reply but showed her contempt with a snort. After a deafening silence, she asked again:

'How's this place spelt you want to go to?' I told her. She flicked through her book. I could only see it out of the corner of my eye.

'What's that, a travel guide?' she didn't look up.

'No, got it from that second hand book shop next to the Tapas Bar; "Irish Myths and Legends," there's a legend about Drochaisling in it.'

'I'd be surprised if there wasn't, everywhere in Ireland has a legend.' She didn't respond. 'What does it say then?'

She scanned through the longish text.

'Years ago, two devoted sisters fell in love with the same man ... became jealous ... grew to hate each other ... younger one poisoned her sister with Wolf's Bane. Wonder what that is?'

'Wild flower, isn't it?'

'The young man was devastated ... retreated into a monastery; stayed for the rest of his life ... young one lost her sister and the man she loved ... committed suicide ... jumped off the bridge at Drochaisling. A troll who lived under the bridge saw how beautiful she was.'

'I'd have staked my life there'd be a troll in it somewhere.'

'Trolls get lonely ... caught her before she crashed to her death ... turned her to stone for 200 years so he could gaze on her beauty... promised to bring her back to life and wipe her bad memories away and...' Georgia then seemed to lose interest, stopped, and looked out of the window.

'And?'

'Oh, she complained 200 years was too long. Troll said not for Trolls, but agreed ... said her spirit could live on the bridge and manifest itself four times a year, once every season; then if she could cast someone else off the bridge, they could take her place; same conditions; one spirit out, one in ... her white rock would stay in the river forever. It's still there.

The author says there's always a nugget of truth in these legends.' Georgia flicked the book closed, 'and if you believe that baloney, you'll believe anything.'

'Don't knock it, a good story's a gift for tourism. Look what Nessie's done for Loch Ness.'

'Anyway, what's this place got to do with birds?'

'Dunno, but there's been sightings of an Irish Dipper near the bridge — strictly speaking, it's a subspecies, but I'd still like to see one.' Georgia wasn't listening, she was making a point of staring out of the side window. The Satnav said to turn left and leave the N11 at the next crossroads.

'We should be there by twelve,' I said, rather wishfully. After a further 20 minutes, the Satnav instructed; "at the next roundabout, take the 3rd turning right." 'What? that's never right — it's sending us back where we came from.' I glanced over to Georgia, 'you sure you programmed the thing properly?' she ignored the question.

'Perhaps there are road works or something ahead,' she said, still looking out of the side window. For the sake of peace, I turned as instructed, but as soon as we'd gone around the roundabout, the Satnav went berserk and kept repeating: "recalculating, recalculating."

'For heaven's sake turn the damn thing off! This can't possibly be right. Let's go the original way. We'll find somewhere for lunch and look at the map.'

Georgia put the book in the door pocket. 'There's no point me programming the thing if you think you know better — don't know why I bother.' She put her sunglasses on and folded her arms. We drove on for 15 minutes and came into a village and stopped at O'Neill's bar and went in.

The small pub looked and smelled like an overstocked charity shop. Every available wall space was filled with nick knacks and shelves piled with ornaments, jars, brass lamps, sporting memorabilia of every Gaelic sport there is, or ever has been. Behind the bar was a grandiose mahogany wall unit. In the centre was a large clock with a gothic surround, it had stopped at 3.47. Below and on either side were shelves crammed with bottles. Black bar stools were set against a brass foot rail running along the bar. Sitting at the far end was the only other customer. He wore mud splattered black trousers, braces; had his shirt sleeves rolled up and a small cap perched on top of his large, oval head. The landlady was behind the bar polishing glasses. He stopped talking when we came in and greeted us with 'Howya' and a nod.

'Are you serving lunch yet?' Georgia asked, looking around disapprovingly.

'We are.'

'Could I see the menu please?' The landlady nodded to a small chalkboard on the wall. The menu comprised one item:

LUNCH
Coddle
large €11 - small €7

I couldn't resist the temptation and whispered to her: 'You wanted to see the real Ireland, well here it is.' She didn't reply but continued to stare at the chalkboard.

'What's the Coddle served with?' she asked.

'Soda bread; just made it.'

'Don't know about you,' I whispered again, 'I can't make my mind up, but think I might have a stab at the Coddle.' She suppressed a giggle.

'Me too.' She turned to face the landlady. 'What goes best with Coddle?' Before she could answer, the man said "cider" she nodded. 'Two small Coddles and 2 halves of sweet cider, please.' Georgia was good at making up my mind for me. The landlady gave us the cider and went to the kitchen. We sat at a table near the bar. Not wanting to appear rude and feeling uncomfortable with the silence, I turned to the man.

'Could you tell me the way to Drochaisling please?' The man finished his drink and inspected the empty glass.

'Would you be after the direct route or the scenic one?' Before I could answer, Georgia replied.

'The direct one.' The man continued to inspect his empty glass.

'Well, if I were you and I had a mind to go to Drochaisling, I wouldn't start from here.' The landlady returned with two bowls of Coddle and a basket of rustic bread.

'Would you like another?' I asked him, nodding at his glass. He pushed it across the bar.

'A touch of the black stuff would be grand,' the landlady filled it, he raised it to me, said, 'Sláinte,' then drained a quarter of it before putting it down. 'What would you be going to Drochaisling for, it's not a happy place, people have disappeared there you know?'

'That's only a fairy story,' The man inclined his head as if to indicate to Georgia his reluctance to be quite so dogmatic.

'Thirty years back,' he continued, 'a young priest went there on Midsomer's day to exorcise the bridge — never seen again. The Garda were all over the place; didn't find a thing, even tried to drag the river but it was too fierce for them.' The landlady nodded in agreement and crossed herself. The man leant towards us and dropped his voice a little, 'some say there's a troll up there, others there's a serial killer in these parts, who's to know?'

'I've been told there's been sightings of a rare bird there,' I said, then for the sake of peace quickly added, 'when we've seen it, we're going to Kilkenny Castle.' The man drank some more, then pointing in a vague way towards the window, answered my earlier question.

'Down the road a mile or two, left at the crossroads, take the little track on the right and pass the big farmhouse.'

'Thank you ...' but he hadn't finished.

'Then ask again.' I picked up my spoon and looked at the food. The bowl of boiled potatoes and bits of bacon and sausage didn't look appetising but tasted amazing, Georgia had finished hers already and was demolishing the warm bread. She turned to the landlady.

'Could have the same again and more bread, please?' I wished I could have recorded that conversation, Georgia eating all before her without a word of criticism was rare, in fact in any crowded restaurant, day or night, anywhere in the land, if a customer found a slug on their lettuce, it was certain to be Georgia and everyone, from landlord, Chef, Maître d, MD, bottle washer and window cleaner would be subjected to her eloquent and acetic criticism of themselves and their establishment. In moments of fantasy, I sometimes wonder if she carried a supply of molluscs with her as a catalyst for her memorable performances. The legal profession lost a formidable prosecution barrister when she went into education. Rather than face Georgia in full flight, every hardened criminal from Mafia Don to small town pickpocket would have happily thrown up their hands and admit to any charge put to them including being Jack the Ripper.

After lunch, we left the pub, studied the map, and switched the Satnav back on. It was still saying "recalculate," which was strange; it worked perfectly when we left Dublin. We eventually arrived by asking the way another twice. The road came around a bend, swept left and followed Drochaisling gorge for a while. The bridge was on the right and now was little more than a footpath. Its high, stone arch was perched on two rock ledges, one on either side of the chasm, the far side dwarfed by a further 50 feet of towering cliff face. I parked in a small layby across the road.

'Coming?' Georgia switched the radio on.

'No – and don't take all day.' When I'd crossed the road and passed a sign in Gaelic and English which read: "Welcome to Drochaisling. Once visited, never forgotten," I noticed an old man standing on the bridge. In his youth, he must have been quite tall, but now, was hunched. I placed my reference book on the parapet and as I took the caps from my binocular lenses, I glanced into the gorge. I wished I hadn't left my shades in the car; the sun was bright but little was reaching the narrow gorge and I doubt if it ever did. It was like gazing into the jaws of an ossified monster; the near parallel sides fell forever. Near the top were thin, optimistic saplings clinging to ledges, below them the wicked rocks were green with moss, grey, then black with mould above the angry water which swirled around a large, solitary, white rock in the riverbed. The old man shuffled towards me.

'Hello there, young man. Would you be doing an old man a kindness and help him over the bridge? I'm not as steady as I once was?' Before I could answer, he spotted my book. 'Would that be a Compton's Birds of the British Isles you have there?'

'You know it?' I asked with some surprise.

'We have a lot of bird watchers in these parts.'

'Really? I was hoping to see an Irish Dipper. I've been told ...' He interrupted me.

'Well, isn't that a coincidence now? It was only this very Monday I heard talk of one in the gorge. If you take my arm, I'll show you where.' I went up to him.

'Really! Where?' He lifted his arm for me to take. As I got close, I could see his pale skin and expressionless eyes change as an insincere smile crept across his face.

'A good deed for a good deed?' he said in an enticing tone.

That smile stirred distant memories. I desperately tried to think of something appropriate to say, but nothing came to mind so I stepped back and yelled: 'Do I look stupid?' The old man stood motionless with a look of shock on his face. I turned and strode back to the car. When I got in, Georgia didn't look up.

'See the birdie you wanted?' I banged my hands on the steering wheel in exasperation and before I could tell her a few home truths, she added 'what did the old man want?'

'He wanted me to help him over the bridge, but he ....' She turned and gave me a furious look.

'And you didn't help him? you left him there? Neil, you're pathetic at times.' She wrenched the door open, stormed out, slammed it and power walked across the road to the bridge. I wound the window down.

'Georgia,' I yelled, 'come back, he's not what you think.' She ignored me. 'Georgia!' She strode on. I shrugged my shoulders. 'Very well, dear ... you know best,' I said as I closed the window then looked through my Compton's Birds of the British Isles for another place to spot rare species.

NO TRESPASSING

Craig Harding checked himself in front of the hall mirror. With shoes polished, hair immaculate, teeth whitened, suit brushed, and drenched in aftershave, he was good to go. He picked up his keys from the hall table and opened the flat door. Eddie kissed him goodbye, again, then handed him his briefcase.

'You take care. Where does everyone think you are today?'

Craig looked to the ceiling and pretended to think. 'Liverpool, following up a new lead.'

Eddie giggled. 'Phone me when you can,' then watched him go down the stairs, blowing kisses as he went. After washing the dishes, making the bed, and tidying the flat, Eddie went into the workshop and set up the engraving machine and set to work. A few hours later, at nearly noon, the doorbell rang. Eddie opened it to a stranger. The remarkable woman was toothpick thin with lifeless hair and a pale, haunted face. Her coat was old fashioned and she wore gloves.

'Mr Edward Russell, please? I've called for my engraving.' Her Micky Mouse voice seemed to come from some distant part of her. She offered Eddie an engraving receipt. Even through her gloves, Eddie could see her hand was long and bony.

'There's no Mr Russell here, I'm Miss Russell.'

'But you're a woman.'

Eddie looked down at her curvaceous front. 'So, I am.'

The woman ignored the comment and looking puzzled, pointed to the plaque by the bell. "Eddie Russell. Engraver." 'Not short for Edward?'

'No, Edwina.'

The thin woman's face showed a surprising emotion. 'I see … Edwina. Well, I've called for my husband's trophy; Craig Harding.'

It was Eddie's turn to show emotion. She took an involuntary pace backwards and started to blush. 'Oh! Mrs Harding … the trophy … yes, I've just finished it. I'll get it for you; it's in the workshop.' She turned, only to find that Mrs Harding had followed her in. With her mind racing, she pointed to a chair. Mrs Harding didn't sit and was not as her lover had described; not in any way. He described his wife as a younger, more vivacious person altogether. Eddie fumbled as she wrapped the trophy in a piece of newspaper. When she'd finished, the package resembled a bag of chips but Mrs Harding didn't notice, she was looking around the room.

The small room had been a servant's bedroom when the Victorian house was first occupied. The engraving machine was set on a heavy bench in front of the window and the walls and alcoves by the chimney were covered with shelves piled with cups, trophies, and plaques. Although she clearly hadn't seen an engraver's workshop before, it wasn't those that held Mrs Harding's interest but a cheap, framed certificate hanging on a nail by the door.

'I see you're a member of the same Athletics Club as Craig?'

The question had loaded undertones; Eddie didn't know where this was going and attempted to sound dismissive. 'Yes, Craig's our star athlete. I do all the club's engraving, keeps me busy.'

'So, how long have you known Craig?' Eddie knew to the day but felt it would be unwise to be precise, especially as Mrs Harding's demeanour was changing and her voice was becoming more assertive.

'I've been a member for a couple of years or so, since then, I guess.' Eddie tried not to look at Mrs Harding.

'A couple of years ... I see,' Mrs Harding repeated in a distant way as she continued her inspection. Then, for no apparent reason, she laughed and the sound sent a chill through Eddie's whole being. The laugh stopped abruptly and she left the room and strode into the kitchen, sniffing as she went. 'Do you live here alone, Miss Russell?'

Eddie followed her. 'Yes, quite alone. Just me and my cat Athena.'

'Athena?'

'Greek goddess of art.'

Mrs Harding laughed again. 'And of war strategy as well, I believe. Why Athena?' She turned and stepped close to Eddie and looked her full in the face. 'Why, Miss Russell?'

Eddie stood back and replied with eyes wide open. 'I teach art, part time.'

'Life drawing?' Eddie sensed yet more danger. Having your lover's wife visit you and ask leading questions was more than a little unsettling, especially when you're unprepared.

'I have done,' then she spotted a trap and quickly added: 'Not recently though,' but before she could go further, Mrs Harding interrupted her.

'My husband's handsome, isn't he?' Her voice was becoming harsher and she held Eddie in her fixed stare again. Eddie struggled to avoid it. She pointed to the lounge hoping Mrs Harding would step away from her.

'Yes...yes, he is, very handsome. You're a lucky woman.'

'Lucky? You think so?' Mrs Harding stepped closer again. 'Before we were married, my mother said, "You think carefully about this, my girl. When you marry a handsome man like Craig, you'll need eyes in the back of your head. Every little tart will be after him." At first, I didn't believe her ... we were so happy. When he went away on business, we'd both look at the moon at 10 at night, so we could share the same moment and he used to phone me during the day for no reason, just to talk. Now he rarely speaks when we're in the same room, except to complain.'

Eddie backed away and went to switch the light off over her bench. Floorboards creaked as she walked which made her wince, but she couldn't think why. Mrs Harding wasn't distracted; she was warming to her subject. 'He said I'd changed; I wasn't the woman he'd married. I told him, 'course I have; you have; we all change, it's inevitable. He accused me of becoming odd and obsessive.' Mrs Harding looked surprised. 'Me? I only vacuum and dust twice a day, I like to keep our home clean.' She raised her eyebrows further as if soliciting a sympathetic response. None came. Despite that, she pressed on. 'You have to be so careful about germs, haven't you?' Eddie still kept silent. 'It wasn't long before I realised my mother was right, he started having affairs.' Eddie desperately tried not to blush, but needn't have worried. Mrs Harding laughed again for no apparent reason, then nodded, as if she was agreeing with herself about some secret issue. The sound sent shivers down Eddie's spine and she went pale. 'Yes, I told him, your little tarts think they can do what they like — I expect it's all a game for them but they're forgetting something; you're mine, not theirs and I'm not about to be traded in like a used car.' Mrs Harding straightened herself in an attempt to look formidable. Then she rasped: 'Not without a fight.' Eddie snatched at the first topic that came into her mind and with all the Am Dram acting skills she could muster, she tried to sound caring.

'Have you a cold Mrs Harding?'

'Cold... me? no; hay fever. I have tablets but they don't really work, but they do dry you up. Give you a very dry mouth — you have to drink a lot.' With raised eyebrows, she gave Eddie a knowing look.

'Oh, would you like a glass of water?'

'Water? no, 'fraid it doesn't help much, but tea does. Mrs Harding raised a gloved finger. 'But only if you're making one.' Eddie didn't waste a second and pushed past Mrs Harding and filled the kettle.

'Funny you should say that, I was about to make one.' Woken by the noise, the cat got up from under the table, yawned and stretched. 'There's Athena. Do you like cats Mrs Harding?'

'Cats? I can't abide them. Far too sly. When they look at you, they can read your thoughts. Did you know that?'

Eddie smiled thinking it was a joke and before she could answer, she realised Mrs Harding was being serious. As she took two mugs from the stand, she replied. 'No, I didn't know that.'

'Oh yes. No doubt about it. My oak tree told me.' Eddie spun round to face Mrs Harding and dropped the tea bag she'd taken from the box, then without taking her eyes from her, took out another two.

'Your…oak tree?'

'Yes, it tells me a lot of things.'

'You mean — you talk to a tree?'

Mrs Harding glared at Eddie as if she was a slow witted school child. 'Don't be stupid, of course not.' And then she softened her tone in an attempt to humour her. 'They haven't got ears, now, have they?' Eddie shook her head, not daring to say a word and attempted to slide towards the door. She hadn't got far when Mrs Harding laughed again. Then stopped, suddenly. 'But it talks to me. It told me my Craig was having another affair. Can you believe it? he's got another floozie on the go, my husband!' Eddie smiled weakly and carried the tea tray to the lounge, followed so closely by Mrs Harding that she could smell the coal tar soap she used. Mrs Harding sat on the edge of the brown sofa.

'Would you like to take your coat and gloves off, Mrs Harding?'

'Take my coat off?' She seemed to be considering the suggestion, then came to a conclusion. 'No, I think I'll just unbutton it, that's what you would do, isn't it? You wouldn't take your coat off, would you?' Eddie thought it wise to agree. 'No lady would remove their gloves, now, would they?' Eddie was about to say she didn't own a pair of gloves to put on or take off but thought that information might not help the discussion.

'No, I'm sure they wouldn't.' Eddie sensed that Mrs Harding had now tired of the subject of outer garments and wondered what the next one would be, but she was unprepared for the one that came.

'My Craig's a sales representative; he travels all over the country.' Mrs Harding smiled at Eddie in the manner that a hungry snake would smile at a mouse. 'I think he might have a girl in Coventry. Have you ever been to Coventry, Miss Russell?' Eddie tried not to sound like a mouse.

'No, I never have.'

'Why haven't you been there, Miss Russell — don't you like Coventry?' But before Eddie could reply, Mrs Harding continued, 'and he's got another floozie besides. My oak tree told me that as well.' Then, immediately, her smile froze as if switched off. 'But I'll stop that little game, I've done it before and I'll do it again.' Eddie's hand shook and she tried not to spill the tea as she placed the mug on the coffee table in front of Mrs Harding. To her relief, Mrs Harding charged off in yet another direction. 'I don't sleep you know. Do you sleep, Miss Russell?' She didn't wait for a reply to this question either and ploughed on. 'I don't sleep in case I have a dream. I couldn't bear a dream of him walking away from me for a younger woman.' Eddie desperately tried not to show any emotion and pushed the sugar bowl towards Mrs Harding. 'I don't take sugar; I use sweeteners.' And as she spoke, she rummaged in her coat pocket and took out a small box. As she was still wearing gloves, she had trouble opening it. As soon as she succeeded, she gasped, looked startled, stared behind Eddie's chair at the door and pointed. 'What was that noise; is someone upstairs?' Eddie instinctively turned and as soon as she did, Mrs Harding lent forward and dropped two tablets into Eddie's tea, then sat back and pretended to stir her own mug.

'No, there's no one above, this is the top floor.'

'No one above … oh good, that is a relief. I must have imagined it; how silly.' Mrs Harding seemed pleased all the same. 'You wouldn't like someone to be above, now, would you?' Again, she didn't wait for a response. 'Well, my dear, it's so nice to be able to talk to someone like you, woman to woman. Someone who understands the way of things.' She sipped her tea. 'You see, these days people think they can be what they want and have what they want, but that's not so. Just because you want something doesn't mean you can have it.'

'No, I suppose not,' Eddie replied, absent mindedly stirring several spoons of sugar into her mug. Mrs Harding then looked vacant and changed to another subject.

'The other day, Craig told me he liked silk underwear, so I got some; red it was. As soon as he saw it, he said he'd gone off that and now preferred black satin — the little imp.' Eddie put her mug down and pulled her jumper around her and crossed the two sides over, hoping Mrs Harding couldn't see through it. She didn't but rambled on. 'Yes, I've decided to go on a diet. Men don't like fat women, do they? it's the cabbage soup diet you know; people swear by it.' She carefully drained her mug; Eddie played for time and drank hers as well. 'Yes, men are so stupid ...' and as Mrs Harding droned on and on, Eddie struggled to concentrate, feeling unusually tired. 'My Craig doesn't think I know he's being unfaithful.'

The statement filtered through Eddie's fog and she struggled to wake up. 'How?' she asked, sounding a little drunk.

'As soon as he comes home, he rushes to take a shower, says it's to freshen up after so much driving. Rubbish! He never used to bother. It's to wash the smell of her off him. I don't need to bug his phone or put trackers in his car, I'm a woman, I've got female 6th sense. I don't need the next generation electronic gizmo to know what he's doing. Yes, that and the nose gets him every time.' Alarms bells now rang on every floor of Eddie's mind. With all the effort she could muster, she asked:

'The nose?'

Mrs Harding warmed to her subject. 'My Craig uses an unusual aftershave. It's very strong and it lingers. I've told him a hundred times he uses too much.' Mrs Harding waited for Eddie to respond. She didn't, she was too busy using all her will power to get up. 'That's right, my dear, I know you're one of his mistresses.'

'Aftershave?'

'Aftershave — your flat reeks of it.' Mrs Harding didn't say more; she watched instead as Eddie struggled to get up, failed and sank back into her chair and fell into a deep sleep. 'That's right, you have a nice sleep.' After waiting a few more minutes, Mrs Harding put her tea mug in her shopping bag, got up and went to the kitchen. She took a pan from the chipboard shelf, filled it with water, put it on the stove, dropped an egg in it and turned the gas on and lit it. As the water came to the boil, she put a plate on the small pine table with a knife and egg cup and spoon, salt, and pepper, took butter from the fridge and placed the loaf of bread beside the plate. Looking satisfied with lunch, she set the chairs straight and glanced out of the window at the panorama of rooftops and factory chimneys, then left the room.

With a disdainful look on her face, she inspected the bedroom, found the bathroom, and opened a cabinet over the basin. It was filled with dust covered pots, bottles, tubs, tins and boxes of lotions, potions, salves, balms, creams and tablets, many out of date. She pushed them together to make space, then took the part empty box from her pocket and put it in the cabinet. They weren't sweeteners; they were Dr Lechner's Max strength sleeping tablets. She turned the box around so it read: "Warning: may cause drowsiness." 'They'd better,' she muttered and closed the door and checked around the flat.

She found her repair receipt in the workshop, put it in her pocket and unwrapped the trophy and put it back on the bench. She returned to the lounge and tidied around and straightened the cushions as if without thinking, then checking that Eddie was still asleep, she said to her:

'Now, Miss Russell; whether my marriage is good, bad, or indifferent is beside the point; it's my marriage and trespassing on it is most unwise. Think on, my dear.' Then with some noticeable colour in her cheeks and a spring in her step, Mrs Harding returned to the kitchen, closed the window, turned the gas up high and blew the flame out. With a last look around, she left; quietly shut the front door and taking her gloves off, went down the stairs humming to herself.

Exodus 20:14

10 STRINBURG PLACE

10 Strinburg Place was a period house set in a large garden surrounded by Beech trees. Once it was imposing and filled with laughter, now it stood unkempt and silent, its soul had long departed and laughter was a distant memory.

Paul parked outside and turned to Amelia. 'Can I see the will again?' She handed him a large envelope containing her grandfather's will. He switched the engine off and skimmed through the pages.

'It took long enough to clear probate.'

'My cousins contested it.'

'"I give, devise and bequest"... left his savings and investments to your cousins; house and contents to you ... and his bureau' — "hope you cherish it ... when you use it, think of me," must be quite a piece.'

'Not from what I remember ...'

Paul wasn't listening, he was still reading. 'Your cousins did well, he wasn't short of cash.'

'His father owned a couple of furrier's shops; they were quite wealthy at one time.'

Paul switched the radio off and handed the envelope back, then looked around to make sure they weren't being overheard and whispered: 'But the will doesn't mention the diamond.'

'Of course, it doesn't.'

Paul looked puzzled. 'Why "of course?"'

'You're forgetting Grandma's family was a bunch of crooks. As soon as Grandma's aunt got her sticky fingers on it, her kids squabbled over who'd inherit it. It nearly caused a family war so to keep the peace she said none of them would have it.'

'She could've sold it.'

Amelia put the envelope back in her rucksack. 'No, she couldn't, it's a blue diamond, they're rare; supposed to be worth a mint, you can't sell them without proper provenance.'

'Then why leave it to your grandmother?'

'She had to do something. She could trust her to keep her mouth shut about where it came from. She got it right; Grandma was so secretive she wouldn't show it to anyone, not even us.'

'With her background that's believable.'

'Dad said Grandma's family could be dysfunctional at times but she was the real deal. To make things worse she had strange habits and smoke — she smoked so much she went around in a fog. You could hear her coming a mile off; she had a gammy leg; she wore one of those built up boots, walked heavily and dragged her foot.'

Paul pulled a face. 'Sounds a real charmer.'

Amelia warmed to her subject. 'She didn't trust anyone either, she hid the diamond in the house and kept moving it around. When we asked her about it, she'd throw her fag into the grate and tell us: "if you lot get your hands on my diamond, I'll come back and haunt you, see if I don't. That thing's bad news. I'm not having no rows over it. None of you are having it, so forget it," then she'd light another fag and clump off, puffing like a train.'

Paul scowled. 'She could've left it to your grandfather.'

Amelia shrugged her shoulders. 'It wouldn't have solved the problem; besides, he wanted her to give it back to the rightful owner. As her aunt was dead and the family didn't know where it came from that wasn't possible. Anyway, their marriage was too rocky by then. I often wondered if they married on the rebound, they were such a miss match.'

'I suppose opposites attract — so how'd they live together then?'

'When she was being difficult Grandpa'd go and do his cabinet making.'

'Was he any good?'

'He thought so. You know, despite Grandma's moods, I liked coming here, it's a great place for kids. We made dens in the bushes.' She pointed, 'those over there and we climbed the trees. We made tents out of old sheets — summers lasted forever in those days. Grandpa made us toy boats, and we sailed them on the pond. Every time we played there; he'd say 'now don't fall in, will you?' but one of us usually did.'

Paul had a dreamy look on his face. 'I had a toy yacht once, wonder what happened to it?'

Amelia didn't notice his comment. 'In the evenings, we made campfires and Grandma gave us sausages to cook and Grandpa told us stories and taught us about the stars and we laughed till we ached and we burned the sausages and got filthy and stank of smoke. It was great. I've fond memories of the days when burnt sausages were a treat. Shame childhood can't last forever. Only fools shorten their kid's childhood to be trendy. I want my kids …'

Paul was indignant. 'Our kids!'

'Our kids to have a proper childhood. I want them to have space to grow up free range, not like the factory bred efforts coming out of the cities now with their heads jammed full of facts and knowing nothing of life. Grief and adulthood will keep, there's no need to meet them early.'

'Yea, you could be right.'

'Grandpa read a lot; he talked about things Dad never did. He was special — you would have liked him — miss him still.'

'You're lucky, I don't remember my grandparents.'

'Dad said Grandma and Grandpa had a rough start; their son was killed in an accident. Sounds like Grandma doted on him; she held séances to contact him. Grandpa didn't approve of that, they had endless rows about it. He wanted a divorce back then but she wasn't having any of it. Apparently, she used to tap her wedding ring and say "that there's mine and you aint havin' it back."'

Paul took the keys out of the ignition. 'Which lamp do you want?' She didn't answer.

'We came once, he'd nearly finished his bureau. When we were alone, he said to me "your Grandma'll leave her diamond to some Dog's home, I'll be bound. If I had my way, you'd have it, you're level headed for a young 'un," then he left the bureau unfinished for a long time. He told me several times, "One day girl, the bureau'll be yours, don't you part with it and don't let anyone take it off you — promise me?" Then just as he was finishing it, they had the row which ended their marriage and he left her.'

'And that's when the diamond disappeared?'

'Grandma told the police he'd stolen it.'

Paul looked amazed. 'She said what?'

'Well, she told them he'd stolen her jewellery. He travelled about a lot but they eventually found him in Leeds but didn't prosecute him.'

'Do you think he stole it?'

Amelia shrugged her shoulders. 'I don't know; doubt it.'

Paul looked amazed and turned to face her. 'So, if he didn't steal it, where is her jewellery, it's not mentioned in the will?'

'That's a mystery; she might've sold it; Grandpa might've stolen it as she said. There's always the chance she hid it and did forget where. Grandpa might have hidden it and it's possible that one of her family found it and stole it along with the blue diamond.'

'So, none of it ever turned up?'

'No; mark you, most of her family were dead by then. They weren't the sort to make wills; don't think Grandma did either; so there wouldn't have been a trace of any of it anyway. Grandpa was adamant he hadn't stolen anything. He told the police Grandma had dementia and hid things and forgot where. The police told Grandma what he'd said and she tore the place apart. Maybe she thought he'd found it and re hidden it to spite her.' They picked up their rucksacks. 'They must have hated each other in the end, Grandpa even sent her letters taunting her; it got really nasty.'

'If their relationship was that bad, it's not surprising there wasn't any maintenance done on the house.'

'Grandma had been ill for some time. It was around then she was told her illness was terminal. That did it; she never could handle illness. Think she was going loopy by then anyway. It pushed her over the edge and she committed suicide.'

Paul looked aghast. 'In this house?'

'Guess so. Eventually, Grandpa heard she'd died. The house was in their joint names so he moved back. The first night he was here something happened, he had a massive stroke; hadn't even finished unpacking. He was in a terrible state, had to go into a nursing home where he died.' Amelia wiped her eye and didn't say any more.

'You all right love?' Paul put his arm around her shoulder, Amelia nodded. 'come on, let's look at this legacy of yours.'

The gloomy shadows cast by the huge trees were creeping towards the house. The gate hung at an angle and the path was overgrown. A breeze blew leaves in swirls around them. They'd got halfway down the path when Amelia stopped and looked around; rapidly.

'What's the matter?'

'Strange — there was a summer house over there, wonder where it's gone?' They pushed their way down the rest of the path and Amelia opened the front door, switched her lamp on and picked up the mail from the mat. The top letter was marked "urgent" and was addressed to "The Occupant." She opened it and read it aloud.

'"Dear homeowner. We at Walcott Developments are urgently seeking properties like yours where we can build our luxury retirement apartments. Call us right away for an informal chat. You'll be amazed at what we can offer ..." The vultures are gathering,' she said, flicking the light switch. Nothing happened. Paul turned his lamp on as well, then Amelia took them on a tour of the ground floor. The house had large rooms, most were decorated with floral wallpaper, some of which hung off the walls. The furniture that wasn't piled in heaps was strewn around in disarray. The kitchen had an uneven tiled floor and assorted obsolete equipment. When they'd finished the tour, they returned to the first room and examined it in detail. After they'd finished, Paul sat in thought.

'Have squatters been in, most of the furniture's wrecked?'

Amelia shook her head. 'Probably Grandma looking for the diamond. She was a tenacious old bat. An old bat with a short fuse.'

'She wrecked all this on her own?' Paul looked shocked, 'I wouldn't like to have got in her way.'

They worked systematically inspecting each room and its contents. The only cupboard they couldn't open was in the kitchen. Paul gave Amelia a hammer and chisel to prise it open. Just as Amelia started to open the cupboard, Paul picked up a coat stand and pulled some wallpaper from the wall.

'What are you going to do with that?' she asked.

Paul held it at arm's length. 'Burn it, it's got woodworm.'

'For goodness' sake check it carefully.'

He took it to the garden and started a fire with other broken furniture. When he'd returned, Amelia had opened the cupboard and was reading a letter; it was addressed to her grandmother.

'Look at this,' she said reading it to Paul. "Remembered where you hid your bauble yet my dear? no? oh dear, that is a shame ..."' She put it back in its envelope and handed it to Paul. 'Burn it, it's not the Grandpa I knew.'

After they'd worked for several hours, they stopped for a break. As Amelia eat her sandwich, she rubbed the dirty window with her sleeve, then pointed. 'I used to climb that tree; I got stuck up it once; it was ages before anyone came to get me down.'

Paul glanced at the tree. He raised an eyebrow. 'Have you noticed there aren't any carpets?'

Amelia frowned. 'There were, Grandma, must've taken them up.'

When they'd searched the ground floor, they went upstairs, their footsteps echoing on the bare boards. Amelia showed Paul the bedrooms. Garlands of cobwebs hung from light fittings and the window sills were sprinkled with dead flies. Amelia tried to open a bay window but the sash cord was broken. A skirting board had been ripped from the wall in the master bedroom. The second bedroom had a bird's nest in the fireplace and black mould by the window. One end of the curtain rail had come away from the wall and the curtains hung in a heap on the floor. They went into one room which was in a better state than most.

'This would make a lovely nursery.' Paul didn't answer. They went further down the passage; Amelia opened another door. 'This was Grandpa's study.'

A floorboard by the fireplace had been pulled up and thrown aside. There was a large bookcase against one wall, the books had been dumped on the floor. Shelves were fitted to just about every other free wall space, one of which still held books and a broken pair of glasses. The bureau was beside the window. Paul put his lamp on a shelf beside an open Bible. He pointed, making a poor effort at hiding his disgust.

'Is this your bureau?'

'Yes.' Paul heaved it into the room. A large spider ran up the wall. The smell of damp permeated the room; Amelia opened the window. Paul turned to her. 'Why did he say this was special? it's awful, the proportions aren't even right,' he held a lamp closer to it, 'and he was no French polisher either.' Paul sat on the only chair. 'Look, love, I know you dream of living here, but this place needs a fortune spent on it, it's way beyond us and this bureau — well it's just ghastly.'

'I know,' she said rather apologetically, 'but Grandpa wanted me to have it; I'd like to have something of his.'

Paul screwed his face up and raised his shoulders in exasperation. 'We're struggling with the flat mortgage as it is, we can't borrow more to do this up.'

'I don't see why not. We could sell the flat, move in here, then do it up.'

'That's all very well love, but we've hardly any equity in the flat and ...'

Amelia scowled. 'And whose fault's that?' she demanded.

'Oh, for crying out loud, don't bring that up again. This place needs a load of major work, it'll cost a fortune. We can't live here while that's going on.'

'Paul, this is a proper family home. I'm sick of the flat, we can't have children there; it's like living in a broom cupboard — it feels like our lives are on hold.'

Paul got up and paced around the room for a few minutes. 'Ok, how about this then: we find your diamond ...'

'If it's here.'

'We find the diamond, sell it, do this place up; sell the flat, pay off the mortgage. Then we'll have a tidy asset to borrow against. We'll be well set up. What do you reckon?' Amelia gave him a blank look. 'And if we can't find it, then we'll talk to a developer like Walcott. Maybe one of them could build houses here and we could do a deal and have one.'

Amelia was quiet for a while as she considered Paul's idea. 'Paul, I'm not letting this house slip through our fingers in another of your harebrained get rich quick schemes. Anyway, it'll take two or three years before the new houses are built. You know what planning permission's like. We could have this place done up in a few months. My clock's ticking, I want a family; is that too much to ask?'

'No one gets every deal right.'

Amelia picked a copy of Ulysses from the floor and put it on a shelf.

'Grandpa only said "if he had his way," he'd give it to me. You're assuming he did have it. We'll look for the diamond and if we do find it, we'll see what it's worth before we do anything else.'

'Oh, come on, he must have found it. This is a once in a lifetime's chance.'

'That's why we're not rushing it.'

Paul changed the subject. 'A lot of the furniture's wrecked, the rest looks like junk, let's clear it out.'

Amelia raised her hands in protest. 'Some of it might be ok.'

'All right,' he said emphatically, 'if any of it is worth keeping, we'll put it in the lounge then. I'll put the rest on the bonfire. Can you bring all of your grandpa's tools here and we'll check over the bureau?'

When they'd searched all the rooms on the first two floors, the only place left was the attic. As neither wanted to go alone, they went together. The entrance was down a long passage and up a steep staircase. The door at the top was stiff and screeched when Paul opened it. The attic was empty except for a wasp's nest and a packing case under a beam. Paul looked around and inspected the roof.

'Got a bit of a leak by those tiles ... got some mould over here ... no insulation on the tiles.' He went on to a corner by the chimney, held his lamp closer then jumped back. 'Rats! Rat droppings — we've got rats!'

Amelia wrapped her jacket around her and shivered. 'You sure they're not mice?'

'I don't give a damn what they are, we've got 'em.' Paul gave the rest of the attic a cursory inspection as Amelia edged back to the door.

'Can we go now; I don't like it up here?' Paul followed her to the stairs and slammed the door shut behind him. When they'd reached the study again Amelia poured herself another coffee.

'Out of curiosity, how did your grandmother commit suicide?'

'Hung herself.' It didn't seem appropriate to say more, so Paul picked up more books until Amelia had regained her colour.

'We've looked everywhere for the diamond, you sure there's nowhere else?'

'Only the garden.'

'We've no chance of finding it if it's there. Look, I've been thinking. Your grandfather seemed to be fonder of you than your cousins.'

Amelia nodded. 'Yes, I think he was.'

'So, look at how much he left them, probably more than this place's worth.'

Amelia considered the thought. 'Maybe.'

'Whether it was or not, your cousins contested the will, which means they think the diamond or the jewellery's still in the house which would also mean they didn't steal them.'

'Yes, but one of their parents might have and not told them. Too many dodgy people knew about that stone, anything could have happened.'

'So, you're saying none of it might be here? but if it is and your Grandpa intended you to have it, he could've sent you a note telling you where it is, and he didn't. He would hardly risk you not being able to find it, now would he? Let's face it, presumably, your Grandma didn't find it and we've looked and we can't.'

'Yes, but even if it's not here, for peace of mind, we've got to be certain we've looked everywhere to make sure. If we do sell the place and a developer finds it, it would belong to them.'

'I still think something's wrong. Your Grandpa wanted you to have the bureau, he made no mention of the jewellery, but he did the diamond; the odds are if it's here it's in the one thing he insisted you keep — his bureau. Shall we take it downstairs and look over it tomorrow in better light?'

Amelia shrugged her shoulders. 'Might as well.' They took an end each. The sun was now behind the trees and dusk was setting in. The fire was well alight in the garden. As soon as they tried to move the bureau, the fire spat a manic shower of sparks high into the air sending shadows flickering across the wall and a hollow, eerie noise came from the attic. Amelia jumped. They both froze.

Amelia frowned at him. 'Did you close the attic door?'

'Of course, I did.' She grabbed his arm. 'Paul — something's up there!' They both held their breath and listened. The sound started again and with disturbing resolve, shuffled and thumped unsteadily across the floor. 'It's the rats — there must be thousands of them — they're coming towards the door!'

Paul snatched up the poker in one hand and a lamp in the other.

'Get that lamp, let's see what it is — come on.'

Amelia glared at him in horror. 'Are you mad? I'm not going up there.' She backed against the wall.

'If something's up there, I'm not waiting for it to come down here and that's final. Anyway, the attic's empty; we checked it, didn't we? come on.' Not wanting to be left alone, Amelia clamped hold of Paul's arm and keeping slightly behind him, they tiptoed down the passage and stopped at the bottom of the stairs. He turned to her and whispered; 'You ok?' she replied with an uncertain nod, then holding their lamps high, they started up the stairs. They'd reached halfway when Amelia wrenched Paul's arm back.

'Look! The door's open!' They stood still, scarcely daring to breath and looked at each other for a few seconds, then Paul shook her hand free, rushed up, kicked the door wide open and with the poker raised, charged in. Amelia followed. The attic was empty.

Void. No rats. No one was there either. It was as they saw it earlier. They searched over and over until they were satisfied they really were alone, then after carefully closing the door behind them, they returned to the study.

'Paul, I'm getting a bad feeling about this place.'

Paul nodded. 'Me too.' He pointed to the bureau, 'let's get this thing downstairs, then lock up and come back tomorrow.' But try as they could, it was too cumbersome and heavy to get down the staircase in the gloom, so they pulled it back into the study. Paul poured them the last of the coffee and thought for a moment. 'Look, if the diamond's in the bureau, it's got to be possible to find it. Give me the tape, let's have another look.' Amelia sat on the chair and drank coffee as Paul took the drawers out, inspected them and put them in a pile against the wall. He took the copy of Ulysses from the bookshelf and as he measured the bureau, inside and out, he wrote the measurements on the flyleaf. After a few minutes, he turned to Amelia.

'That's odd, all the joints are dovetailed and they've got a peg glued through them.'

'So?'

'That isn't necessary; the only way you'd get this apart is to break it up, why'd he do that?' He took

Ulysses and studied his measurements. After a few scribbled calculations, he did a little jig.

'What?' Amelia demanded. 'What?'

'Some of the measurements don't add up. There must be something in the middle. It's quite small and I can't find a way into it.'

'Are you sure?'

'Absolutely, I can't see any reason for it to be there unless it's another compartment or, or — it's a box — a small box! Right love — it's your call. What do you want to do? if the stone's in the box thing and we break the bureau up to get at it, we could have it professionally restored and keep it as a memento. If it's not inside, your grandfather's playing a sick joke on you, so what the heck, we just burn the thing. What do you reckon?' Amelia snatched the book from Paul and read his calculations.

'You sure you haven't made a mistake; you know what you're like?' Paul grabbed the tape and getting on his knees, remeasured, calling out the measurements as he went. Amelia checked them off. When he'd finished, he looked at her quizzically. 'Ok,' she said, 'they're the same.'

'Thank you. Thank you very much,' he said in mock agitation, 'so?'

Amelia fidgeted with the zip on her jacket. 'I'm not sure, I'd like to think about it.' The second she'd finished; the wind blew and the open window rattled. Before Paul could say a word, Amelia raised her hand to stop him. 'Did you hear that?'

'Yes, the window rattled.'

'Not the window, didn't you hear that squeaking sound upstairs?'

'No,' Paul listened intently again. 'Get a grip, it's an old house. There's no one here except us. You know that, don't you?'

She looked at him attentively. 'Do I?' she turned all three lamps fully up, 'Paul, I want to get out of here — now. Just break the thing open and let's go.'

Paul took the rip saw and rendered the bureau to pieces, eventually removing a small wooden cube from its centre. It was a box, but it didn't have a lid, the sides were glued down. He shook it, then carefully cut one end off. 'There you go love,' he said pushing the dismembered bureau aside with his foot, 'you open it — positive thoughts now!'

They brought the lamps closer. Paul crossed his fingers and Amelia gently tipped the box up. Out slid a piece of folded paper. She held the box to the light, there was nothing else in it. It was empty. She unfolded the paper.

'It's a note from Grandpa.' Amelia read in silence.

'What does it say for pity's sake?' she didn't reply. A lone tear trickled down her face as she handed it to him.

He read aloud. "Dear Amelia, If you are reading this, I'm deeply disappointed in you, I expected better. It means you have destroyed my bureau to find Grandma's diamond. Well, it isn't here. I appointed a company of solicitors to keep it safe. I won't tell you who they are, or where they are. Had you kept my bureau for just one year, they would have contacted you, inspected it and given you the stone to do with as you wish. However, by destroying it, you have forfeited the diamond, it will now go to the dog's home as your grandmother wished. I made the bureau so it can't be mended so don't waste your time trying to fool the solicitors. I hope you learn well from this lesson. Farewell, my dear. Grandpa."

As he read, the fire died down and the house seemed to relax and be at peace. The only sound was of Amelia sobbing. She took Walcott's letter from her rucksack and pushed it into Paul's hand.

'Let them have it,' she said, then walked past the bureau and out of the room.

THE OCCUPANT OF BENCH 24

Autumn is my favorite season since the bomb test. I love watching the golden leaves turn purple as they fall from the trees; they look so pretty on the pink frost and on a good day, you can hear them fizzle. A lot of strange things have happened since the bomb was tested in Shetland. It was experimental and supposed to make local people vanish, but something went wrong and instead, it scrambled time and worked in reverse. Even though the effects were beginning to wear off, it was still a pain having the seasons shuffled. To make matters worse, I'd been hitting the bottle and a few days after the test, I got breathalysed. The magistrate said that alcohol would be the ruin of me, and took my driving license away; I guess I have been overdoing it a bit, so I've been really trying to give it up.

I cycle to work now and cut through Victoria Park. The main avenue has a bench under every tree and each bench used to bear a memorial plaque to some dead local worthy but the Council replaced the plates with numbers. On either side of the road are manicured lawns, colour coordinated flower beds and clipped trees. It's the pinnacle of municipal gardening and man's attempt to control nature.

Nature's simple response in autumn is to bury man's attempts under an untidy duvet of leaves.

It was late autumn when I first saw him and I paid little attention, but after I'd passed him a few times I began to take more notice. Every morning he was lying on bench number 24 and in the afternoon, he'd gone.

The town was a magnet for rough sleepers and buskers, some had talent; most didn't. Although the tramp on bench 24 was one amongst many, there was something about him that troubled me. As the nights grew colder, I became increasingly concerned and I couldn't get him out of my mind. He even invaded my dreams and stared at me, rubbing his eye with the back of his hand, just like I do and each night he grew older and more haggard; then I'd wake up in a cold sweat. The more I thought of him, the more strung out I became. There was something weird and exasperating about him; it was like we'd met, which we hadn't, or he was some sort of relation, but I haven't any male relations. Whoever he was, he'd become the fingernail on my chalkboard. Screwed up seasons, lack of sleep and a rough sleeper squatting in my head all got at me and on one particularly bad night I decided to act before I was tempted to drown it all out, so the following morning on my way to work, I stopped off and bought a coffee to go with three of those pathetic paper twists of sugar. I cycled into the park with my heart racing. He was there again, lying on bench 24, asleep. He wore ex-army clothes and was covered with a sheet of polythene. He was surrounded by carrier bags; one was his pillow. A seagull pecked through his scattered rubbish. I figured that if I spoke to him and maybe slipped him a few quid, at the very least he'd get out of my head and let me sleep. I lent my bike against a lamp post and crossed the avenue.

'Hello,' I said and waited as he turned around. When he'd focused his bloodshot eyes on me, he gasped and sat back with a jolt. 'I bought you a coffee,' I said and handed it to him. After a while, he took it from me and with a slow, theatrical sweep of his hand, dropped it into the rubbish bin next to the bench and then waived his dirt engrained finger at me.

'You — you get away from me,' he rasped in a hoarse voice, then rubbed his eye. 'You can't haunt me, you can't haunt anyone, you aint dead yet.' I span around thinking he was talking to someone behind me, but there was no one there. 'Bugger off, I don't want nothin' from you; no sermons, nothin'.' His aggression took me off guard.

'I thought I'd say hello. Cold, isn't it?'

'Did you now?' he rasped, then belched and waved his hand at me again, 'so you thought you'd wake a law abiding citizen to tell 'em what they already know.'

He pulled a half empty bottle of cider from his coat pocket, drained it, then dropped it over the back of the bench. 'Got any fags?' and before I could reply, he continued in a mocking voice. 'Oh, don't tell me, you've given it up again.' He was right, I had given up again; I was horrified. How on earth did he know?

As he spoke, I noticed his centre tooth was crooked like mine, and I was about to say 'what a coincidence' when I thought better of it. Instead, ignoring his gut wrenching stench, I held my breath and lent closer to take a better look at him. His face was weathered and furrowed; life had been savage with him. Meeting him was beginning to look like a mistake, but for sanity's sake, I had to make sure he was ok.

'Have you got somewhere to sleep at night?'

'Hostel — they chuck you out in the morning.' I was desperate to know why he thought he knew me but sensed not to ask. 'If you haven't any fags, don't just stand there — clear off,' he said, waving me away. He pulled his coat collar higher, his hat lower, then laid down, turned around and went back to sleep. As I gazed at him, I began to realise what had troubled me. My heart hammered as the horrifying truth sank in. I now knew who I was looking at. My head swam and I needed a drink like never before.

TWO RUNNING MEN

Edward Bishop's phone rang. He answered and heard a familiar but very agitated voice.

'Eddy? John's got remission and he's found out about us.'

Bishop was confused. 'But I thought he'd found someone new and couldn't care less what you do now.'

The caller was becoming increasingly distraught. 'His floozy dumped him and he's furious.'

'But he doesn't get out of prison till next year, so what?'

'He got remission for good conduct. Him — can you believe it? I'm out of here; I'm going back home, it's safer there, Eddy, he's after your blood.' The caller started to cry. 'I'll phone you some time.'

Bishop raised his voice to be heard over the sobbing. 'June — does he know who I am?' Eventually, the sobbing died down.

'No, but he'll find out.' Neither could think of what to say now, so said goodbye.

Messy relationships were the norm for Bishop and it didn't worry him when June Gray originally told him about her husband's criminal past and violent temper, but now he was highly disturbed. Not because of Gray's temper, but because the emotional playing field with June no longer seemed as level as he thought. Over the following days, he became increasingly rattled and convinced he was being followed. Unaided sleep evaded him and as empty booze bottles piled up in his bin, so did used packs of pain killers for the hangovers. He became paranoid, changed his route, turned around, went in opposite directions, and took cabs when he'd usually walk, but he didn't see anyone acting strangely, that is until one Tuesday evening.

Bishop had just come out of Westminster underground station when he felt he was being watched again. He spun around and stopped dead. It was as if he had seen his own reflection. His double was staring at him. Bishop stepped towards him, but his double raced across the road, dodged traffic, and vanished. Bishop chased after him but eventually gave up and went to his flat. He spent the whole evening desperately trying to make sense of his double and the events with June, but not coming to any useful conclusion, fell asleep.

Bishop woke early as he had appointments out of London in Ely. He had a hurried breakfast, went to the station, and boarded the train. The engine was old and belched smoke and smuts. Bishop read the leader story in his paper for a while, then stared out of the window. The sun cast long shadows on the fields and as he watched, he realised he was part of the flickering image. It only took a cloud to intervene and he was snuffed out. A nebulous nothing getting in the way and he disappeared without a trace. The carriage soon became stuffy and he fell asleep. He woke when the station announcer called "Ely, this is Ely." Bishop got up and as he turned to let a large man get on, he spotted his double on the platform, walking away. By the time he'd pushed his way out, the man had disappeared.

After Bishop had finished his first meeting, he went to lunch at the Stable Bar of the New Inn and ordered a lager and steak pie. The bar was old, it had a flagstone floor, black painted beams, and horse brasses on the walls.

'You like chips or mash with that?' the barman asked. Bishop shook his head then went to a table near the wall. Eventually, the barman brought him his pie. No sooner had he put it down than Bishop's double entered the bar from the lounge, approached and sat uninvited at the table, facing him.

'Nice to meet you Mr Bishop — remarkable, isn't it?' Bishop was taken off guard.

'What is?'

'Us, looking so much alike, we're absolute doubles, could be twins, but were not.'

'How do you know?'

'We have different parents.' He coughed and seemed rather flushed. But before Bishop could speak, his double raised a finger to his lips and lent forward over the table. He spoke quietly. 'Aren't you curious why I'm interested in you — I would be?' Bishop was about to reply, but the man continued, 'it's said that everyone has a double somewhere, a doppelganger.' The man smiled and nodded, 'I first saw you in London, quite by chance.' The man stopped, took a handkerchief from his pocket, and patted his brow. 'Please, don't let me interrupt your lunch.' Bishop looked at his pie, then pushed it aside. The man coughed again and continued. 'Yes, I was struck by how similar we looked and realised how opportune it was.' He seemed very short of breath but wasn't overweight.

'Why opportune, who for?'

'Oh, both of us, me especially,' the man sipped his brandy, 'you see, it would be to my advantage if I could be in two places at once in a few days' time, one officially and one not if you get my drift?'

Bishop was confused. 'No, I don't.'

The man looked around then spoke quietly. 'I would like to conduct some discrete business in one place and need to have certain people think I'm elsewhere.'

'Sounds illegal.'

'Oh no, not illegal, I assure you, but useful to me.' He leant forward a little more. 'Let me put a small proposition to you.' He looked disapprovingly at Bishop's lager. 'Would you care for something else, that doesn't look very exciting?' Bishop shook his head.

'I am prepared to give you £200, plus expenses to go to Bath Spa, pretend to be me, spend the day and night there and return to London the following evening.' He sat back looking extremely self-satisfied. Bishop was taken off guard.

'How much?'

'That's right' he said nodding, '£200, in cash. Half, plus expenses before you go, the rest when you come back.'

Bishop looked amazed. 'What on earth do you want done for that?'

The man smiled in a patronising way. 'Just be noticed; that's all. Start at Putney Bridge, be there about 6.00am, take the underground to Paddington then a train to Bath, you'll be there in a couple of hours.' He raised his hands in an expansive gesture. 'See the sights, go to Sally Lunn's tea room if you wish, have a Bath bun, try one with marmalade, they're delicious. Go to the Roman Baths, don't drink the water though, it's revolting. Book everything in my name,' and then he spoke in a firmer voice, 'and make sure you're remembered. Drop things so the waiter has to clear them up, complain, be demanding, that sort of thing. Now, this is important, on the second day, check out of your hotel after breakfast and take a trip into the country, even if it's raining. Go somewhere nice and quiet. In the evening, come back to London. That's all, have a couple of pleasant days in the country. I'll give you £25 for expenses,' he waved his hand in a dismissive gesture, 'keep any change.' He patted his face with his handkerchief again, coughed and drank more brandy. Bishop was trying to get his head around the strange offer.

'Why Bath, what's so special about Bath?'

The man shrugged his shoulders. 'Nothing, it's just a convenient distance from where I wish to be.'

'Why do you need an alibi so badly?'

The man's face dropped. 'That's my affair, you don't need to know, just do exactly as I ask. No one will trouble you, after all, they'll think you're me and who knows, maybe I may be able to return the favour one day.'

'When would you want me to go to Bath?'

'Next Thursday and Friday will do.'

Bishop sipped his lager, playing for time. 'I'll think about it, I'll see what my wife thinks.'

The man smiled and shook his head. 'You won't have to think for long, you haven't got a wife.'

Bishop looked surprised. 'How did you find that out?' he demanded.

'It's not difficult.'

Bishop struggled to keep his anger under control. Although he was used to his life being chaotic, this was taking things to a whole new level, but £200 was very tempting. He went on the attack. 'So, who are you? did John Gray send you?'

The man looked confused. 'Who?'

Bishop lent towards him. 'John Gray,' he demanded.

'No, who's John Gray?'

Bishop watched his reaction and was satisfied that he didn't know Gray. 'Don't worry about it.' The conversation stopped and Bishop studied his double. It was strange, like some sort of out of body experience, the face opposite looked just like the one that started out from his mirror in the morning. He thought for a few seconds, then went on the offensive.

'Ok — we're doubles, so how'd you know my name and why have you been following me?'

Bishop's double hesitated. 'I needed to be certain you're right for my plan,' he looked around again before continuing, 'I'll arrange where we can meet again. I'll give you all my details, the expenses and the first half of the money then. I'll put a note through your door.' Bishop's double finished his brandy, got up and took a pace away from the table.

'Hey — I haven't given you my address.'

'Don't worry, I know it.'

Bishop's double gave him a cold smile, then left. Bishop sat in a daze. This whole business was bizarre, but worst of all, his double knew too much about him which was disturbing. He ignored his pie, drank his lager and then went back to work.

Bishop returned to London that evening, bought fish and chips and went home, still mulling over the day's events. He'd just unwrapped the soggy newspaper and was adding more salt when an envelope was pushed under his door. Inside was a note: "Meet me at the Regent Hotel, off Shaftesbury Avenue tomorrow at 7.00 pm. The room's in the name of Evans." By the time he'd opened the door, there was no one there.

Bishop didn't sleep well that night but eventually decided to go to the hotel, he had little to lose in seeing what this was all about. The following day was cold and misty and with his mind in a whirl, he managed little work. That evening he went to the Regent Hotel. Even in its hey day, the hotel wasn't good, but after years of neglect, it did well to rent by the hour. He went to reception. The scruffy receptionist was reading a newspaper and didn't look up.

'Yes?'

'Mr Evans please.'

The receptionist glanced at the guest book. 'Room 207, up the stairs, on the right.' Bishop went up the wide stairs; everything was worn and shabby. The neon light on the landing was flickering. He found 207 and knocked, a few seconds later, his double opened the door.

'Excellent, come in, sit yourself down.' Bishop sat by the dressing table. The room smelled stale; there was a damp patch by the window. A framed print of

Buckingham Palace hung over the bed. Bishop's double kept coughing and patting his face with his handkerchief, was more breathless than before.

'So, Mr Bishop; do we have a deal, £200 cash for two day's work? two days don't forget; tax free — it's more than most would earn in two months.' The offer was certainly tempting and he could easily take the time off. Bishop didn't hesitate for long.

'We have a deal, but out of curiosity, how will you know if I go?'

'Oh, I'll know exactly what you do. You must carry out my instructions to the letter. Book everything in my name and give me the receipts when you return.' He handed Bishop an envelope. 'Here's the £125, take my coat and hat and wear them to Bath, bring them back here at 11pm on Friday. When you go, don't take anything of your own with you, not even your door key if you can help it. May I see your lighter?' Bishop handed it to him, 'it has your initials on it, don't take it, use matches.'

'I'll have to take an overnight bag.'

'Of course, but remove any luggage labels.'

'This is all a bit extreme, isn't it?'

'Yes, and so's £225, but it's necessary. One slip up and my alibi will fail which would be most inconvenient. Here's a letter addressed to me, memorise my name and address and carry it with you at all times.' It was addressed to Mr Henry William Evans. Bishop studied it for a few seconds then put it in his pocket. Evans was now looking quite unwell. He didn't speak for a while, then sat heavily in the armchair and rubbed his chest. 'My heart ... not good these days.' he rummaged through his pockets, found a bottle of tablets, unscrewed the top and poured them into his hand, spilling some. 'My heart ...' As he tried to get to his feet, he made a gasping sound, his eyes rolled up and he slumped to the carpet, scattering the tablets, then lay completely still. He'd stopped breathing. Bishop tried to find a pulse, but there wasn't one to be found. Evans was dead. Bishop rushed to the door to get help but stopped, fate could be handing him the perfect way to disappear. He stood back, feeling both excited and guilty and thought for a while.

Bishop was shocked and a little frightened, but by changing identity with Evans, he'd be free of John Gray and all the other loose ends in his life. He eased his conscience by telling himself that Evans wanted him to swop identity anyway. He checked for a pulse again, then emptied his own pockets onto the bed. Evans was lying awkwardly. Bishop gently turned him onto his back, emptied his pockets and made a second pile on the bed. He picked up the bottle and tablets, then put his own possessions in the dead man's pockets.

Bishop was about to put his keys in Evans' pocket when he realised that he needed them to get back into his own flat. Leaving Evans without a key was suspicious, but he had no option. When he'd finished, he put Evans back into the position he was in when he died and took the envelope with the money, Evans' keys, the tablets, his comb, lighter, wallet and his silver cigarette case. He put Evans' hat and coat on and re checked the room. He even crawled over the dirty carpet again to make sure that he'd got all of the heart tablets and checked Evans again, opened the door, hooked the "Do not disturb" sign on the outside handle, stepped into the corridor and crept down to the lobby. The receptionist wasn't at his desk so Bishop strode into the street and as he went, he kept saying to himself, 'I'm Henry William Evans.'

Bishop took a taxi part part of the way home, then walked to his flat, made a coffee then sat and thought. It was too risky to stay for long, as soon as Evans was discovered, the police were bound to call. He decided to go to the Wellington Hotel in Waterloo until he could make further plans, it would make a good central base. He knew that he should visit Evans' flat immediately, but he couldn't face the thought of going now and even less of sleeping there. He decided to have a meal, get some sleep and visit Evans' rooms first thing in the morning. Having made his plan, he pushed the paraffin heater aside and took the smaller of his two suitcases from the top of the wardrobe and carefully selected a few clothes so it didn't look as if he'd moved out. When he'd finished, he inspected Evans' wallet, it contained a driving licence, a dry cleaning receipt and a dog eared cheque book. The used cheque stubs were blank. The more Bishop thought about Evans, the more he felt uneasy; Evans was too anonymous.

Bishop left the flat, walked briskly for a while, then turned a corner into a dark, badly lit road. Half way along there was a pub, as he approached it, a tall man wearing a trench coat and a cap low over his eyes came out of an alley. He had an unlit cigarette in his mouth and was searching through his pockets. Bishop was just about to pass him when the tall man addressed him with an Irish accent.

'Excuse me there, Sir, could I trouble you for a light?' Bishop put his suitcase down and tried to get Evans' lighter out of his pocket, but the comb caught in the lining. He took out Evan's bottle of tablets, freed the comb and had just got hold of the lighter when he dropped the bottle. The Irishman picked it up. 'So, how is the heart Mr Evans?' he asked quietly. Bishop looked aghast.

'My name's not Evans,' he said without thinking, 'it's ...' but before he could continue, the Irishman stood squarely in front of him.

'Oh, that's grand — you really do look like we've never met before, that Special Branch trainin' is truly grand.'

'You must be confusing me with someone else,' Bishop said, desperately trying to think of what to do next.

'Is that so?' The Irishman handed the bottle of tablets back to Bishop with the label facing up; it read Henry William Evans. 'Well Mr Evans, we meet again. You'll recall now that we told you when you and your Special Branch friends were in Northern Ireland meddlin' in our affairs that there'd be fatal consequences.' He looked around before continuing. 'You know, you've been a very careless fellow, we've been watchin' you for a long while now, you're not tellin' me you weren't aware, not with all your trainin'?' The sound of laughter came from the pub doorway. 'But we're truly grateful, we've learnt a lot.' Bishop grabbed his suitcase and tried to step past, but the Irishman blocked his way. 'It's way too late to be runnin' now.'

'Look, I'm not Evans, I can explain …' but the Irishman wasn't listening, he looked around again, then as he slipped his hand inside his coat, three men came out of the pub and pushed past them. The Irishman turned away and kept his head down, then as the men walked away, a car sped down the road, stopped and the rear door opened. The Irishman was about to say something but changed his mind, touched the peak of his cap, got into the car, and raced off.

Bishop grabbed his case and took a taxi to the Wellington Hotel, ordered a meal but only picked at it then went to the bar. Although he was a little more composed now, he felt isolated. Everyone in the bar seemed to be in some sort of parallel world of which he wasn't part, they were enjoying their lives, he was running from his. As he drank, Bishop reflected on his relationship with June, unlike other relationships, instead of moving on when they started to unravel, he seemed powerless to leave this one, his heart was hauling him north and his head tugging him south. The more he thought, the more he realised that his life had become a chaotic mess; he hadn't planned it that way, it had just happened, and the mess had piled into a mountain. As he put his glass down, the reality sank in; the mountain was now collapsing in an epic avalanche. He struggled to think clearly, everything seemed so unreal; either this was a nightmare, or he was going mad. He desperately wanted to talk to June but couldn't risk where the conversation could go. Bishop took Evans' envelope out of his pocket and read the address again; it was a flat in Putney by the Thames. The envelope contained a theatre program. The more he thought, the weirder it seemed. It was as if he wasn't looking at the real Evans, just an image, a staged presentation, something of smoke and mirrors, but why? How did Evans keep disappearing and why did he want him to be busy and obvious one day and alone in the country the next? Was the Irishman connected to any of this? He tried to take stock. By changing his identity with Evans, he avoided a violent confrontation with John Gray, but the Irish matter was deeply worrying, it looked as though Evans had somehow tangled with the IRA. He considered going to the police, but it was too risky, they'd never believe him, then he decided that it would all look different after some sleep and he'd visited Evans' flat. He had another drink, requested an early alarm call, went to his room, and fell asleep.

The following day, Bishop had an early breakfast and left the hotel, only to find thick fog had turned buildings into ghosts and had reduced traffic to a crawl with headlights on and horns honking. Pedestrians shrouded their faces in scarves and looked like the undead as they shambled out of the gloom, into the dim light of shop windows and away again. It all seemed unworldly but despite that he was grateful, conditions were perfect for a little clandestine activity.

The yellow acrid air tasted foul. He took a cigarette from Evan's cigarette case and lit it but it didn't help, so he flicked it into the gutter, then caught a tube to Putney Bridge. Trains were crowded but he pushed his way on and stood next to a man who'd been eating garlic. When Bishop arrived at Putney the fog was even thicker by the Thames. He asked for directions to Evans' address at a newsagent, went down a street of terraced houses and up the steps. He entered a dim hallway, squeezed past a large pram then went to the second floor. The cold flat had the charm of a dentist's waiting room. It consisted of a bathroom, a kitchen, and a bed/sitting room. He decided to search it from top to bottom.

The kitchen had a grubby electric cooker, cupboards and a table covered with a plastic cloth. The water heater dripped into the stained sink. The pedal bin and ashtray were empty. Cupboards only contained tea and tins of soup and the living area had a bed and a wardrobe that smelled of mothballs. The bedside clock had stopped. A dressing gown hung on the bathroom door. When Bishop had finished searching, he'd only found a few clothes and other basic odds and ends. He was extremely troubled about Evans now. It wasn't what he found that worried him, it was what he didn't find. The flat was too bland, there were no photos, personal effects, no pictures, letters, bills, no dirty laundry, not even enough food. This clearly wasn't where Evans lived, but Bishop couldn't find anything to indicate where he did, other than there were more keys on the key ring than were needed for the flat. After a final check around, he returned to the street.

A boat on the river sounded its hooter as it crept under Putney Bridge. The eerie, mournful sound sent an icy shiver down Bishop's back. He was on the edge of panic and had an overwhelming sense of foreboding and that sensation was back — he was being watched again. He was desperate to get away and hurried to the underground station and had just passed a small derelict dock when a shadowy figure stepped out from a gateway and walked toward him through the fog. It was the Irishman.

'Well, it's hello again Mr Evans, oh, and goodbye,' he said in his soft accent, taking a revolver out of his pocket.

SOFT BROWN EYES

The reception started a couple of hours before I got there. Drinks were free, the bar was heaving; the noise level rising and most people had reached the stage when whatever was said resulted in raucous laughter. I picked up an Americano and managed to get most of it to a quiet part of the room where I switched my phone off, leaned against a pillar and watched. Nobody asked why I was there although the odd person smiled politely as they passed. After maybe a quarter of an hour of people coming and going, she came to the edge of the crowd, stood, and looked around. Although she was on the sad side of 35, she was slim, unfashionably elegant, and stunning. She spotted me and walked over in a rather lazy way.

'Hello — are you a solicitor?'

'No. Why do you think that?'

She thought for a moment. 'The suit. You look like one.'

'No, not a solicitor.' She ran her fingers through her hair.

'What's your name?' I asked. She looked me in the eye and giggled; it was a beguiling sound. The sort of sound that could easily become an addiction.

'Catrina.'

I raised questioning eyebrows. 'Really?' She giggled again.

'No, not really. I never tell a man my real name at parties.'

'Now, why's that?' She leant towards me; too close. I could smell her perfume. She straightened my tie like we'd been dating forever. 'It gives a girl an air of mystery.' She finished her drink and handed me the glass, 'what's your name?' she asked. It sounded as if she was interested.

I looked around and pretended to make sure we weren't being overheard. 'It's a secret.' Someone across the room dropped a glass and it shattered on the stone floor. Laughter.

'Oh, do tell.'

'It's Lord Lucan.' She grinned and steadied herself by placing her hand on my chest. Her nail varnish was a subtle shade of champagne. She raised her eyebrows and gazed deep into my eyes and way beyond. Her soft brown eyes were the most beguiling

I'd ever seen; the sort you could spend a lifetime getting lost in. It was all I could do not to put my arms around her right then.

'So, what do you do Lucan?' she asked in a near whisper.

I didn't answer and had little difficulty in changing the subject.

'Has Catrina found any interesting people here tonight?' she smiled, bit her lip, and thought. A psychologist could have written a thesis on the contents of that smile.

'The fellow over there,' she said waving vaguely, 'was talking about life. Says there are two sorts of people, those who follow their feelings and those who follow their heads. Which are you, Lucan?'

'Head.'

'Me too — for all the good it's done me. You plan, figure things out, take care, be sensible and life still comes unstitched at the seams. Might as well live by the heart and hang the consequences. Is your head making you happy?'

'I'm too busy to think about it.'

'Sounds like you're on a treadmill; the faster you go, the faster you'll have to go.'

I held up her glass. 'Something like that. Your glass is empty; like another?'

She shook her head. 'No, I'm trolleyed; I should go, I've got a long day tomorrow.'

'What do you do during your long days?'

'Art director — advertising agency.' I was disarmed by her self assurance and captivated by her personality and what else we spoke of I don't recall. Time stopped and the room faded to oblivion. As we talked and laughed, she became unsteady and her speech slowed a little and I realised she'd drunk way too much and without realising it, I felt concerned about her; she shouldn't drive.

'Would you like a lift?' the question eventually soaked through and she shook her head.

'I live near.' Then for some time, she didn't speak and eventually opened her bag, took out a note pad and felt tip, wrote her number, and tore out the page. Her writing was bold and confident. Then looking deep into my eyes again, she smiled. 'Phone me, Lucan. Come around and we'll have a glass of wine.' As she handed it to me, I noticed a band of pale skin on her fourth finger where a ring had been. She turned and walking a little unsteadily said 'Ciao' and headed for the exit, then stopped and looked back. 'By the way, you didn't say what you did, Lucan.'

It was the last question I wanted to answer and uncertain of where it could go, I answered with a deal of reluctance.

'I'm a Private Investigator.' She stiffened, turned to face me, and took a couple of paces back. Her tone changed.

'And are you working now?'

I couldn't think of a way of stalling, so I answered. 'Yes.'

'And are you good at what you do?' As she looked at me, I sensed she'd prefer the reply to be 'no.'

'Very.'

'And can one ask who you're working for at the moment?' Before my head could hide behind client confidentiality, my heart let it slip:

'Your husband.'

She thought for some time before she spoke again.

'Do you like your work?'

'Mostly yes, sometimes not.'

'And now?'

Right now, one of the two.'

Looking at me with a straight face, she said in a firm voice:

'So, Lucan, what are you going to do?' Of all the women who had passed through my life, she set my pulse racing like no other. My head and heart went into blitzkrieg and not wanting to see which would win and after years of doing the sensible thing, I handed the note back.

'Nothing.'

She stood absolutely still, those bewitching eyes not leaving mine for a second. After an Aeon, she handed the note back again.

'Phone me, Lucan, come around and we'll have a glass of wine.'

OVER CHEESE HILL

(In homage to Under Milk Wood by Dylan Thomas.)

Sadly Broke New Town is never silent. As the moon steals behind the Bus Station, not all slumber. Manky foxes trot their hungry way down ill lit, bin lined, yellow lined, white hatched streets eyeing tasty cats slinking homeward from their nocturnal lawn scratching, post sniffing road signs instructing: Turn left; Turn right; Turn it in; whilst a weary goods train grumbles its way over the rails to the oil depot.

Sadly Broke rests cradled in the gentle bends of the M7 Motorway whilst early day Seagulls wheel and screech, chip searching around Miss Tilly's Battered Chicken Emporium as a cloud looks down on the small, soulless, graffiti coated town and searches for refreshing darkness, but finds gloom; seeks the perfume of spring, but smells fumes; hunts for reviving streams but only finds mud and fly tipped trash, and it weeps. As yesterday dies and St Mary's clock tolls the last stroke of midnight, babies snuggle, young girls dream of boys and wedding cars; young boys dream of girls and fast cars and Gerry Atric, manager of *Dun Carin,* the old people's home, lies the whole night long, tormented, guilt racked and sleepless, wishing the dreadful incident had never happened.

Alarms ring, kettles boil, cereals soak, pans fry full English cholesterol; one leg in, tea slurping, toast burning, second leg in, sock seeking, desperate children memorising undone spelling homework; 'The world is a sphere: s-p-h-e-r-e.' Mothers, one hand on wheel, the other tablet holding ear clipping their unruly broods as they drive the full half mile from home to school whilst Garry Baldi opens the shutters of his Gent's Hairdressing Salon. His first customer awaits.

'Good morning, My Lord.'

The Hon. Longstretch-Jones, High Court Judge, pushed his way past.

'Would be if you opened on time for once.'

'Soon have you on your way — usual Sir?' the judge grunted. 'Have you heard about the dreadful business at *Dun Carin*? would never have thought it could happen here.'

The judge grunted again. 'Nothing surprises me — so what did happen?' Scissors snipping, razor stropping.

'Well … I don't actually know the details yet, but I will before the day's through.' Talc puffing, mirror waiving, coat brushing; the judge paid and left; his hair looking exactly as it did when he arrived.

'Next please?'

Count Fornothing took the chair. 'You'd better not have put your prices up again, not paying a penny more than last time, times are hard, damned hard. So, what were you saying about Gerry Atric at The Care Home, not that I approve of gossip you understand?' Hair spraying, combe flying.

'Dreadful business, it's all over town; such a scandal, Police will be involved for certain; that sort of thing's got to be stopped.' Humming clippers; falling hair.

'What sort of thing?' question dead batted.

'Would you care for conditioner on that?' A much practised "gimme a tip" smile to the mirror, cape flicking away, seat descending, side turning. None forthcoming.

As the day progressed in morning cake shops, lunchtime restaurants, bus stops, check out queues, afternoon cafes; reports of the incident grew with every telling until, by evening; it had grown to such magnitude that questions in Parliament were inevitable. The population of *Sadly Broke* was incensed and those demanding action gravitated to the pub. Mo the Grass, the Police informer and his friend, Di Nasty the

assassin, were the first to arrive at The Dog &
Toothbrush. The landlord, Nosmo King, polishing
glasses with a "huff," greeted his regulars. Bar wiped;
pints poured.

'I can't abide abuse of old folks, makes my blood
boil. That's £7 to you,' hand waiting. Mo, note
offering, pint slurped. Change given.

Nosmo asked: 'Will the law do anything? no. Will
the police take action? no chance. That devil Gerry
Atric should be strung from a lamp post.' The pub
filled with others of a similar opinion. Di, cap over
eyes, pushed a reluctant Mo onto a chair.

'So, mates, is anyone with me?'

General Lea Wrong, pushed to the front. 'This
needs Military planning – gentlemen, arm yourselves.'
Billiard cues handed around. 'We'll march on *Dun
Carin* in two columns, one up Elm Street, the other
down Lime Street, catch him in a pincer action. Come
along you men, England expects and all that, we'll
teach the blighter a lesson, then drive him out of
town. Detailed planning's the thing,' he hesitated,
then whispered to Nosmo King, 'what's his name?'

'Gerry Atric, sir.'

'That's the fella. We'll drink a toast to the success
of the operation.'

'You buying?' General's hearing aid developed a fault. The eight vigilantes readied themselves, white feathers from the bar cushion were handed to all including Mr Watkins in his wheelchair and as the General was about to raise a toast, the bar door swung open and a beleaguered Gerry Atric staggered into the pub.

'Gimmi a large scotch — quick.'

Nosmo King raised eyebrows. 'But you don't drink.'

'I do now. Worst days of my life.' Large gulp. 'Gave the residents roast turkey for a treat; all the trimmings. As soon as it was served Mr Smith thought it was Christmas and shouted: "stuff the turkey, where's the mistletoe" and tried to kiss Mrs Wigmore-Hall. She screamed, swiped at him with her walking stick; missed and laid out Mr Stone. In no time, there was a riot; Complan in all directions, gravy dripping from the ceiling. Major de Feet grabbed the breadbasket, took cover behind the drugs trolley, and shouted "send for back up and get more rolls and make 'em stale ones," then started to take a bite from each and lobbed them all over the place, grenade style.' Gerry shuddered. 'Noise was horrendous. Matron banged the table with a ladle with such force, a turkey leg flew through the air and broke the Queen's photo. Mrs Wigmore-Hall shouted at Matron: "Right, you old crow, that's it, this is where you get yours" and beat her over the head with a French Stick. Matron's been hospitalised with concussion since.'

Someone from the crowd asked, 'So, who's in charge now?'

'No idea; when I left, Mrs Leftwing had tied her red knickers to a broom handle and was marching up and down the corridor chanting "Unite comrades, time for a worker's collective." She can run it. I can't take any more, I'm a broken man.' There was a stunned silence as the scene sunk in.

Di Nasty was in a daze; he took a swig of his pint. 'But Mrs Leftwing's 19 stone!'

'I know, it was a large flag.' Mo the Grass put his pint down with a thump, unable to drink more as the dreadful scene replayed in his mind like an endless loop. In case he hadn't pleaded a strong enough defence, Gerry Atric turned to the stunned crowd, raised his hands in exasperation and added:

'And to cap it all, so much food had been thrown into the piano, the piano tuner said he didn't know whether to use a tuning fork or a knife and fork. I'm finished. I'm going for another job; think I'll go back to the building game.'

Evans pushed through the stunned crowd with a copy of The Gazette in his hand, placed it in front of Gerry and pointed to an advert.

'You're in luck, you are.' Gerry read.

"Bodgit & Scarper – we build, you regret," have a vacancy for a bricklayer, no experience necessary."

'That's for me!'

Nosmo leant over the bar and patted Gerry on the arm. 'We were just saying what a wonderful job you all do at *Dun Carin*, weren't we boys?' There was hiding of cues, nodding of heads and mutterings of "absolutely" and "yes we were." Nosmo beckoned Gerry nearer and so no one else could hear, mouthed 'have that on the house, you deserve it.' Miraculously, everyone else instantly acquired the ability to lip read and the whole bar emptied their glasses in anticipation. Nosmo seized the opportunity, called time, and closed the pub before he could be charged with Riotous Assembly.

The moon rose over Cheese Hill, the town settled, boy racers raced, ambulances left; fire engines returned; girls dreamed of popstars; boys dreamed of fame, foxes left lairs to go late night shopping in the waste bins of Rookums Supermarket and Gerry Atric started another nightmare featuring gigantic red knickers and flying bread sauce and as St Mary's clock tolled the last stroke of midnight, a goods train rumbled over the tracks to the oil depot.

THE ROSE OF TEWKESBURY

Andrew Harington parked his rusty 4X4 by the towpath. He and his passenger, Steve unloaded their kit and provisions and then carried them to the bridge. Steve stopped and lent over the parapet. Pieces of masonry fell into the canal. He turned to Andy.

'The canal's in a rough state. That was a good move of yours, slipping Smithers a few quid to bring the narrowboat here for us.' He stepped back and brushed stone dust from his shirt. Andy pointed to another part of the parapet.

'This bridge is pretty knackered too — look at that crack. Maybe that's why Smithers wasn't keen on his hire boats being here.'

Steve took his rucksack off. 'If he did say, I didn't catch it, his accent's so thick I had a job following him but he did ask me twice why we wanted to come here.'

'I could understand him ok.'

'When I told him we're doing some archaeology, he said "rather yuw than me" and gave me the St. Christopher thing off his key ring, look.' Andy didn't look, he was cleaning his sunglasses on his tee-shirt. 'He insisted I took it, "go pokin' around that canal at noight an' yuw'll be glad yuw got it."'

From the bridge, they could see the horizon shimmering in the intense heat. The once busy countryside was now deserted; there wasn't a man, animal, or crop to be seen, just grass being charred in the blistering sun.

Andy pointed to a field next to the canal. 'That's where the dig is; the farmer says it's known as Millfield on every record he's ever seen and he thinks the canal could be on the site of the leat. Can you tape it out; we need to find the wheel and gear pits first; hopefully we'll be able to date it from them. The mill predates the canal; hopefully, the canal construction didn't wreck too much of the site.'

'Does everyone know who the Finds Manager is?'

Andy put his Ray-Bans on. 'Should do; it's Bob. When they arrive, get Anne to organise the tents; she knows what she's doing then crack on with the geophysics and keep an eye on Mitch, don't let him wander into the field with his metal detector, we haven't permission and don't let anyone put anything on social media. Clive couldn't get time off, so he's had a sudden attack of 'flu — don't want his boss seeing him in full health nibbling Fran's ear.'

'I thought their affair was over?' Andy didn't reply, he'd walked off towards the boat; Steve followed. They stowed their kit, made an early lunch, and sat on the rear deck throwing bread crusts to a brood of moorhens. Andy laid back to get a tan.

'I've got sunblock if you want it?'

Andy ignored him. 'What could be better, a summer break on a narrowboat and doing a dig with your mates? all we need now is a decent pub; must be something in Flaxbury.'

'Flaxbury? Flaxbury can be full of pubs for all I care,' Steve got up, 'you won't get me there.'

Andy looked surprised and followed him to the gally. 'What's wrong with Flaxbury?'

Steve made coffee and handed him a mug. 'My Great grandfather was a fireman on the Gloucester Railway.'

'Sugar?'

Steve pointed to a cupboard. 'His driver was Cliff Parker; full of himself, thought he was railway royalty. Our families lived near each other, most railmen did, we were all pretty close in those days.'

Andy stirred his coffee with a ball pen. 'Wasn't there a rail crash at Flaxbury?'

'1926, Parker and Great grandfather were driving that train.'

'And they survived?'

'Yea; bizarre, isn't it? it was foggy, they crashed into a freight train at Flaxbury Junction. The crash wasn't too bad, but their train was lit by gas. Some gas bottles exploded, set light to the carriages and the whole lot went up. Great grandfather was convinced the signal was green; everyone else said red. Parker blamed Great grandfather.'

'Think I read something about that,' Andy said as he packed an overnight bag. 'A load injured, umpteen burned to death and two kids who were never identified.'

'There was an enquiry, Parker was sacked; couldn't get a rail job after that. Having your reputation stuffed for crashing your train's bad enough, but he became fixated with the two dead children; became an obsession.'

'Weird nobody reported them missing; suppose their folk were killed as well.' Andy licked his pen and put it in his pocket.

'It was all over the papers, no one came forward and the enquiry thought not. My family said Parker became so messed up nobody'd work with him. He couldn't keep a job down so he and his wife got a barge, The Rose of Tewkesbury and worked canals all over this area but the older he got, the more screwed up he became; blamed Great grandfather for ruining his life.'

'Nice.'

'He even cursed Great grandfather — sent him abusive letters.'

'He did what?'

'One curse was that anything good for our family would come to nothing.'

'They believed that bunkum?'

'Absolutely, a lot did. That was it — the families fell out big time. The squabbling eventually died down, but I might've stirred it up again; I'm dating a Parker and older Parkers aren't amused.'

'Your Gill's a Parker?'

'Yeah.'

'You've known her for ages, why hasn't her family kicked up before?'

'I didn't tell them my surname until last month.'

Andy pushed a toothbrush into his bag.

'Good move — what'd you say she did?'

'Psychiatric nurse. Tell you something Andy; I'm having sleepless nights about her; she's got to get another job. Took her ages to qualify and now her patients are pushing her over the edge. She's too soft, can't leave work problems in the hospital. It only needs one more bad case and she'll be in there with them.'

'Sound like she needs to chill out a bit.' Andy picked up his car keys. 'I'm off to collect Bob and the digger.'

Steve put Andy's mug in the sink. 'You insured to drive the digger?'

Andy shrugged his shoulders. 'No idea — it'll be alright — don't panic — we'll be back at first light. Throw another rasher in the pan for us. Hasta la vista.'

When Andy had gone, Steve walked around the mooring site. In its youth, the canal had been busy; now in its dotage, it was useless, smelled dank and was seldom visited. Nature resented it from its creation and was making steady progress in reclaiming the site. Irises and reeds grew along the stagnant, green water. The towpath was covered in grass and saplings. Banks had subsided tipping trees over till their branches touched the water. As Steve looked around, he could see every shade of green he could imagine and many he couldn't. When he'd finished, he checked out the narrowboat and chose a bunk. The vessel was well equipped and had hot and cold running water and a shower. He pulled the curtains; secured the boat, took his camera, and went to the dig site.

Stonework from the mill had been stolen long ago and little remained. Like many mills, it had been rebuilt several times and wasn't easy to interpret. Steve spent that afternoon surveying and taking photos. By late afternoon everyone had arrived and he worked till early evening taping out geophys grids. The team settled in; prepared a communal meal on camping stoves and sat around drinking cider. Steve left when they started to sing folk songs to a guitar and wandered back to the narrowboat. He microwaved a meal; opened an iced can, sat on deck, and listened to the silence.

After another day's impressive performance, the sun took a bow; slid behind the trees then as an encore, turned the sky gold. Steve watched in awe, his lungs savouring their change of diet from city fumes to bittersweet, pollen filled country air whilst his mind wandered free from distractions. He thought about the Flaxbury crash and its aftermath and another subject that had been on his mind for too long. As dusk became night, shadows gained ground and trees turned to silhouettes, he decided it was time to be decisive, so he called Gill Parker on his tablet.

'Hi, love ... Bob and Andy? they've gone to Northampton to get a digger ... wish you were here.' Gill said something, but he interrupted. 'Love ... Tuesday night we're going to the West End for dinner, I've got something to ask you, something I've wanted to ask you for some time.' He couldn't make sense of anything else she said, Gill Parker had burst into tears. Despite Gill's repeated questions about what he wanted to ask her, he managed to finish their conversation, then sat in the dark till the midges started to bite. Eventually, as he went inside, he remembered Smithers' strange comment and to his surprise, the hair on the back of his neck stood up. Although they'd never met before, Steve got the impression that Smithers wasn't a man to be easily spooked.

Steve went below, made a coffee, set his alarm, and read his Kindle until he fell asleep. Although he normally slept through trains, planes and artics thundering past his flat, he wasn't prepared for the country being so noisy at night. Each time an owl screeched or a fox screamed he woke, but besides them, he became aware of something else, something disturbing and intangible.

So far, the canal had been motionless, but now, the boat began to gently rock. At first, Steve didn't pay it any attention, but as the rocking continued, he became more uneasy. He got up, searched for Smithers' St. Christopher, found it in his rucksack, dressed; grabbed a lamp and a mooring pin as a weapon and cautiously went on deck, only to find the darkness was treacle thick. The moon and a good many stars were cloaked by the trees. Even the hedgerows were barely visible. The night had a strange, chill demeanour and it was wasting no time in turning the crow black trees into sinister monsters while an unworldly mist twined itself around their roots and hovered over the water. It wasn't the eerie nightfall that set Steve on edge; it was a feeling of being utterly alone; it was as though all of humanity had left the planet leaving him behind. Besides that; every now and then he could smell smoke. It didn't come from the campsite, they didn't have a fire. He checked the narrowboat over. Everything was as it should be, so with his emotions scrambled, he went back to the cabin. The rocking stopped and as Steve hadn't slept in a boat before, he dismissed it but as a precaution, sat fully clothed with the mooring pin by his side until he fell asleep again.

Sometime later, the boat started rocking again, only now more vigorously. Steve woke again; switched his lamp on, picked up the mooring pin and crept back on deck. He saw nothing, but as he listened, among the sounds of the night was another; one he couldn't identify. It was steady and insistent and he could smell smoke again, only stronger now;

then he realised what the new sound was. He clutched the rail and started to sweat. It was the labouring plod of a horse approaching along the towpath. He shone his lamp towards it but all he could see was a moth flying to the light. With his head swimming, Steve backed away and collided with the cabin wall. As he tightened his grip on the mooring pin, a shape slid along the canal and the smell of acrid smoke became intense. The plodding of the horse grew louder and the rocking more violent. He stared in disbelief. The shape became the flickering outline of a barge. As it emerged from the mist, it steered towards him with smoke billowing from the galley funnel. Steve gasped. A bargee stood on the bow; sleeves rolled up; cap low over his eyes, pointing to two small coffins laying on its roof.

Steve gasped and pressed against the wall as if his life depended on it. After an eternity, the horse trudged passed his narrowboat, oblivious to its presence. When it seemed inevitable the two boats would collide, the bargee, pointed away from the coffins and straight at Steve. The frayed tow rope tightened and swept over the narrowboat like a cheese cutter. Steve tried to duck, but couldn't move. Then he saw a name on the bow. It was The Rose of Tewkesbury.

Andy and Bob arrived early next morning with the digger. The team had finished breakfast and some had made a start on the geophysics. Not finding Steve at the dig, his friends went to the narrowboat to wake him up and make breakfast. When they arrived, the day had started as usual; dragonflies hovered, skylarks wheeled over the meadow and although the sun was already drying the mist, the air was cool and still. Rooks called; swallows did aerobatics over the water and robins sang. It was like any other summer's day, there was nothing unusual. Nothing, except for two small coffins floating towards a reed bed and Steve, his face drained of colour, crouching on the rear deck with a weeping rope burn on his neck, staring with unseeing eyes at the water. He rocked endlessly back and forward muttering incoherent rubbish as a pair of swans swam on by.

DYING FOR A DRINK

Our college reunions were usually boisterous affairs, but this one was subdued. Subdued that is until the cocktails soaked in. As usual, everyone milled around the displays of old photos, pointing, laughing, and talking loudly, then stood in silence before the new Great War Roll of Honour plaque listing those chaps who had died for their country. The Master of Ceremonies stood in the doorway of the panelled dining room.

'Gentlemen, dinner is served.' We filed past him, some awkwardly with sticks and crutches and found our places around the mahogany table. As luck would have it, I was next to my old pal, Blenkinsop. As we stood and waited for everyone to settle, I whispered to him.

'I thought more would have made it.'

'Me too. I said that to Cavendish. He reckons they didn't because so many of our lads were subalterns. Become an officer, lead from the front, and get shot for the privilege.' I decided to let that comment go.

When everyone had found their places and we were all still standing, a piper started playing in the Hotel's foyer and with the volume of a steam whistle, processed with unmerciful slowness into the room followed by the maître d' carrying a Baron of beef. They circled the table in a clockwise direction. When they had passed us and with our ears still ringing, Blenkers lent towards me and whispered, rather loudly:

'Imbecile; should have been anti clockwise.' The beef was set before the Chairman who took a slice, nodded then said Grace in Latin and we sat. Blenkers nudged me with his elbow. 'Tell you what, old lad, these new American cocktails are the cat's pyjamas; I'm half blotters already.' He then unfolded his napkin. 'That Roll of Honour makes grim reading — didn't see Stanbury's name on it; is he here?'

'No, he married a divorcee in 1912 and they moved to Australia.'

The entre was served and the waiters discretely removed the plates of those who could only use one hand, cut their food into small pieces, and silently returned them. It was a new duty, already well established. War has unforeseen consequences.

'Shame, he was a brick; liked him; were you at the last reunion?'

'What, when Atkinson was taken short during the speeches and peed in a champagne bucket under the table?'

Blenkers snickered. 'It was yours truly who gave it to him. Never drinking fizz here again, I can tell you.' And with that, he drained his soup bowl with the alacrity of a bilge pump. He was never one for finesse, 'rather partial to Sherry Consommé,' he added as he put his spoon down with a clatter, 'never asked before, old lad, what were you up to during the War?'

'Gallipoli; absolute disaster from the off. And you Blenkers?'

'Me? Reserve Occupation. I inherited the family engineering firm. Years back, my grandfather, bless 'im, decided we should specialise in making springs. We landed some very tasty Government war contracts; I can tell you.' He noticed my disapproval. 'Oh, got my War Service badge — wore it all over the place. I couldn't have joined up if I wanted to; business would have folded without me. Feel a bit bad about it all the same.'

The fish course was served and we didn't speak until it was cleared. The maître d' poured our wine. When he was out of earshot, Blenkers spoke again.

'Who's the fellow sitting to the right of Cavendish; don't recognise him at all?'

'Nor me. Need to hear him speak to know who he was. That's the trouble with these shindigs; none of us are the people we were; we don't even look the same and everyone's putting on an act; bet they're all claiming to have made good.'

Blenkinsop looked around to make sure we weren't overheard. 'Not me. Want to buy an engineering company?'

'What, yours, why?'

'Bally orders are drying up since the war and we keep losing what contracts there are to America; we can't compete. To make things worse, the men are getting bolshie; think they can run the show better than management.'

'Why can't you compete?'

'Americans have mechanised and reduced labour costs. They've got modern electrical kit everywhere.'

'So, do the same then.'

He shook his head. 'Costs a fortune and we can't borrow at American interest rates. Even if we did, our orders are too small; need another war to make it pay. After the last lot, no one'll be mad enough to start another; we've lived through the last war, never be another.'

'Very true.'

'And I'll tell you something else,' he stopped to empty his wine glass and raised a finger for more, 'I reckon the writing's on the wall for British firms if things continue as they are. Thinking of selling up and investing in American industry — import American cars or put the lot into US stocks — make a fortune. That's where the future is; America, you mark my words.' I didn't know what to say, so said nothing. The noise level of chinking cutlery and babbling voices rose as the third and fourth courses and their wines were served.

'Think I'll give the torte a miss; had it here before, too dry for my liking. Bye, the bye, is that Cooper over there with his collar backwards?'

I looked where he was indicating. 'The Reverend Cooper, if you please?'

'Would have staked my life he'd take the cloth; his scrawny neck was made for a dog collar.'

I placed my hand on his arm. 'Easy, old chap, he might hear you.' I checked to see we weren't being overheard. 'Have you noticed he only drinks apple juice?'

'What, never touches laughing fluid?' Blenkers seemed to have difficulties comprehending the idea. 'Strange fellow.'

'Absolute teetotaller; big on temperance and Band of Hope. Claims booze is evil and never did anyone any good.'

'Really?' It looked as if an idea was attempting to surface in Blenker's mind. Eventually, it did and he turned to face me. 'Fancy some sport?'

'What type?'

'My £5 says before the evening's through, I can get him to accept that not drinking is as dangerous as drinking.'

'He'll never go for it.'

'My fiver says he will.'

I offered him my hand. 'You have a wager.'

There were speeches, more speeches, anecdotes, reminisces; each more embroidered than the last time they were told; jokes which wouldn't have been funny if we weren't all well oiled, toasts to this, that and the other then cutlery rattled and wine glasses clinked as they were cleared from the table and coffee cups clattered as they were laid in their place, all indicating the meal had entered the final furlong. The maître d' offered a box of cigars; Blenkers choose a Bolivar, and the maître d' clipped it and roasted the end. I declined them.

'May I have a Black Russian?' The maître d' raised a finger to the waiter who followed with the cigarettes.

'Mr Frobisher will take a Sobrane.' As I took one the waiter took his new lighter from his pocket with a flourish and lit it. The flame didn't look as if it had decided whether to cooperate or give up. As Blenkers blew a cloud of smoke, its heady aroma, the smell of fresh coffee and the fragrance of expensive aftershave all seemed out of place. They were from a lifestyle that had been slaughtered in the trenches. The Master of Ceremonies stood and brushed an imaginary speck from his red tailcoat; it was new, made of best, Yorkshire Barathea wool. He was proud to be the only person wearing colour in a room of black and white.

'Gentlemen' he announced; 'the cricket first X1 wish to take wine with the second X1.' There was laughter and ribald comments. Waiters ignored the banter and placed baskets of nuts and ashtrays on the table.

'Now to bait the hook!' Blenkers raised his voice, 'Cooper!' Cooper looked around to see who called, then spotted Blenkinsop. 'Would you care to take a brandy with Frobisher and me?'

Cooper cupped his hand behind his ear. 'Brandy, did you say?'

'Yes.'

'No, thank you, I eschew alcohol in all its forms — stuff of the devil.'

Blenkers patted his lips with his napkin. 'Hook baited; he eschews alky; pompous twerp.' He dropped the napkin and addressed Cooper again. 'Tell me, Cooper, doesn't the Good Book say somewhere: 'drink no longer water but use a little wine for thy stomach's sake?"

Cooper nodded. 'It does, but one suspects the Blessed Apostle, Paul was laying a heavy but unspoken emphasis on the word 'little."

'So, you see no virtue in it at all?'

'Absolutely none, it ruins lives.'

'Ah, would it surprise you to know that a man lost his life because he refused to drink alcohol?'

Cooper lent forward and pushed the candlestick aside to see better. 'Do inform me.'

'The incident was documented in the Reverend. R. Cutler's book "Original Notes on Dorchester."' Cooper smiled and nodded. 'The event occurred in 1830 or thereabouts. A condemned man was to be hanged in Dorchester and as usual for the time, his execution was set for 1 pm to give time for the Royal Mail coach to arrive from London in case it carried a last minute reprieve.'

Cooper nodded. 'I'm familiar with Cutler's work and the custom.'

'However;' Blenkers stopped to take a sip of wine and as he put his glass down, he whispered "get your fiver ready." 'Where was I? oh, yes, the poor devil was so traumatised, he wanted to get the miserable business over as soon as possible so as he was being brought to Dorchester, despite the urgent pleas to the contrary of the Constables who were with him, he urged them to hurry and refused the traditional parting drink at the Bell Inn and so arrived at the gallows early.' Blenkers whispered again: 'an ace coming up. As he was so insistent, despite his misgivings and it not yet being 1pm, the hangman prepared him, pulled the lever and down he dropped, but just as he fell, the Postmaster rushed up the hill shouting and bearing a reprieve. The hangman immediately hacked through the new hemp rope as best as he could and fetched a surgeon, but it was too late. The poor fellow was dead. What do you say to that?'

Cooper was still smiling. 'I recall the incident now. You have failed to finish the Reverend Collins' account. He recorded that the crowd who had been in the tavern since dawn, had no sympathy for the felon and shouted, "Sarved him right — 'e should 'av stopped for his drink."'

Blenkers was a little taken aback. 'And?'

'If memory serves me well, the surgeon was reported to have commented, with rather ill timed levity I might add: "I will stake my reputation on the fact; the poor fellow has taken a drop too much."' And with that, Cooper raised his glass of apple juice in a mock toast.

I held out my hand for the fiver. 'Think that's game, set and match to Cooper, old man. Care for a port?'

BYE COMBE VALE

Estate Agents described Bye Combe Vale as a desirable location. I was about four when we moved there and it certainly was a quiet, leafy suburb, but very isolated. The older residents said that nothing ever happened there, but that wasn't true.

The Bye combe ran around a small, but steep hill. On the higher side was a row of detached, Edwardian houses. We didn't live in one of those, we lived in the new Council Houses on the lower side. The folk who lived in the Edwardian houses looked down on us, both literally and figuratively and resented our presence from the start. Before the Council houses were built, the open ground was used as a dump for their garden waste, with us there, they had to take it up the lanes to the woods.

The folk who lived in the Edwardian houses were established, mostly older professionals; respectable people, doctors, and things like that. The men wore blazers and belonged to clubs and all the women seemed to be members of the W.I. Their houses had names, mature gardens, garages, and wood gates and a number had phones and some even had cars. Most had "daily helps." Our houses were in plots divided by a wire and were as the builders had left them. The older neighbours seemed to keep themselves to themselves, but one thing did unite them; they were damned sure their children weren't going to mix with the likes of us. That didn't give us children a problem, we just played together anyway, although it was a pain when the Jewish kids couldn't play on Saturdays and the posh kids couldn't come out in the evenings until they'd done their prep, whatever that was.

All in all, I guess there must have been about ten children in our part of the combe. Residents who were disturbed by us called us a gang, an accolade we were glad to accept. There were usually about five in the gang at any one time. Our exploits depended on who led the group on the day. The overall leader and oldest of the gang was Streaky Stedman who lived in one of the Edwardian houses. Streaky was tall, lanky, and big for his age. He didn't have siblings but acted like a big brother to us younger boys and like most of the children of the professionals, he went to prep school and was expected to go to Grammar School, then University. I felt deprived because nobody gave me any prep, although I accepted it as the way of things. The wealthy sent their children to private schools and then into the professions. For us, the boys got jobs and the girls were taught domestic science, country dancing and got married.

When Streaky wasn't around, the gang was led by Big Annie and heaven knows what she was into, she insisted that we trotted everywhere like ponies and frequently took us to a large, rather ugly house on the hill which she called "High Tops." She was convinced or at least tried to convince us, that fairies lived there, although, on the many occasions that we crawled around its large kitchen garden, eating their gooseberries, we never saw any.

Most of the hill was covered with trees and the derelict remains of a small farm. Lanes twisted, looped, and meandered all over the place, their original purpose lost to memory. They were dark, muddy, overgrown, and menacing places used during the day by dog walkers and the foolhardy who wanted a short cut to the road over the hill and at night by those with no good purpose at all. Streaky told us that the folk who lived on his side of the road were convinced that burglars hid in the lanes planning on breaking into their houses, but that didn't seem to happen, burglary was rare. Everyone else thought that "men" loitered in them.

When Streaky led the group, the activity largely centered on us playing dare. We would group at the end of one of the lanes and take it in turns to run as far up as we dared; the winner was the one who could stay the longest. Kenny, who was somewhat in awe of Streaky and acted as his henchman, claimed that Streaky had gone all the way around, in the dark and stopped for a fag at the style into the bargain.

'It was a Gauloise an' all, 'e got it off their French au pair.'

When it came to my turn, even though I was one of the youngest, I wasn't in the least afraid, after all, Streaky would look after me. I ran as hard and as far as I could and eventually, feeling a hero, returned, and sauntered around the final bend, trying to look nonchalant, only to find that everyone had gone home.

On the whole, we kids accepted most of our neighbours at face value, but there were some of whom we were wary. Old Dafty lived in a Council house further along the road. Something happened to him during the war and he'd go wandering about aimlessly, wearing his hat and raincoat, summer and winter and get lost. He had a high pitched squeaky voice and would close one eye and open the other wide when he spoke, a habit we mimicked endlessly. Old Dafty was often rescued, standing by the main road, unable to move and crying, he could neither cross nor return home. Not only that, he had "funny turns" which got worse after his wife died and were something to behold, not only would he shout and swear and wave his arms about, he'd get violent as well. Once he attacked the coalman.

The gang's main enemy was a neighbour we called Sparrow legs, a widow of substantial means who lived in one of the larger Edwardian houses. Sparrow legs was ancient and held old fashioned views even by Victorian standards. Streaky reckoned she was a hundred when she was born. She was five foot nothing, wore expensive hats, expensive fur coats, expensive perfume, expensive jewellery, expensive makeup and had the thinnest legs ever issued to a human. Everything was an outrage to her and she was forever demanding that we stayed on our side of the road and if we didn't, she was going to complain to our fathers, which she did, frequently. After a particularly indignant rant one November, Streaky who was very brave, put a banger through her letterbox and ran away. She phoned the Police. I don't know what happened, I hid for the rest of the week.

When I lived there, Bye Combe Vale still showed signs of its rural past. Besides the lanes and styles, there were small clusters of old cottages dotted around the district. Those were the final days when silence was alive and well and was soon to be driven to near extinction by progress. We lived before mobile phones and TV, if you had one started at 9am and closed at 11pm, often with a break in between. Those days were before we became addicted to the internet and became busy fools. Before technology started to assault us with everyone's opinion about everything, we were aware of the world around us and content with our own thoughts.

On those hot, never ending summer days, I used to lay in bed in the early morning, watching the sun rise through the open window, listening to the silence being disturbed by the cracked Angelus bell from the convent on the hill. Often, its echoing, discordant, three by three call to the devout was accompanied by cuckoos and when the wind was in the right direction, the cockerel from White's dairy farm in the distance. All these were part of a life that seemed to be unchanging, eternal, and secure, none of which was the case.

Not only did time seem to stand still in the Vale, but there was also an ordained rhythm to life as well. Without fail, each day had its allotted tasks. On Wednesday evenings, the scouts sang nonsense songs in the corner of the field whilst incinerating sausages on their campfire and Friday was shopping day. My heart sank on Saturday mornings when I had to take the shopping basket to the local shops for the weekend bread. Inevitably, the gang would see me and ask jeering questions about where my dress was and when was I going to start country dancing. But worse was to come. One of the Jewish families owned a colossal Great Dane who had the run of their garden. The postman often left the gate open and it would escape. The beast would wait for laden baskets to return from the shops, then hurtle into the road and pounce. All the baskets were at his head height and he would snuffle, lick and dribble on the purchases. Rumour has it that one shopper panicked and tried to outrun him, although I never met anyone who had witnessed the event, or the outcome.

Despite being isolated, on occasions, beret wearing Frenchmen would cycle around the area selling onions and the rag 'n bone man would drive his horse and cart at walking pace down the road calling "rag bone?" Even though I was young, I was aware that this was the end of an era.

Each of the days of the week had its high and low points, but Sundays had more than its share of low. Sundays never seem to end; I swear there were 36 hours in a Sunday. Besides everything being closed; for reasons I never understood, my mother refused to hang washing out and I was forbidden to play in the road.

When I was a little older, on Sundays I was sent to the grey stone chapel and spent the services staring out of the window over the gravestones erected in memory of people now long forgotten, to the allotments in the distance, whilst the preacher worked himself into a lather telling us that the broad road led to destruction.

It was one late summer morning when things started to happen. Mrs Cochran's baby was stolen in its pram; it was a top of the range Silver Cross. Luckily the gang were at school or we certainly would have been blamed. In those days people did things for themselves rather than expecting the authorities to do it for them. In no time, a posse of mothers was formed with some "daily helps" from the posh houses. Their first call was to Old Dafty's house. Although he was confronted by a fired up lynch mob, he fervently denied knowing anything about the baby, so the posse split into twos and threes and searched the area. Later that day, the baby was found in the scout's field, unharmed but yelling for a feed and in need of a nappy change. The pram was never recovered. As the baby was unharmed and nothing could be proved, the matter was dropped, but from thereon, there was a noticeable change in the mood of the residents and all the mothers, mine included, started to insist that we kids were not, under any circumstances, to talk to strangers. At the time, this instruction created a problem. Few people were stranger than our teacher, Mr Johnson and I wondered how long I could go without talking to him before I had a serious problem on my hands.

Change came to the gang with slow inevitability. We grew up and became more competitive. We built go carts from scrounged wood and pram wheels bought from Eddie's scrapyard. Eddie was an affable man who seemed to have an uncanny knack of being able to satisfy the insatiable demand for pram wheels. It wasn't the casualties or crashes which stopped our go cart races, nor the complaints from terrified motorists who were greeted by hordes of brakeless go carts hurtling down the hills towards them, it was Eddies' scrapyard being closed when he was jailed for receiving stolen goods.

The big change came when the nights drew in and men were seen loitering in the lanes again and Old Dafty went through a particularly bad patch and wandered about aimlessly all night. Kenny came through the lane which joined the combe to the only bus route when he was assaulted. Whatever happened and for whatever reason, he was seriously frightened. The police were called and Kenny's parents overreacted. He was grounded and not allowed out on his own.

The description of Kenny's assailant was vague, but at best, it was of a tall man wearing a raincoat and a hat. Over time, the description became embellished. Two versions prevailed; one fitted Dracula, the other Frankenstein. The police not only interviewed Kenny but also Old Dafty, who couldn't offer an alibi and who freaked out at the questioning and then had "one of his turns." He attacked a police officer with a kitchen knife which resulted in him being put in a straitjacket and taken away in a van. He never returned.

A day or two after the incident, Streaky disappeared. He didn't say goodbye, he just vanished. Mrs Stedman announced that Streaky had won a scholarship to a very prestigious school in Birmingham. Strangely, no one could recall her ever saying the name of the school, but overall, there was a general feeling of relief. The posh folk said it was safer with Old Dafty out of the way and the

Council House tenants said the same with Streaky's departure, but both sides agreed on one aspect of the whole affair, it was good to know that it was safe now.

A week or two later, one evening when the days were at their shortest, I met Johnny, one of the gang who was sucking a luminous green lolly.

'Give us a lick,' I asked.

'No, get your own,' he said, sucking furiously.

'Where'd you get it from?'

'Off a tall bloke up the lanes. Don't you go tellin' though — our Ma'll kick up 'ell, she don't like us eatin' between meals.'

Psalm 46:10

NO DOUBT ABOUT IT

Dedicated with fond memories
to K.B.Hancock
(1925–2014)
The last of the Impressionists painters

No one will ever find me. Even if they search through all the dead end towns in all the world and get lucky, they won't identify the alley, locate the correct building or get the right floor as my rooms are hidden and anonymous. My name isn't by my doorbell; no one need ring it anyway; I don't answer anymore as every caller is the bearer of grief. I live alone and visitors to my studio are banned. People, the lot of them, come with their hands out wanting something, a piece of me, or my vote or to sell me something I don't need for money I haven't got, or worse, they'll be irate customers after my blood or cops wanting my liberty.

On rare occasions when I want company, my imagination creates guests for me, like you. Don't look so surprised; you are a figment of my imagination. All my creations, at their worst, are more agreeable than reality, but I warn you, when I'm done, I snuff them out, and you'll be no exception, so don't start whinging. Right, move my dinner plate off that chair and sit over there.

'You want to know what? Well, ok, I'll tell you, but it's strictly entre nous — understood? right, I'd better check around first, you can't be too careful, there are ears everywhere, what with the police for one and "them" for another.'

I peeked out of my front door then closed and locked it, closed the windows, and pulled the curtains. 'Ok, keep your voice down and move closer. Now, days were when my paintings commanded five grand a time, but do they now? no chance; cultural desert out there these days. A few years ago, a top London gallery viewed my work; they said it was technically accomplished, but reactionary — bloody cheek. They wanted cutting edge like paint dribbled from the tube or blown from fire extinguishers.

'Why are the police after me? Well, a few years ago, fashions changed and my sales slowed. I was in a bit of financial bother and as luck would have it, a dealer asked me to paint something in the style of Cealey. What do you mean, who's Cealey? Frederic Cealey — the impressionist painter; that's his portrait on the wall, the one next to Manet's. Anyway, it didn't need to be signed; he gave me an advance, so I studied Cealey and his work. The man was a genius; obsessed with light and shadow; liked to paint in the open air; lived most of his life in France. He became my hero. I mixed my paint like him, copied his style and techniques 'till I could produce nearly identical work. The dealer sold the painting and asked for more, all unsigned and perfectly legit; they weren't copies of Cealey's, simply works in his style.

'After I'd done a dozen or so, he offered me a load of cash to forge an existing Cealey, but I turned that down flat, the risks are enormous but unknown to me at the time, he'd been getting signatures forged on my efforts then selling them as genuine Cealey's. That's given me sleepless nights since I found out. Trouble is, I think I know who added the signatures and there's nothing I can do about it. He was a lad I met, not long out of Art College, utterly brilliant, a genius if ever there was. I gave him a bit of encouragement, showed him some tricks of the trade, introduced him around and even gave him my gesso formula to prime his canvases. I was short of cash in those days, but he was utterly broke. One day he gave me a bottle of wine, nice one at that. I asked him where he got it. He said one of the dealers I'd introduced him to had paid him a ton of cash to do some small jobs, no questions asked. He hadn't been married long when his wife had a baby; it had some disability, can't remember what. With that sort of start in life, he definitely didn't need the law breathing down his neck, so I kept that to myself, not realising it would come back to haunt me.

TONY BILLINGHURST

'Eventually, the Met's Art and Antiques Squad arrested the dealer. He swore he didn't say who painted the rogue works, but he must have; I've seen cops give me funny looks, and they've got plain clothes people after me, no doubt about it. They might not get me for forgery, but they'll stick conspiracy to defraud on me for sure, which can't happen, I'm too old to do time. Anyway, that's all history now; I don't do impressionists anymore; I can't be associated with them; it could prove disastrous.

'What do you mean, who were the irate customers? well? Ok. When the dealer was arrested, his customers realised they'd been conned. There was one in particular who was spitting blood. He couldn't get at the dealer, he was in jail, so he's looking for me instead. The police are one thing, but a buyer with an injured wallet is something else, so I keep on the move.

'No, I don't consider copying someone's style is immoral; some say it is; Cealey did; said it was plagiarism. He could get vindictive — really nasty about it; paranoid some say. I think he was insecure, bit unhinged. He was a depressive, lived life in a minor key and had a short fuse. Most who met him couldn't stand the man. He could be alone in a room and still start a fight but most who saw his work loved it — still do. Now, copying a finished piece is something else. Every painting's a work of art, copy or not. Admittedly, some are better than others, but what's immoral is going hungry when so many people have too much of everything. Anyway, there have always been copies, look at Monet, he painted umpteen "Haystacks." Granted, any artist will kick up if someone forges their work – 'course they will; mark you, I'd be tickled if someone forged my work, means I've arrived. All the same, I'm glad Cealey's dead; who needs his sort of aggro?

'Although I say it myself, I've produced some good stuff but still haven't made the big time, but it'll happen, it's got to; it's damn well got to. Heaven knows I've tried hard enough. I tell you, I've been so desperate I've been to the crossroad at midnight to do a deal with the Man, but he was out, but I'll do it; with or without him; no doubt about it. Anyway, I've got a feeling my current painting's the one that's going to make me famous. Ok, I've work to do, now back into my imagination you go and breath a word of this and it'll be the worse for you.'

I went to the kitchen and made a sandwich with a bit of cold meat I found at the bottom of the fridge and poured a glass of wine from an opened bottle. After pushing the jugs of brushes aside, I eat at the small table by my studio window. The room still smelled of Turps where I'd spilt it last Tuesday.

The women in my life have long gone and my rooms are bachelor pads now. There was a pile of unopened mail on a beat up sofa. A pine table was heaped with tubes of paint, bottles and old mugs filled with brushes. My apron hung on a nail in the bookcase. Packs of frames and canvases leant against the bureau and there were piles of books everywhere. A bowl of cereals was on a biography of Man Ray, my pipe rack lived on the window sill, empty wine bottles were all over the place, full ones in the First Aid cabinet on the wall. A broken clock was on a shelf beside the radio and near my easel, the waste bin was surrounded by a halo of rubbish. I'm a lousy shot.

My current painting featured a schooner in a harbour. Why I chose that beats me, the sea gives me the creeps, I can't swim and how anyone sails for pleasure escapes me. When you're on the sea you're a speck in a void and if the waves get you, you disappear as though you never existed. Who needs that?

The sandwich was dreadful so I binned it, filled my pipe, and painted and smoked and painted and drank wine until becoming so tired and drunk, I ground to a halt. I inspected the painting; it was coming along nicely so decided to call it a day. As I pulled out plugs and checked locks, I glanced at the portraits on the wall. I swear it; Cealey gave me an evil look. I turned on him, but in a split second, he'd returned to his usual pose. With booze filled bravado, I squared up to his portrait. 'You can pack that up right now! Everyone needs to make a living; you know what it's like when the plebs won't buy your stuff, don't you? needs must. It wasn't personal, just business.' Feeling better after putting him in his place, I got into bed and made a mental note to wash the sheets sometime and tried to sleep, but it was no good; I had to get up and re check all the locks and windows, you can't be too careful.

After falling asleep I dreamt that Cealey was wagging his finger at me. I told myself he was dead, but it didn't stop me from having a nightmare. He chased me as I ran in slow motion through thick water and I couldn't get away. Eventually, I woke in a sweat with the duvet tangled around my feet, got out of bed, switched the lights on, brewed a cafetière of strong coffee and not finding a clean mug, poured it into a jug and added enough sugar to turn all humanity diabetic. With my mind befuddled and my head aching, I shuffled to my easel to be greeted with a scene so surreal I dropped the jug. My painting had changed! The colours were now muted and applied impasto; I touched it; the paint was dry. Try as I might, my bewildered mind couldn't decide if this was reality or if I was still dreaming. I staggered to the kitchen, rinsed the largest mug I could find, filled it with more coffee and kept drinking until my head cleared.

At length, I went back to my easel, only to plunge into another nightmare. The painting had changed yet again. 'For crying out loud,' I screamed, 'what the hell's going on?' My cloudless sky had become overcast, and the schooner was now a steamship. I had absolutely no recollection of making the changes. Were the culprits all the empty bottles lying around the studio — for heaven's sake, how many had I drunk? even scraping the surface with a pallet knife didn't work; it barely took the top off which was impossible, the paint had gone too hard for such a short time. I dragged a chair up to the easel, collected the cafetière, baccy and matches with the intention of not moving until I'd figured out what was happening. Having finished my first pipe, I was faced with three alternatives; either I'd been sleepwalking, or someone had broken in or something had happened which was not of this world. I covered myself with the duvet; put the poker beside my chair and willed myself to stay awake to see if I could catch the culprit.

Eventually, morning came. I got up feeling stiff and wobbly, drew the curtains and with great reluctance, inspected the painting. It was unchanged! I've rarely been so relieved and to celebrate, decided to tidy the place up. My head was pounding, so swallowed some pain killers then emptied every opened wine bottle into the sink. As I watched the stale liquid swirl down the plughole, the thought occurred that this was lunacy; the stuff cost £7 a go; it would be cheaper to get a couple of crates of beer in. My wallet warmed to that idea, but my creative karma baulked at the alliance of beer and paintings. Maybe it was right. Who could imagine Van Gough painting "Sunflowers" while getting outside a pint of brown ale and eating a bag of salt and vinegar? I collected the mugs, plates, and cutlery, stacked them in the sink; found the sweeping brush and swept the broken jug into a corner then watched mesmerised as dust glittered like diamonds in the sunlight. If I painted that, no one would believe me. Maybe I will someday.

After a shower, I felt somewhat better, so went to make breakfast, only to find the butter was rancid and there was too much mould on the bread. On checking the cupboards, it was clear I needed to go shopping, so locked my rooms, went to the high street, and returned a couple of hours later. Feeling more than a little jittery, I dragged myself to the easel. It was as I'd left it, even the portraits on the wall looked the same. I made lunch and drank the energy drink I'd bought. It looked like fizzy pee and smelled like drain cleaner, then got stuck into putting the painting back as I'd planned it. I made excellent progress but eventually ran out of energy. I was unaware of time and hadn't noticed it was dark, so cleaned my brushes, checked the locks and windows again and still having the mother of all headaches, swallowed more pain killers and went to bed.

Sunlight shone through the worn curtains and woke me the following morning. Holding my breath, I rushed into the studio and to my relief the painting was unchanged. I was famished and decided to have a shower, a good breakfast and finish the confounded thing once and for all. I even shaved my beard off, got dressed and went to boil some eggs, only to find they were a month out of date. I was tempted to take the dratted painting with me, but it was too big, so left it and reluctantly, slipped out to the shops again.

As I returned, I had a premonition something was wrong and as soon as I opened the door, my worst fears were realised. An accordion was playing "La Mer" in the studio. I looked in the mirror and a haggard face with a bloodshot eye stared back at me. Was this what insanity was like? was I going mad? I picked up the carving knife, crept to the studio door, kicked it open and charged in to find the music was blaring from the radio. I dashed over and ripped the plug from the wall. Then I saw it; my painting had changed dramatically. It was no longer an unfinished, semi abstract. It was a nearly complete, impressionist study of a ship beside a quay. I wanted to scream at the ridiculous situation, but fortunately, didn't, it would only have attracted the neighbours. Instead, I went to the bathroom and poured cold water over my head until I'd recovered my self control.

On leaving the bathroom I passed Cealey's portrait. I stopped dead. I looked again in disbelief. There was absolutely no doubt about it; he had an evil smirk on his face. That was the last straw. I ripped his portrait off the wall and smashed it over the back of a chair with all the venom I could muster, then threw the mangled frame onto the floor. The broken glass crunched under my feet. Having returned to my painting; the situation had become worse than ever; it had changed yet again. I beat my head with my fists; I must be going mad, there could be no other possible explanation.

Now, people were on the quay, waving; smoke billowed from the funnels and noise and steam seeped into the studio. The painting was both haunting and hypnotic. In front of the vessel were tugs in steam. Then it hit me; my blood ran cold — the painting was pure Cealey through and through. It had his brush strokes, pallet, subtle muted colour, and exquisite light on water. It was magnificent, and as I studied it, I was drawn to it and became one with it. Then I saw the signature, large and clear — my signature: Alfred James. I snatched at a knife and scraped and stabbed at the signature but without the slightest success. I couldn't even mark the surface so grabbed a tube of Burnt Umber to obliterate the whole thing, but some strange power prevented me from changing a single brush stroke. The studio was now filled with noise, it was surprising the other tenants weren't complaining. The ship was crowded with excited passengers. I'd given anything to burn the wretched painting right there, but I was under its spell and powerless. If that wasn't bad enough, the objects in the painting started to move. The ship blew three blasts on its whistle and the tugs took up the slack from the hawsers. My mind screamed at me; this was only a painting, but somehow my imagination had gone berserk with a twisted plan to drive me mad. Now as my studio walls faded away, I became drawn to the scene itself. Shortly, when all of me was part of the scene and it of me; against my will, I took a step closer, and without realising it, found myself on the aft deck where I was joined by excited passengers from the lower decks.

I was carried with the crowd to the rail and started waiving with everyone else but to no one in particular. As we got underway, the passengers thinned leaving me all but alone. I was desperately trying to hold on to my sanity. Was this a hallucination? I searched through my pockets, found my penknife, and jabbed it into my forearm. The pain was real and so was the trickle of blood. I clutched my arm and turned, just as two young ladies walked towards me, arm in arm.

'Excuse me, ladies, what vessel is this we sail on?' I asked, trying to stay calm.

They giggled. 'Oh, Lizzie, what a hoot! I think we've got a stowaway. Can't wait to tell the others; they'll never believe this fellow doesn't know he's on the Titanic.'

IS THAT YOU, DEAR?

Mrs Henshaw, grey haired and ancient before her time, resting her rheumatic twig fingers in her pinny lap, sat facing a large wall mirror and rocked the gloom away. Her frame was bent by discontent, missed opportunity, and twisted by rejection. The once sweet child was now a sour old woman who could curdle the milk of human kindness with a mere glance. Come good days she rocked and thought, come bad, she just rocked but on this middling day, she rocked and nursed her obsession with the past as though it was newly born. No longer recognising her own reflection, she shared her musings with the only one to pay her attention; a deaf-mute woman who appeared in the mirror and rocked with her each morning. All the people who'd been in her life had left and not one with as much as a wave goodbye. Since Mrs Henshaw had joined the unwanted generation of the elderly, she'd become an embarrassing vexation and something to be ignored.

A man in a boiler suit dug the garden and a heavy hand knocked on the front door.

'Is that you, dear?' she murmured in time to her rocking. 'Wipe your feet, bring in the milk, and let out the cat.' She closed her eyes. 'Teddy bear, teddy bear, turn around ...' and she, in her mind now seven years old, skipped with her friend, Pigtail Mary through tarmac melting summer days doing handstands against the school wall showing knickers to all. 'Did you marry your sweetheart; did he make good? did your dreams come true? do you pay me any mind?' As if it was yesterday, she recalled school friends; school bullies, tests, and exams, "could do better" reports, then big school, new friends, bigger bullies, "must do better" reports till one day, an old teacher in a worn grey suit marked the final day's register and with a warm smile, wished everyone "good luck and do stay in touch" but no one ever did.

Mrs Henshaw's childhood seemed to stretch to infinity and was a life of immutable routine. It was chip shop scraps as a treat on Saturday nights, church and roast beef on Sunday, clothes washed in a galvanised gas boiler larger than a dustbin; dragged from the garden shed every Monday morning, and set in the middle of the kitchen to fill the house with steam; the same boiler that cooked the Christmas puddings in November. Ironing Tuesdays, shopping Fridays; fruit in season, butterflies in summer, bright days, moth filled nights, fogs in winter, curtains frozen to bedroom windows, heat bumps, growing pains, tonsils and adenoids, Carol singers in the snow, Christmases with Aunties and Uncles who were no relations at all doing the Hokey Cokey in the parlour, fewer each year till none came anymore. 'Am I still your favourite, Auntie — am I?

Then first dance, first date, first kiss, first love, first broken heart till you, dear Donald, swaggered into my life, blotting out everything and setting my world ablaze. Mrs. Henshaw focused tear filled eyes on her mute visitor. 'Are you a part of someone's past?' Her visitor didn't reply. 'I loved him dearly — I really did. His mother found out about us and insisted he break off our engagement. She said there was Tuberculosis in my family. He did — he always did what she said. She didn't like me anyway and I cried 'till there were no more tears in the world to cry. Why can't we change our past, why can't we change our "could haves" and "should haves?" She closed her eyes as though she was weary and murmured under her breath: 'Friends ... sweethearts ... husband ... children ... grandchildren ... all washed in and out of my life like flotsam on the tide. One day I will be a thing of the past as well and for others to weep over, whether with joy or sorrow will be for them to choose.'

Two men in boiler suits now dug the garden behind the privy.

Plodding footsteps with the pace of an undertaker approached the back door. A heavy hand rapped and opened it without being bid.

'Is that the plumber?'

'No, Inspector Pritchard.'

'Oh, how nice of you to call again. I see you've brought a friend, how jolly. Has he come far? perhaps we can have a party.'

'No, Mrs Henshaw, this is Sergeant Watkins.' This was Watkins' first visit. He glanced around. The run down, grubby farmhouse looked the sort of place where you'd need to wash the soap before it could be used. 'We've made enquiries and no one has seen your husband for several weeks now. I have to ask you again, where is he, madam?'

'I expect he's in the garden, he spends so much time out there you know; loves gardening.'

'Don't you know exactly where then?'

'Are you married, Inspector?'

'Yes, last year, Madam.'

'When you're newly married you spend every possible moment together; when you're old like me, you spend most of your time apart; it happens to all of us; you'll see. Mr Henshaw's not far away; when you find him, send him in for his tea.'

Inspector Pritchard nodded to the Sergeant who didn't understand.

'What, Sir?' he whispered. The Inspector whispered back.

'Well, go on, have a look around.'

'But we haven't got a warrant.'

'Sergeant!' the Inspector hissed, 'we could get 10 warrants, it wouldn't make an atom of difference, look at her; her mind abandoned ship years ago; now go and look around the house, I'll keep her here.'

As the Inspector drew Mrs Henshaw's attention to the garden, Sergeant Watkins slipped past and crept up the ill lit stairs. He tiptoed towards the landing, froze, and drew a sharp breath. Two unworldly green eyes stared at him out of the gloom. He gasped and instinctively stepped back, missed a step, and narrowly saved himself from hurtling downstairs by grabbing the handrail. The bannisters creaked and swayed but no one came to investigate and all the while, the green eyes continued to stare, unmoved. He desperately searched in his pocket for his tablet, put it to torch mode, found the landing light switch, and flicked it on to reveal that the eyes belonged to a large, stuffed cat with a manky coat standing guard over the staircase. He inched past it and rapidly checked through the musty bedrooms. It appeared that nothing had changed in years; the walls in each room were covered frame to frame with pictures. Worn, floral rugs were set in the middle of all the rooms and heavy furniture filled every space. Evidence of Mr Henshaw was in abundance, but there was no Mr Henshaw.

Watkins crept downstairs and peeked in the larder; its walls were lined with pine shelves. There were rows of rusty tins and Kilner jars filled with preserves and pickles, all covered with cobwebs and dust. The room had a disturbing, sickly smell that he'd smelt before, but couldn't recall where. He was still desperately trying to remember when he saw a large bottle of liquid at the end of the middle shelf. The label read; "Formaldehyde;" he'd last seen it in the path lab. He rapidly backed out and briefly searched the kitchen. The walls and air were alive with flies. The room had little modern equipment except for a large chest freezer. His blood ran cold when he got near it. Flies were swarming over the lid. With difficulty, he prized the frozen lid open to be greeted by Mr Henshaw, frozen rigid and partly decomposed, staring up at him with his mouth open, surrounded by packs of deep frozen home grown vegetables. The kitchen garden had been particularly productive that year. Watkins recoiled and let the lid drop, sending a cloud of flies buzzing around his head. With one hand clutching his stomach and the other clamped over his mouth he hurtled past Mrs. Henshaw and the Inspector, wrenched open the back door and projectile vomited into the garden with full sound effects in stereo. The two men in boiler suits stopped digging, gave a rousing cheer, and applauded. Colleagues can always be counted on to give solace in times of trauma.

The Inspector followed him to the garden and waited, exuding irritation and impatience through every pore. Watkins moped his face with a grubby handkerchief. Looking more dead than Mr Henshaw, he faced his boss, desperately trying not to vomit again. It was his first day working with Inspector Pritchard. Not the way he'd planned it to go.

'So ... sorry, Guv ... he's in the freezer ... looks as if she tried to embalm him. The cat's been stuffed too, it's at the top of the stairs. Guv, she's a nut job.'

'Embalmed, with what?'

'Formaldehyde.'

'Where is it?'

'The formaldehyde? In the pantry.'

'Where else? You didn't touch it did you?' the Sergeant shook his head. Inspector Pritchard signalled to the two men in boiler suits to stop digging which came as a relief; the clay soil was heavy going and it looked like rain at any moment. The older man dumped his spade against the privy wall and sat heavily on a tree stump, lit a roll up, took a can of beer from his colleague's 6 pack, tore the ring pull off and drank it without a stop. Pritchard addressed Watkins who'd been watching. 'We'd better see if we can get a statement from her then, hadn't we?' he turned to go, then turned back. 'For heaven's sake throw a bucket of water over that and tidy yourself up then come in and take notes. Phone the factory for the usual backup and some female help. Well, get on with it then.'

The Inspector marched in to the kitchen, peeked in the freezer cabinet, closed his eyes, and gulped, then strode back to Mrs Henshaw.

'We've looked in the freezer.' Mrs Henshaw ignored him and started to rock again. 'Tell me what happened.' She didn't respond. 'Mrs Henshaw, when did your husband die?' The question was disregarded. 'All right then,' he demanded, 'how long has he been in the freezer?' Silence. Sergeant Watkins returned looking greyer than Mr Henshaw. Inspector Pritchard nodded, indicating he should take notes. 'How did your husband die Mrs Henshaw?' No reply. Then Sergeant Watkins gingerly walked around to face the old lady as if he was approaching his grandmother. 'Mrs Henshaw,' he said gently, 'you do know there will be an autopsy, don't you? did you try to embalm him?' she stopped rocking.

'You don't look very well, dear — upset tummy?' he nodded, 'tea, that's what you need.' She got up and shuffled to the kitchen in her worn slippers. Inspector Pritchard indicated to Watkins to follow her. She boiled water and stuffed handfuls of assorted herbs and leaves from a wicker trug into a large brown teapot. It had a chipped spout. She stirred vigorously with a wooden spoon; then put it on a tray with a huge stained blue mug and two cups, a sugar bowl and a milk jug and handed it to Watkins to carry. As soon as they returned, she filled the blue mug without adding milk or sugar and drank it straight down and poured herself a second and drank that. 'What were you saying, young man?'

'When did Mr Henshaw die, Mrs Henshaw?' she smiled at the Sergeant.

'Oh, not long ago.' She started to rock again.

'Why didn't you report his death, you know you should have told someone?'

She looked angry and stopped rocking. 'They would have taken him away from me.' Mrs Henshaw sat forward. 'He kept saying he wanted to visit his brother in Australia. I knew what that meant. He was always going on about Australia, said he wished he'd emigrated when his brother did. He wouldn't have come back, that's for sure. I wasn't having that.' Her demeanour softened. 'Would you like some tea; it was Mr Henshaw's favourite?' Watkins glanced at Inspector Pritchard who shook his head with gusto.

'In a minute maybe, thank you.' He waited as Mrs Henshaw drank more tea. 'Preventing a lawful and decent burial of a dead body is a serious offence, you can go to prison for that.'

Mrs Henshaw stopped rocking and as she started to get up, she spied the deaf-mute woman leave the mirror. 'No!' she screamed. 'You're not going to leave me either.' She grabbed the milk jug and hurled it at the mirror, sending the shattered glass flying in all directions. 'Now you'll have to stay forever.' She sank back and started to rock again, crunching the glass into the worn lino. 'I'm not going to prison, young man. I'm not going anywhere.' Smoothing her pinny with her twig fingers, she turned to the Inspector with a hint of a twinkle in her eyes. 'Are you sure you wouldn't like some herbal tea, Inspector, it's my own special recipe? I make it with the very freshest deadly nightshade.'

CLOSURE BY PROXY

My father died shortly after I was born. Mum's latest partner was a pig; he didn't like me and I didn't like him. To make matters worse, I think Mum was afraid of him; whenever we had arguments, she'd side with him. It all finally blew up on my 16th birthday with another row and I'd had enough. I told them to shove it and left. The last time I saw Mum she was standing at the garden gate crying. I didn't know what I wanted to do in life so I drifted from one dead end job to another, I even briefly considered joining the Navy but didn't and I did bar work instead.

In this pub, it always happens when it rains. The bus stop outside doesn't have a shelter. Those waiting put up with rain till it gets heavy then overcome their misgivings and come in and wait. Most keep their backs to the bar and face the window. The more brazen sit at the tables and don't give a damn. A few buy something small like a bag of nuts to ease their consciences. It's a biker pub and at night and weekends, it's jammed with petrol heads. It's a beer out of the bottle, full throttle service, shots of whisky, ear shattering, hard rock, head shaking, hot, stale, dingy place with leathers and tattoos at every turn and the largest, most aggressive jukebox on the market. The only thing drawing breath that isn't tattooed is the landlord's dog, Vincent, and even he doesn't go near the toilets they're so dire. Most of the time the place is awash with testosterone but get a biker alone and you often see a messed up hurting life. This game taught me most people put on an act but eventually, the real person breaks through the charade. When that happens, most want to talk and some find it easier to talk to a stranger; as a barman, being that stranger is part of the job.

That day, it was raining hard; passengers waiting for the bus crept in, desperately trying not to catch a barman's eye. Amongst the crowd was an older guy; he definitely wasn't our usual sort of customer. He wore a suit, tie, raincoat, and a Trilby. He looked around, hesitated, took his hat off, shook it, put it back on again then started towards the bar, got halfway, stopped dead, drew a breath, went pale and stared at me, wide eyed. One of the other barmen greeted him, but he didn't respond; I don't think he heard him. Eventually, he came up to me, still staring intently, then looking past me at the shelves behind the bar and pointed.

'Could I have one of those, please?'

'What, a pickled egg?'

'No, the pork things.' He picked up the packet, took out his purse and paid. He clearly wasn't going to eat the scratchings. 'Is this your regular job?' he asked putting them in his pocket.

'Yes, here most days.' I straightened the bar mat.

'Have you always worked in pubs?' The question didn't seem like small talk.

'No, I've had a go at a lot of things. It's all zero hours contracts now. When the boss fancies someone new the hours dry up then he chucks you out to make room.'

The old man looked indignant. 'But surely that's not legal?'

'Maybe not, but work's erratic when you're at the bottom of the heap. Trouble is, the bills aren't.' A bus came and most of those sheltering rushed out.

The old man turned to the window, then looked at his watch. He hesitated. 'I must go, it's been very nice talking to you ... Glenn.' It seemed he was making an effort to remember my name. 'Glenn. See you again soon.'

I thought no more about him, but the following day he came back. I was serving a Knucklehead and a rough cider chaser. Knuckleheads take a while, especially when you can't find a clean tumbler, so another barman asked the old guy what he'd like. He blanked him and waited for me to finish.

'Hello ... Glenn. Nice to see you again. Remember me, I was here yesterday? Is there any chance I could have a coffee ... do you sell coffee?'

'Hello. Sure, we can do you Americano, Short Black, or Latte.'

He looked confused. 'Oh, I don't mind. What sort do you drink?'

'Americano.'

He looked relieved. 'Americano it is then.'

'Small or large?'

He thought for a moment. 'Large please; life's all decisions these days, isn't it?' Two other customers came in, so I gave the old guy his coffee and left to serve them. The old guy put his newspaper and coffee on a table near the bar and sat. Every time I glanced at him; he was staring at me; it was unnerving. He waited until it was quiet again, then got up, caught my eye, and pointed to a half empty bottle behind me; I thought for a moment he'd chosen it at random. 'That one looks interesting, pretty colour; do you know what it tastes like?' I looked where he was pointing.

'The Calvados? it's a type of brandy — tastes of apples; it's nice.'

'Could I have one then please?'

'Would you like to go large for another £2?'

He didn't respond for a while as if the question was too hard for him. 'I'd better not, small will do. So, have you worked here for long?'

'Four months.'

In bar work, if a customer wants to talk, you hear what they're saying, serve others and keep the conversation going with bland chit chat. An experienced hand can have two or three conversations going at once. The skill is to leave each customer thinking you were talking to them alone. People come to bars to talk, few come to discuss and most leave with the views they came with. The old guy was different; he could talk on a wide range of subjects and always asked for my opinion. If I sidestepped a sensitive topic, he wouldn't let it go, he insisted I told him what I thought. He became a regular and only wanted to be served by me, and as time went by the conversations started to change. Other than asking how I was that day or was there much traffic on my way to work, he stopped asking me my opinion and started to tell me odd things. I didn't realise what had happened for a while until one Tuesday I spotted the change. He started as usual.

'Morning Glenn; how are you today? I'm a bit later this morning, I've been planting parsnips in the old strawberry bed, the one by the fence.'

I wiped a spill on the bar. 'That's nice.'

'Yes, tricky blighters, I've tried everywhere and they won't grow, so I thought I'd try there. It might work. The grass has started growing early this year, the patch by the kitchen window is still too wet to cut so I took the mower to bits and found why it was squeaking instead.'

I replied, scanning the room for unserved customers. 'Did that fix it?'

'Yes, a bit of fence wire was caught in it.'

The old guy was always polite and often didn't drink what he ordered and always left a generous tip. But every time he left, I felt uneasy, but not for any reason I could pin down. He'd been coming in for nearly three months and I thought he hadn't been looking too good lately but I didn't like to mention it. One day he got off his barstool a little more unsteadily than usual and instead of saying goodbye, he stood still. I looked to see if he was ok and I thought he had a tear in his eye. After a while, he lent over the bar, swallowed hard and patted me on the arm. 'Well, goodbye ... take care of yourself,' and he left, turned at the door, waved and never came back.

A few weeks later, an older lady came in, very cautiously. She wasn't our type of customer either. As she searched around the room, she spotted a large wall poster of a biker chick who'd forgotten to dress draped over a Harley. She recoiled, clutched her handbag tightly and took a rapid step back. She saw me, looked relieved and came over, rather hesitantly.

'Excuse me, are you Glenn?'

'Yes. What can I get you?'

Ignoring the question, she opened her handbag and took out two photos. 'Oh, I'd better buy something. Do you have tea?'

'No; I can do you some coffee.'

She clearly wasn't used to being in a pub. 'Better not, it doesn't agree with me. Can I have an apple juice then please?'

I found a bottle at the back of the chiller cabinet and as she watched me pour it, she seemed to be coming to a decision.

'Glenn, you don't mind me calling you that do you?'

I tried to put her at her ease. 'Glenn's fine, I answer to a lot worse.'

She didn't smile. 'Glenn — I understand a while ago my husband used to come in here.' She put one of the photos on the bar and pushed it towards me. It was of the old guy.

'Ah yes, I haven't seen him for a while. How is he?' She didn't reply, but took the photo and put it back in her bag. Looking at me closely she nodded and said something so quietly that I couldn't hear it, then she put the other photo on the bar, facing me.

'I wanted to come and thank you. You were a great help to my husband — a very great help.'

I tried not to look surprised. 'Was I?' She nodded to the photo. I picked it up. It was of a young man, my age and build. It was uncanny, we were so alike we could have been twins. 'Good heavens.' I couldn't take my eyes off the photo.

'Yes, this is our son. He was a Corporal in the Army. He was killed in Afghanistan last year — stepped on one of those improvised bomb things. He was terribly injured and died two weeks later. He and my husband had a silly row at the end of his last leave. He went back to Afghanistan and they never had a chance to make up. Talking to you helped him come to terms with our loss. It gave him a lot of peace. I think in his heart he was finally able to say goodbye to Jonathan. I just wanted to say I'm grateful to you — very grateful.'

She looked at me, tears welling in her eyes and picked up the photo. I didn't know what to say for the best. 'Do tell your husband I always enjoy our chats. I look forward to seeing him again soon.'

She shook her head, almost imperceptibly and as she turned to go, she whispered: 'Goodbye, dear.'

I watched her go and just said: 'Goodbye ...' but couldn't say more.

Ephesians 4 v. 26.

A MAN OF HIS WORD

It felt like I'd been walking all day and I still couldn't find the place. I asked two people but neither spoke English so woke a dosser sleeping in a doorway an' asked him for Greek Street. Eventually, he pointed down the road.

'Down there,' he mumbled, pointing left, ''s on the what's it — right.' As I left, he held his hand out, 'spare some change, Mister, I haven't eaten all day?' nor had I. I eventually found Greek Street; it was in the opposite direction. The restaurant was across the road; Chez something unpronounceable. I checked the note I'd been given; it said Doug Bailey had booked a table there for two at 1.00 pm.

The place looked top of the market and even at a distance oozed condescension. When I got closer, I found the framed menu hanging in the window like a work of art. I had £16, barely enough to buy a starter. It was a poncy outfit, all quasi-French; no prices, just a number by each item; not my sort of place, I'm a pie an' mash man, me, proper grub, not this foreign muck; I went in anyway. Bailey wasn't there although it was 1.15. I can tell you, to start with I wasn't too concerned; I thought maybe he'd been held up. The lights were low and they were playing Miles Davis quietly over the P.A. cool. A waiter appeared, he was wearing black trousers, waistcoat and bow tie; smart. He looked at me like I was a toenail in a takeaway an' I swear was about to say "deliveries at the back door," when he changed his mind; gave me a fake smile an' a slight bow. Fair do's, I didn't fit, I know; my clothes were wrong, my worn trainers were wrong an' I doubt if their customers usually have a scar on their cheek an' "hate" tattooed on their knuckles but I thought; 'aint life a bitch,' an' stood my ground. The waiter hesitated; calm dignity prevailed.

'Good morning, Sir, table for one?' I nodded an' he led me to a discrete table behind an enormous plant, fronds everywhere; monstrosity, it would have blocked my view; I wasn't 'aving none of that.

'No, this'll do,' an' before he could object, I sat at a table where I could see the whole restaurant. He handed me a large, leather covered menu an' asked if I would care for a drink whilst I decided; I ordered a large Macallan; no ice. The time was now 1.20. Anyway, I had a good look around; casing a place was a bit of a habit an' it was better than I'd expected so I decided to play for time an' sit it out. The room was a sort of rectangle with a flash bar at the end, four large mirrors behind an' an alcove stacked with bottles; expensive. The round tables had linen tablecloths, large turquoise plates with rolled serviettes, King's pattern cutlery an' polished glasses; classy. The punters were the types you'd expect, Henrys, suited, booted an' being ever so nice to popsies, probably their secretaries. I read the girl's body language an' thought, 'you lot are wasting your time; they've got your little number' but they wined an' dined without a care anyway; all on expenses no doubt. Bet they went back to their offices to sleep it off 'til it was time to go home an' tell their missus about the stressful day they'd had.

On the other side of the room was an elderly couple, straight out of Jeeves and Wooster; fossils, county types, cut glass accents, loud voices, talking tosh. He was lanky with buck teeth; she was so fat her skin struggled to keep everything in; gross. I thought, "blimey, girl, go easy shovelling more in, the wrapping can only take so much." The old trout wore a screamingly awful luminous pink hat at the table, nearly as loud as her voice which could be heard all over the room an' in the kitchen. At no time did buck teeth get a word in edgeways, doubt if he ever could; the wimp, bet she was a laugh a minute at W.I. meetings. Any wannabe dictator could take a master class from her on how to talk down the opposition.

The waiter sidled over but I blanked him an' he left but didn't give up an' a few minutes later came back an' didn't move this time. I couldn't make sense of the menu, so took a chance an' pointed to the second item on the entrée list. The waiter wrote on his pad. The mains list was a mile long, all goujons this, confits that, lardons and noisettes. I wasn't about to order any of that lot an' give the waiter a laugh, so handed the menu back. 'What you got that's not got garlic, can't eat it, wrecks my guts?' He showed no emotion — perfect poker face, opened the menu, handed it back and pointed to a section.

'Of course, Sir, I understand. May I suggest turbot meunière if you would care for fish or the sirloin is especially good, Aberdeen Angus, we dry cure our own; not so much a meal, more an experience.' Sounded good so I ordered steak, medium rare. 'Everything is cooked to order, so it does take a few minutes I'm afraid.' Suited me.

He made another note. 'And to accompany your steak?' I couldn't give a monkey's as long as it wasn't none of this al dente rubbish so I shrugged my shoulders. 'May I suggest petit pois, Pommes Frites, sautéed mushrooms and green beans perhaps?' I was impressed, this guy was the biz. Although I'd rather have a load of chips with a steak, I agreed. I couldn't see tomato sauce anywhere but didn't ask, I didn't want to look a total prat. My nerves were on edge now, beginning to get frayed 'round the edges — know what I mean? So, I downed the whisky in one for a bit of Dutch courage. The waiter had X-Ray eyes an' spotted my empty glass, floated over an' handed me the wine list. 'Would you care to order wine, sir?' I glanced at it, nothing I recognised so turned to the reds, located the French, found the most expensive ones an' ordered a bottle, no point mucking about. The waiter hesitated an' looked troubled; I guessed what he was thinking; 'could I afford it?' that was an easy fix; I told him it was one of my favourites, he looked relieved and now showed interest. 'Very good, sir, an excellent choice, if I may say so.' He then unrolled my serviette an' lunged for my crotch. I was a split second from giving him a smack in his teeth when I realised, he was only spreading the serviette on my lap; things people do for a tip; narrow squeak.

The waiter left and shortly returned an' presented a bottle with a flourish, label up; he would have played a fanfare if he'd had one, I nodded; he carefully uncorked it, placed the cork by my plate an' poured a little into the largest of my wine glasses. I knew the routine here; seen it on YouTube; I picked the glass up by its stem, swirled, sniffed, and sipped; no doubt about it, it was red wine so nodded an' the waiter wrapped a napkin around the bottle an' half filled my glass; stingy sod. As soon as he'd gone, I filled it to the top. Eventually, my starter arrived. It looked lost on the plate; square thing with cheese stuff on top; if I'd wanted cheese on toast, I'd have ordered it; bunch of con artists. I was getting hungry by now so knocked it off in a couple of bites then got stuck into the wine. After I'd necked three glasses, I began to get the point of this wine game, all the same, it wasn't a real drink; not like half a dozen pints of decent bitter.

I checked the time again; it was 1.45; had something gone wrong? maybe Bailey wasn't coming; caught Covid or something; plan B was beginning to look like a goer. I pushed my chair back to give me room to leg it if the proverbial hit the fan. It scraped on the floorboards, the whole restaurant must have heard an' figured out what I was doing, but no one took any notice; 'course they didn't, the sound was drowned out by Miles Davis, humming air con, scraping plates, rattling cutlery, murmuring voices all topped off by Mrs Face Ache-Jones opposite who'd aired her views on female Bishops, the European Union, the Ukraine an' Vlad the Invader, immigration, declining standards in public life and was now demolishing the Government. I told myself, don't panic, hold your nerve, you've done it a hundred times before, so I counted to ten an' hung in there. Just as well, a few seconds later the waiter brought my steak, asked if I would like anything else, wished me "bon appetite," topped my glass up then Doug Bailey made a grand entrance followed by a face I didn't know.

I'd got Doug at last; he was difficult to find of late, never around our old haunts, always on the move, didn't associate with the likes of us anymore, even dressed differently; he now wore a long coat over his shoulders; vintage Crombie with a velvet collar an' cherry red lining, looked bespoke, 400 notes of anyone's money, carried a brief case tooled with his initials; Gothic gold letters; he'd joined the manicured nails an' whitened teeth brigade; the burke. He glanced around, didn't clock me which was no surprise, I wasn't expected to be released yet. So, at last, here he was; Doug Bailey, MBE; Mr Celebrity, reformed career gangster, turned to God or so he says, done good, top guest on T.V. chat shows, now on a nice little earner with 10 grand a pop for after dinner speeches, more than we pulled for some jobs, best-selling autobiography, consultant for gangster films, sought after for conventions, self satisfied regular nice guy, and an old partner in crime. As he slipped his coat off an' held it at arm's length the diamond in his pinkie ring glittered in the light, so did his new gold tooth, always was one for a bit of glitzy tom. He'd got stockier; his close cropped hair was greyer and he'd either acquired a beer gut or was 5 months pregnant. Two waiters materialised gushing charm an' greeted him, he was a regular; one took his coat, the other ushered the two of them to their table an' presented them with menus.

This was the weak part of my plan; it was the flaw that could nause everything up an' put me behind bars again. I moved my chair to the left a little to give me a completely clear sight line and bolted the steak down mega fast, all the time keeping an eye on Doug. Shame to rush it, it was ace. The face with Doug was fawning all over him; made me wanna chuck up an' they didn't stop yakking, they were giving it some, ten to the dozen. Timing was crucial if I was going to get away with this. I called the waiter an' asked for the menu again. He enquired how my steak was; you gotta be fair, it was the best lump of cow I've ever had so I told him, 'outstanding,' not that I'd had one in years. He cleared the table. The dessert menu was easier to get my head around, although what on earth Balthazar chocolate truffles and glaces et sorbets Maison were, I had no idea, although I did recognise chocolate profiteroles; Ma used to make them at Christmas; hers looked a mess but tasted wonderful, I went for them. I really fancied a mug of builders an' a fag but opted for filter coffee and petite fours; daren't ask for tea, I knew it would turn into a flaming quiz show; 'which would you prefer, black, green, herbal, decaffeinated, chai, Assam, Darjeeling or ruddy Earl Grey?' can't stand twenty questions about food. As I waited, I willed Doug's mate to push off, drop dead, vanish, evaporate; I wasn't fussed which; I needed Doug to be completely alone, but he didn't; just kept nattering. I finished my coffee, slowly.

Shortly, the waiter approached an' asked if everything was satisfactory. I needed more time, so ordered a glass of Hennessy an' the bill. Shortly, they both arrived; the brandy in a cut glass balloon, the bill on a small plate. I read it, my head swam — it was ten times what I'd ever paid for lunch before, I checked it again; you could nearly buy a whole caff for that down our way, it was an eye watering amount; great!

Here it was, at last, the time had come to settle our old score. I carefully looked around; no one was watching; good, so I slowly slid my hand to my inside my jacket pocket.

After a final check around, I took the document pouch out, folded the bill in half, then slowly sipped the brandy. I'd bought the pouch that morning from a charity shop, it was dog eared but had a strong zipper; champion. As I was about to tell the face to push off, he got up, laughed an' headed to the loo for a jimmy; perfect. With my heart pounding, I drained my brandy and got to my feet; the waiter spun around an' stepped towards me then stopped when I strode over to Doug's table an' sat down. Doug dropped his bread knife with shock; wicked.

'Good heavens — Charlie!' he gasped, then whispered, 'when did you get out — how are you — what you doing here?' I could see the cogs spinning; then he changed gear an' played for time. 'Good to see you — how've you been...?'

I stopped him by raising a finger. 'Hello Doug, you pathetic runt, thought I'd come an' give you a couple of little prezzies.' He looked confused. I handed him the pouch an' my bill. As he picked the pouch up an' looked inside, I asked him who the face was.

'My literary agent, not that it's any business of yours; wants me to write a follow up to my autobiography.'

I sniggered. 'That's nice, I enjoy a good laugh — gonna be another work of fiction, is it?'

He ignored the jibe an' showed me the empty pouch. 'What's this for?'

'It's for my 40 grand cut from the Chester Street job.' He looked like a cornered rat, then leant over the table towards me.

'I haven't got it...'

I interrupted him again. 'Don't tell me, you put it on a collection plate somewhere.'

'Don't be so bloody stupid; I haven't got it because Kenny Yates had it away on his toes.'

'So, find him and get it.'

'I can't,' he said, 'I tried, he vanished, no one knows where he is; word is he might have had it away to the Maldives.'

'The what?' I asked, 'Why there?'

'No extradition treaty; it's an Islamic country but they sell booze an' accept US dollars at their holiday resorts, he might have gone there; plenty of female Brits on holiday for company as well, know what I mean? anyway, I'm straight now, forgiven him, I'm a new man, I have the Lord in my life. I've never earned so little but I'm rich in blessings; besides, I never carry that sort of dough about, too many villains around.'

'Oh, don't give me that old pony,' I said, 'you're on a good earner here, best-selling book, guest on T.V. chat shows every 5 minutes, after dinner speeches 8 days a week an' we all know when we did jobs you skimmed off our cuts as well — you've got the dough — there's a bank on the corner, get it, I'll wait.'

'Charlie, I'm telling you, I haven't got it; I'll buy you lunch for old time's sake, but that's it, no more' an' he handed me the bag back.

I pushed some glasses an' cutlery aside so I could lean closer to him. 'I done 5 years for that job an' I kept shtum about you, kept you out of it 'cous you told me you'd see me right, I took your word, you owe me, big time. I don't wanna blow this stroke for you but this is business an' I gotta have my cut, my lad Sam needs some expensive medical treatment; urgent like; it's not available on the NHS and I'm gonna get it ... whatever it takes.'

'Sorry to hear that,' Doug didn't show any emotion which was no surprise, he'd always been short on humanity, nothing new there then. He turned towards the loo, clearly hoping the face would come out so he could change the subject.

'I promised Sam we'd get him better an' when I give anyone my word; they know they can stand on me, even a kid.' I've seen Doug's stubborn look before, he didn't look like he was going to cough up easily, so I played my ace an' took a photo out of my pocket. 'An' we're all lucky that night watchman didn't croak, what you shoot the old geezer for, we could have handled him, no trouble?'

Doug shrugged his shoulders. 'I told him to freeze, he moved, it was his fault.'

Now wasn't the time to argue the point. 'The law an' the court lent all over me to grass up whoever did it but I never told anyone; kept my mouth shut but that story must be worth a fair few bob, especially now…'

He bent over the table, knocked a glass over an' pointed a finger at me. 'Don't even think of pulling that one,' he said. 'Anyway, who's going to believe you, a jail bird fresh out of nick or me, Doug Bailey; I even met the Queen, she gave me an OBE and this isn't a gig, I have found the Lord, straight up.'

'Yea, yea, yea….' course you have, so when did you get religion then?'

'I can tell you exactly, August 8th, six years ago.'

I sat back an' savoured the moment. 'Well, isn't that strange; you were still at it with the rest of us after you say you found God, we did the Chester Street job on November 20th six years back. You're pulling a stroke.' I leant forward again and pointed at him, 'but I won't blow your cover if you cough up.'

That threw him off balance. 'Maybe I am a bit confused about the dates;' his answer was pathetic, 'anyway, it's all behind me now.'

'Doug, it's me you're talking to, not some media mug — I don't buy it.' I handed him the piccy, it showed a stub barrelled .38 revolver, mean looking bit of kit. I looked around to make sure we weren't being overheard. 'Meet my under the Man in The Clock outside Padding station, day after tomorrow, 11 am. with the dosh or this piccy goes to the filth an' my story goes to the highest bidder. People will believe me 'cause the shooter's got your dabs all over it…'

'No way have you got it,' he spat, 'you're bluffing; I gave it to Lee Grant and he told me he'd got rid of it.' Lee Grant was the fourth member of our firm; we did a lot of blags together, he was our treasurer, raised the working capital an' got rid of artefacts that could link us to the crimes. Doug sat back looking pleased with himself. 'Besides, if I go down, I'll take you with me.' That was the old Doug. The face came out of the loo.

I was half expecting Doug to say something like that so I had another card up my sleeve. 'No, you won't, I've already done time for that job, I'm fireproof, besides, take a closer butchers at the photo, the shooter's on a copy of yesterday's Racing Post, Lee did get rid of it, he gave it to me for safe keeping an' if you don't cough up you can watch your world go down the pan an' that's a fact, stand on me.' I got up, beckoned to the waiter who came over as rapidly as dignity would allow. I told him, 'Mr Bailey has kindly offered to pay my bill, isn't that nice of him?' I turned to Doug who'd just lost his appetite. 'Give the man a nice big tip, Doug an' think on,' He regained some of his bravado, quicker than I expected an' opened his brief case; took out a bunch of booklets which he handed to me as the face reached the table.

'I have found the Lord, straight up, I turned my life around. I'm done with the past, I'm out and I'm not going back, no more running from cops, locking horns with wannabe mobsters and no more nick, I've done all the time I'm gonna do and you know what? at last, I can sleep easy at nights – you need Jesus in your life too, Charlie — read those.' I put them in my pocket as he turned to the face. 'This is Doug, an old acquaintance, Doug — Simon Harrison.'

I shook his hand. 'Nice to meet you.'

Doug picked up his bottle of wine and filled the face's glass. 'Unfortunately, Charlie's got to go, haven't you, Charlie?'

No point in staying, job done. 'Yes, things to do. Think on what I said, Doug.'

I wasn't going to leave my bottle for the waiter to have away so as I nipped back to neck the last of it,

I caught Doug out of the corner of my eye as he unfolded my bill, I thought he was going to have a 911, 'How much?' he yelled; I enjoyed that moment as much as the steak; good 'un. I left, went into the street, around the nearest corner, lent on the wall of an empty shop an' got my breath back. That whole thing was kinda weird, 'aving a free nosebag, putting my plan into action, not getting nicked an' meeting Doug again even though he'd changed. I couldn't put my finger on quite how he had, but he was noticeably different. Maybe I had as well, after all, prison does strange things to you an' it was five years or more since I last saw him. We used to know each other well, had the same roots, went to the same school an' time was when all four of us were brothers in crime, thick as the proverbial, bit unsettling.

Doug didn't cough up the dough, time was running out so I raised it from a loan shark an' got a job as a long distance lorry driver. Doug continued to behave like nothing had changed, he even had the neck to visit jails telling the lads why they should stop being naughty boys.

I was home one evening in front of the box channel hopping when he was there again on the biggest T.V. chat show of them all, The Matthew Foster Show; laying back on the guest sofa like he owned the place, all the big names were on that show at one time or another, D list celebs, soccer players caught in bed with someone else's squeeze, media numpties who'd said the wrong thing to the wrong person at the wrong time, whole load of them, you know the form. He exuded charm with his butter wouldn't melt look, took everyone in, but I knew there was a different side to him. Way back, our firm started to do bigger jobs an' other gangs began to poach on our manor, Doug went ballistic an' vindictive as hell — it was outright war for a time, got so bad I had to sleep with a gun under my pillow; what a way to live; when you're not doing time, you're running from the law and waiting for a petrol bomb to come through your window an' what do you get out of it? a broken marriage, screwed up kids, dead mates an' little else while gormless actors make fortunes portraying crime as glamorous, it's not, it's grief all 'round; really tiddles me off.

One evening a few months later after a long day, I was binning my junk mail an' working through a 6 pack, when there was a ferocious banging on my door. My blood ran cold — I'd heard that sort of knocking before; there's only one sort of low life who hammer on doors like that; I opened it and was right, two stuffed shirts were there brandishing police warrant cards. 'What do you two comedians want?' They asked if they could come in. Experience has taught me you might as well so I pushed the door open and left them to close it. I didn't invite them to sit.

'Charles Arthur Hall? Can you tell us please, where were you on the night of Thursday 19th last month?'

I thought for a minute. 'Driving, long distance, spent the night at Tebay services, Cumbria.'

'Anyone who can corroborate that?' I got up, went to my file an' took out a receipt. The cop made a note without thanking me and as he turned to go, he asked, 'do you happen to know Dan Mellors?'

'Who?'

'Danny Mellors.'

I thought for a while. 'Name rings a bell. Think we had a kid at school called Mellors, not sure what his first name was, bumped into him once or twice since; that the fellow your thinking of?'

The cop made another note. 'When did you last see him?' he asked.

'A few years back.'

'Sure, not more recently?'

'No, why?'

The cop gave me a straight look. 'Thank you, Mr Hall; see you again, no doubt.'

'Not if I see you first,' I said, slamming the door. Course I knew Dan Mellors, he's one of your own, but I wasn't about to tell them that. The same thing happened three times or more in as many months; the last time they tried to fit me up for a blag in Kent just because one of the faces involved used a sawn off 12 bore loaded with rock salt, same as Lee used when we were at it; he preferred it 'cause it would mess you up a bit an' probably wouldn't kill you an' there was no need to aim as everyone in the room'd get their fair share; thoughtful. Actually, I knew all the geezers they were asking about; odds are they were all at it, 'course they were an' it started to play on my mind big time; it got to the stage I'd sit every night waiting for their knock, I was becoming a wreck. I'd done my time; I was trying to earn a legit living for once but it was typical of the filth; do a stretch and they think you've done every similar job since. I'd had it up to here, looked as if they were going to harass me every time some toe rag so much as nicked a hub cap. Was this what my life had come to? I decided to go down the pub an' drown them but as I put my jacket on, I found Doug's leaflets in my pocket, don't know why, but I sat an' started to read them.

I'd often wondered about this evolution lark and one thing always puzzled me, if things did evolve, where did the original stuff come from? saying it came from nothing doesn't bring it home for me, I mean, try telling a judge your loot came from nothing an' see where it gets you. After I'd read the second booklet, I started to think a creator God made a lot of sense. It was 2 am. when I put the last booklet down an' my head was spinning. Maybe, just maybe there was something in this religion stuff. Trouble was, I now had a load more questions than when I started an' I wanted answers.

The following morning, it came to me out of the blue, there was a guy on the manor called Holy Joe, bit of an odd ball; he'd been to theological college or something but wasn't a vicar or priest, maybe he could answer my questions. That night I found him in a back street drinker leaning on the bar. I explained about my questions. He emptied his glass of lager, told me answering questions was thirsty work but if I kept him topped up, he'd have a go. We went to a table and by closing time he'd answered pretty well all of the things on my mind, but for some questions, he just said "dunno, ask God, he might tell you."

As we were leaving, Holy Joe said, 'Charlie, go on the way you are and in ten years' time you'll either be doing life or dead. You're asking the right questions and you've got a good brain but think on this: either there is a God, or there isn't. When you get home, ask him to make himself real to you; he will and when he does, you'll know, believe me, then get yourself a decent education. He'll guide you what to do next, trust me,' so I did both an' that's why I'm here, a changed man with a new life.'

Matthew Foster smiled to camera then faced me as I sat on the guest sofa. 'Well, Charlie, that was amazing, so, your new life was all down to Doug

Bailey?' He held a book up and camera 2 panned in for a closeup. 'You can read all the facts of Charlie's fascinating life in his autobiography, "A Man Of His Word," out now.' He turned to me. 'Do you ever see Doug Bailey these days?'

'Now an' then.'

'Where is he?'

'He's just been moved from Belmarsh to Long Lartin, still doing time for shooting the night watchman on the Chester Street job; he's got another 3 years to go.'

Matthew Foster pointed at me, lent forward in his arm chair, and turned to the studio audience. 'Ladies and Gentlemen, a big hand for tonight's special guest, Charlie Hall; reformed career criminal, after dinner speaker, now working with schools and prisons and CEO of his new charity, "Out" which helps recently released prisoners go straight — Charlie Hall.'

BARNABY VOLE, HERO
OF THE RESISTANCE

The voles in Chestnut Lane were getting excited, it wasn't long before their summer holiday. Barnaby Vole had already packed his suitcase with important things like his bucket and spade and model yacht. He did this every year and every year; Mrs Vole took them out and put boring things in like socks; but this year, not all the other animals were thinking of holidays. The foxes who lived on the other side of Folly Brook were getting excited about something else. A bossy fox had told them they'd be a lot happier if they formed an army and took over every wood in the area. He told them they'd be the mightiest animals in the whole land and all the other animals would have to jolly well do as they were told. The foxes thought this was a very good idea.

When eventually the foxes had practised enough so they could march without biting each other's tails, the bossy fox told them to leave their dens and march down Chestnut Lane to the hedgerow where the voles lived. Voles don't like foxes. Foxes are crafty and have sharp teeth — lots of them. As soon as the voles heard the foxes were coming, they did what voles always do at the mention of foxes, they started to dig. They dug new burrows, longer burrows, deeper burrows and twistier burrows, which didn't solve the problem at all as they kept meeting other voles who were digging their burrows in the opposite direction. As none of the voles wanted to turn around and go back, a lot of fur was ruffled as they tried to push past each other which made the voles very cross indeed.

Mr Vole decided this couldn't go on. He called the voles to a meeting under the oak tree. After a lot of shushing to stop them talking, he told them his idea. 'Fellow Voles, we can't go on like this. We must do something about the foxes. They're much bigger than we are and so to beat them, we've got to outwit them. I say we need to nip them when they're not looking.' Every vole nodded and said "splendid" and "excellent." Eventually, some of the bravest voles offered to join Mr Vole and they formed a secret club which they called the "Resistance." Members of the Resistance wore black berets, coats with their collars turned up and dark glasses, which looked really cool. The only problem was that when the Resistance went out at night, they couldn't see and kept falling over and bumping into things.

It wasn't long before there were fox spies everywhere and it became too dangerous for voles to find food. As their food stores were nearly empty, some voles started to look rather thin. Mr Vole called the Resistance to a meeting in his burrow under the Yew tree. Before any member arrived, Mrs Vole gave the young voles their nightly spoon of elderberry syrup. As soon as they'd had their goodnight kiss, they started their nightly chant of:

'Story, story, story!'

Mr Vole raised his paw for silence. 'Not tonight, my dears, there will be double tomorrow. Now, you mustn't listen to anything that is said at the meeting.' As Barnaby's bed was in the parlour where the meeting was to be held, that was difficult as even under his duvet, he could hear everything.

The members of the Resistance squeezed into the parlour. Soon there was an ear splitting commotion as they tripped over each other's tails and all talked at once. As they had their dark glasses on, no one had any idea who was speaking, except Barnaby who peeked out from under his duvet. After a while, with a lot of helpful heaving and pushing, a rather fat, important looking vole climbed onto a chair. Standing rather unsteadily on his hind legs, he held his jacket lapel with his front paw, cleared his throat and looking at them over the top of his glasses, made an announcement. 'Fellow voles, this is a very serious situation,' everyone agreed. 'Something must be done because right is right and wrong is ... well, it's wrong, isn't it?' They clapped and cheered, but nobody had a clue what it meant. Encouraged by the applause, the fat vole waved his paw in a grand gesture and was about to continue, when he lost his balance and fell off the chair with an undignified squeak. When several voles had helped him up and found his beret, Mr Vole raised his voice. 'Fellow voles! Is it to be a dandelion then?' he looked around rather nervously. To his relief, they all said "yes." Eventually, Mr Green was chosen to go to the meadow and get one. He turned his coat collar even higher and crept out of the burrow. He returned a few minutes later, carefully holding a dandelion puff and looking pleased with himself. They inspected it; then gently carried it outside again. Barnaby could barely contain his curiosity. He tiptoed out of bed and followed them.

Looking rather suspicious, the members of The Resistance sneaked to a corner of the meadow. Barnaby raised his paw to ask why everyone tiptoed when you couldn't hear a vole move anyway, then realized that was rather silly. Four voles were set as lookouts. The other voles crowded around Mr Green who held the dandelion above his head. After more whispering and nodding of heads, they closed their eyes tight, each took an enormous, button popping breath, then started blowing. They blew and blew till they went dizzy and the dandelion seeds floated away on the breeze. The voles seemed very pleased; so, they eat the dandelion stalk, then went home.

The following morning at breakfast, Barnaby thought he'd burst if he didn't ask. '

'Dad, what are dandelion puffs used for?'

Mr Vole gasped, and dropped his acorn cup, spilling his blackberry tea on the table cloth. 'Shush!' he said raising his paw to his lips. 'You mustn't talk about such things … you mustn't even think of them … you …' But he didn't get further because Barnaby interrupted him.

'But what are they used for Dad?'

Mr Vole looked around nervously, waived his paw in agitation, then put his beret and dark glasses on and turned his coat collar up. He beckoned Barnaby to come closer, then whispered quietly. 'Dandelions, my boy, are used to send messages.' He looked around the parlour again, 'secret messages,' he whispered, tapping the side of his nose with his paw. 'If the Resistance gets a dandelion puff and everyone thinks of the same message and all blow together, the message is carried by the dandelion seeds to our special friends, the mice who live in Hester's Wood.'

'So, can anyone read the messages, Dad?'

Mr Vole laughed and shook his head so hard his glasses fell into his porridge and slowly sank below the surface. 'No, of course not, the messages are in a Top-Secret code, no one can read them.'

'If the code is secret, how can our friends read them?' Mr Vole went strangely quiet as he fished his glasses out of his porridge.

'Umm,' he said and absent mindedly put them back on. 'Perhaps we should have told our friends the code. Maybe that's why they haven't answered any of our messages.' Now, this was an important thought, but Barnaby wasn't paying attention to what Mr Vole was saying, he was too busy watching porridge slide down his glasses and drip off his whiskers.

After breakfast, Mr Vole asked Old Crow to call the members of the Resistance back to an urgent meeting. Later that day, they squeezed into the burrow again, berets and glasses on and coat collars turned up. Mr Vole called for silence; then announced in a hushed voice:

'Someone must go to Hester's Wood and tell our friends the mice the code so they can read our messages. It's an important and dangerous mission. Who'll go?'

There was an awkward silence and everyone became busy. One blew his nose in a red hanky and several polished their dark glasses. Four Paws Vincent inspected a valuable jug on the dresser till Mr Vole took it away from him. Eventually, Mr White said he'd love to go, but he couldn't leave the bakery or no one would have any bread. Three others announced they had important appointments. Mr Black said, unfortunately, he'd hurt his paw and he started to limp, which was strange because he wasn't limping when he'd arrived. Everyone else went quiet. No one offered to go. Now, the following day was Wednesday; bath day. Barnaby hated bath day. On bath days, Mrs Vole filled the bath with warm soapy water and put Barnaby and his brothers in together. When Mrs Vole wasn't looking, Barnaby's big brother used to push him under the water, hold him down, then let him go. Barnaby would hurtle to the surface, coughing and spluttering and every Wednesday, Barnaby was sent to bed without any supper for larking about. Barnaby had a brain wave. Without thinking further and standing on his duvet, he piped up in a clear voice.

'I could go, Dad, I'm only a little vole and I haven't got a beret, a coat or dark glasses, so no one will suspect me.' Before Mr Vole could say 'absolutely not,' other voles said 'what a marvellous idea,' and 'how brave!' So, Mr Vole reluctantly agreed. Suddenly, Mr Black's paw got better.

Mr Vole took Barnaby to one side. 'This is a very dangerous mission. I'm afraid you'll have to miss your bath, but if you succeed, you'll be a hero of the Resistance. You must go to the big Willow tree in Hester's Wood, knock three times and tell the mice the secret code. Then they will be able to read our messages.' He held his paw up with a raised claw which meant "pay attention!" Go straight there, don't talk to anyone and be very careful. Now, you know how to get to Hester's Wood, don't you?' Barnaby nodded.

Despite several voles carefully explaining the code to Barnaby, he couldn't remember it. He kept getting it backwards, so Mr White made up a catchy little song to help him. Mrs Vole fussed around and brushed Barnaby's fur one way, then another, then she licked her hanky, wiped his face and for some reason, started to cry. After a lot of wishes of good luck and take care, off he went, humming his song.

The meeting had taken so long that when Barnaby left, it was getting dark. Stars started to twinkle and his whiskers twitched as he sniffed the sweet, scented air. He went as fast as his legs would carry him, scurrying under leaves and bushes and avoiding open spaces. As he scampered through buttercups and ivy, he hummed his little song, but as he went, he got hotter and hotter. Eventually, he ran around a small gorse bush and there, in front of him lay the cool, clear millpond. Moonlight glistened on its surface.

Barnaby stood panting and gazed at it. It was so inviting, so cool, so refreshing. He put his front paw in the water and closed his eyes in bliss; it was even better than he imagined. He thought for a second or two, then forgot his secret mission, and dived in. The millpond was as good as it looked. He swam and swam. No one else was in the water to watch him, so he decided to try a flip dive. He climbed onto a large log and dived in, but the dive went completely wrong and he hurtled down waving his paws and tail in all directions and hit the water with a loud kerploosh!

When Barnaby eventually stopped blowing bubbles and came back up, he found that he wasn't quite as alone as he thought. A large pike had come over to watch him. He was a very friendly fish. 'Well, young vole, in all my days, I have never seen,' he stopped to lick his lips, 'diving quite like that.' He licked his lips again. 'Remarkable, you must show me how you do it.' Now, although Barnaby had been taught it was bad manners to leave when someone was talking, he suddenly remembered his mission. He pointed to the other side of the pond.

'Look!' he shouted. The pike turned around, then swimming for his life, Barnaby tore over to the bank and leapt out before the pike realized he was gone. Panting and feeling very frightened, he shook himself dry; then ran like the wind.

At long last, Barnaby reached Hester's Wood and found the big Willow tree. He knocked three times on the door. Shortly, the door opened a paw's width. A voice demanded: 'Friend or foe?' Barnaby's heart raced and he felt dizzy. No one had told him what to say.

'I — I don't know.' He screwed his eyes closed wishing he'd never offered to come. Resistance work was far more dangerous than he'd thought.

'Oh, that's all right then,' the voice said. The door opened and in he went. A rather stern looking mouse stood in front of him. 'Yes, young vole, what do you want?'

Barnaby told him and sang his song. The mouse motioned with his paw and pointed to a chair. 'Sit there young vole and don't move!' Barnaby sat on the edge of his seat and tried to keep still, which was difficult as he was trembling so much. The stern mouse went away and then returned with a lot of other mice who walked around and around Barnaby, staring at him. 'Tell us your story again,' the stern mouse said, so Barnaby did, trying not to cry. When he'd finished, there was a long silence. Eventually, a thin mouse spoke.

'That explains why we couldn't read the vole's dandelion message.' An older mouse was sent to get the messages. As the mice now knew the Top-Secret code, they could read the messages and they did, one after the other.

As they read, Mrs Mouse came into the room and took Barnaby to a table. She sat him down and gave him a jug of elderflower cordial and a ginormous, incredibly sticky, iced bun. Barnaby was ravenous. He nibbled, chomped, and chewed his way through it, getting sticker and sticker as he went. In the meantime, the mice made good progress reading the messages.

"Please send carrots; urgent." So, they got some carrots and put them on the floor. The next message read: "Can we have some carrots and acorns please?" they got more carrots and acorns and put them on the floor. The third message said: "we're out of blackberries, we're desperate, please send carrots, acorns and berries." Yet more carrots, acorns and berries were added to the pile.

Eventually, feeling near to bursting, Barnaby finished his iced bun and the mice had read all the messages. Mrs Mouse came back into the room and walked around the mountain of carrots, acorns, and blackberries. She stood, looking at Barnaby with her paws on her hips.

'Well,' she said with a smile, 'will you just look at the state of you, young vole! We'd better do something about you before your mother sees you.' Barnaby looking sheepish tried to rub his sticky fur down, but it only made it worse.

Mrs Mouse went away and returned with a huge bowl of warm water and a sponge. Holding Barnaby's neck firmly with her paw, she gave him a good wash. When she'd finished, Barnaby shook himself dry. 'You're a very brave little vole,' she said and gave him a big hug, then brushed his fur with a badger brush till his eyes watered. As there was now so much food on the floor, every mouse in the wood was summoned to help. They got the biggest cart in the wood and carried the food out of the willow tree and piled it in and sat Barnaby on top. They harnessed four dormice to pull it. Everyone was told to put their berets on and turn their coat collars up. The stern mouse gave them strict instructions:

'Now mice! Don't make any noise in case the foxes hear. This is an important mission. Good luck everyone.' He turned and looked up at Barnaby perched on top. 'Hold tight,' and they all set off with two visiting fireflies lighting the way.

The mice didn't stay quiet for long. As they were wearing dark glasses, they kept falling over and bumping into each other. By the time they reached Bluebell Wood, there was such a commotion of squeaks and squeals, it sounded like a huge army approaching, which frightened the foxes, who ran away, never to return. The mice eventually arrived at the hedgerow. It was nearly dawn when the voles had exchanged news and unloaded the cart. As they were all so tired, they fell asleep in a big heap.

When it was daylight, Mr Vole sent the voles home to fetch wheelbarrows and hand carts then he shared the food among them. Everyone was given plenty, and then Mr and Mrs Vole dug a bigger store to hold theirs.

As Mrs Vole and Mrs Mouse were busy baking acorn cakes, primrose biscuits and rose petal buns,

Barnaby licked the bowls until Mrs Vole thought he was going a rather odd colour, so after being sent to collect jam and honey from the larder, he was sent outside with the young voles to play.

The mice prepared a big party to celebrate and after a lot of games, which the mice seemed to win, they had a huge feast in the meadow. Tables were piled so high with food, they started to sink under the weight. Mrs Vole rescued the jugs of cordial and cowslip wine which were sliding to the edge. Before anyone was allowed to have even one nibble, Mr Vole said Grace.

When the voles and mice opened their eyes again the stern mouse banged his spoon on the table. He beckoned Barnaby to come to the front. With a big kindly smile, he presented him with his very own beret, dark glasses and the biggest, juiciest, carrot that ever was. On it, tied with a blue ribbon, was a label on which was written:

"Barnaby Vole, Hero of the Resistance."

And everyone clapped and cheered and Barnaby went a pretty shade of pink.

The Eric Miller Stories

COCKTAILS AT SUNSET

The alley was narrow and dark. Eric picked his way around the rubbish bins, stepped over a sleeping wino, counted three doors on the left, and then rang the bell by a cellar door. It was opened on a chain.

'Yes?'

'Eric Miller, I'm a new member.' A man inside muttered and a woman replied. The door was taken off its chain and opened by a thickset doorman who was putting his black coat on.

'First visit?'

'Yes.'

'Come on in.' He handed Eric two slips of paper. 'That's a list of events and that one's the club rules; the important ones are payment in cash for everything, no receipts given and no credit offered on the tables and you must put your smokes out before you leave.' He strained the buttons as he pulled his coat over his massive chest. He pointed down a steep flight of stairs. 'Take care on the stairs; cabaret starts in fifteen minutes; welcome to The Flamingo Club.' The woman sitting beside him offered a rubber stamp.

'Pass out stamp?'

Eric shook his head. 'Is Anita Tregowan singing tonight?' As she shut the membership book, she nodded.

Eric went down the long stairs into a nether world of hot stale air and tobacco smoke. He squeezed past the queue for the toilets. A man was lounging against the wall, feeding coins into a payphone. He made no effort to move as Eric tried to pass, so Eric jabbed him in the ribs with his elbow, then pushed past to the cloakroom and checked his coat in. He'd only been in the building a few minutes and already could feel sweat trickle down his neck. Eric did a tour of the club, then went to The Atlantic Suite which was cooler. He sat at a small table by the stage. All the waitresses wore black cocktail dresses; a few minutes later, one approached; she looked Asian and illegally young.

'Large single malt and ice please?'

'You like Cuban cigar as well?'

'No.' She nodded. Eric looked around. The cellar club was a maze of alcoves and small rooms, many on different levels, all lit by swirling, flashing lights that changed colour like a migraine attack. In front of him was a stage with drawn midnight blue curtains. On the far side of the room, a bar. People swarmed like ants. The lights dimmed a little, thunder rumbled through the PA system and built to a crescendo, then a spotlight followed the compere as he crossed the stage to the mic stand.

'Good evening, ladies an' gen'elmen. It'll shortly be cabaret time at The Flamingo Club.' As soon as he spoke, the room started to fill with people. Two couples sat at the table behind Eric and didn't stop talking. The compere mouthed a greeting to a couple as they went to their table. 'Time to freshen your drinks whilst I welcome our very own house band, The Dave Hillman Trio.' The curtains opened and as soon as the musicians started playing their signature tune, "Time is Tight," a fruit machine by the bar rang a fanfare of bells, the club lights flashed and there was a premature cheer of anticipation which stopped abruptly when the constipated machine only delivered a handful of tokens. The winner couldn't be seen, she was surrounded by a scrum of customers and waitresses collecting drinks. Eventually, when the room was full, the compere returned to the stage.

'Ladies an gen'lmen, your appreciation for The Dave Hillman Trio. An' now, the part of the evening you've all been waiting for, an' Gen'elmen, wait till you see this dress, it's rumoured there's so little material in it, Anita had to pay for what wasn't used.

A big hand please for the amazing, Miss Anita Tregowan!' The house lights dimmed, the ceiling turned to night and twinkled with stars, then Anita Tregowan, nearly wearing a maroon dress, slowly sashayed across the stage with the spot light flickering on her diamond earrings, stopped beside the mic stand, pulled it over to her as though she was embracing a lover and started to croon a heart rending torch song with such anguish that many had tears in their eyes. Eric was mesmerised by her husky voice; it sounded as if she smoked 40 a day. The waitress brought his drink. He threw a note on her tray and waived the change away.

After an excellent set of blues, torch songs and Piaf classics, Anita closed with "Cry Me A River," then took a well earned bow during which she thanked the band and left the stage. A DJ took over and assorted couples filled the minute dance floor. A while later Anita entered the room and spotting Eric, strolled over to his table.

'Well, hello again — so you joined the club then? Tell me, do you like my repertoire or are you stalking me?'

'If I said stalking you, would it be so bad?'

She smiled. 'Maybe, maybe not.'

Eric pointed to an empty chair at his table. 'That's some dress, gives minimalism a new meaning.'

'You like it? It's a Gallo & Moretti.'

'Could a stalker buy a lady a drink?' she hesitated then sat facing him. As soon as she accepted, Eric became aware they were being watched by a man who was leaning on the bar. His demeanour was hard and dead, one Eric was familiar with. 'So where did all that angst come from; can't see you working the streets of Paris or anywhere else on your way up?'

'Angst from life in general and grief from men in particular.'

'Maybe you need to change your men.' Anita shook her head and her chestnut brown hair fell over her eye. She brushed it aside. Eric would have been happy to watch her do that all night.

'All men cause grief; the only difference between them is the amount.' She picked up a beer mat and read the advert on it. 'You've never told me your name, Mr Stalker?'

'Eric Miller.'

'So, Eric — do you like my songs?'

Eric looked straight at her. 'The songs maybe, the singer yes.'

She smiled again and put the mat down. 'What do you do, Mr Stalker?'

'I'm a Security Consultant.'

'What sort of security would that be?'

'Working for companies finding staff with their fingers in the till; that sort of thing. I solve problems which need to be done on the quiet.'

'Been doing it for long?'

'Too long and the 29th of next month, 'I'm done.' The room changed to red.

'Then what?'

'I've a couple of ideas.'

'Why are you leaving security?' Eric finished his whisky then rolled the ice around his glass.

'The game's changed, security's high tech now. The best jobs are creamed off by kids with degrees who stare at computers all day.'

'It's called progress.'

'Maybe, but I'm left with crummy two bit jobs. These days, I spend my time poking around the dregs of society fixing problems for peanuts.' As they talked, a tall thin man with slicked back hair and wearing a corduroy suit approached the table. He put his arm around Anita and kissed her forehead.

'Hello, love.'

She gave him a deadpan glance, then waived towards Eric. 'Eric Miller, my husband, Andy McKenzie.'

McKenzie looked surprised, but before he could speak, Eric said;

'But, Anita Tregowan?'

'Stage name; Susan McKenzie isn't very Show Biz, is it?'

Eric hadn't met McKenzie before but knew several who had. None spoke well of him. He shot a glance at Anita who seemed more than a little apprehensive. McKenzie didn't notice; he lent forward and snapped his finger in recognition. 'Eric Miller — you're a hard man to find,' and as he spoke, the heavy who was leaning against the bar started to approach the table. McKenzie saw him and waved him away, then turned to Anita.

'Love, go and chat to the big guy wearing a bow tie on table 12, he wants to meet you, be nice — I need him for a while.' Anita got up and McKenzie sat and stared at Miller.

'Know who I am?' Eric was taken off guard and played for time. He replied slowly.

'I've heard.'

'I've been searching all over for you and I've been hearing disturbing things.'

'Like?'

'Like you're planning to retire.'

'Yes, so what?'

'Got a good pension have you, saved a nice nest egg?'

'What's that to you?'

McKenzie took a wad of envelopes from his pocket, selected one and put it on the table in front of Miller. 'Look in there.' Miller took a crumpled piece of paper out of the envelope. 'It's your marker for eight grand and you, sunshine, have till the end of the week to pay me for it.'

'But the marker's with Ron Fraser. We have an understanding. I'll pay when I can. He knows that.'

'Your Mr Fraser's got tired of waiting and sold it to me, it's mine now and if I don't get my money by Saturday night, it won't be a case of wanting to retire, you won't be able to work; you'll be about to catch a bad case of broken legs — capiche?'

'McKenzie; I need some time …'

'Oh, don't tell me you've spent all your hard earned readies on that wreck floating in Weymouth harbour. What's it called; the Saratoga, isn't it?'

'It's not a wreck, just needs a bit of TLC. Anyway, how'd you know I'd bought a boat?'

'I make it my business to know things about people who owe me money, like I know all about the little Security jobs you do and the devious ways you get results.'

'I do what it takes.'

'Course you do; we're alike you and me; go getters; we probably like the same things, have the same friends, but the big difference is on Saturday I'll be eight grand better off and you won't.

'I haven't the cash right now …'

'Ooh, that is unfortunate. You know, the way I see it, you're a man with limited options. Sell your boat, buy a wheelchair, or do a little job for me.'

'What job?'

'Nice easy one, won't take long.'

'If it's that easy, why not get one of your boys to do it, you've got enough of them?'

McKenzie rolled his eyes as though he was talking to an idiot. 'My staff are specialists, extremely good at extracting things, like money from people who won't pay, but this job needs finesse. They haven't much of that.'

'And if I decline your offer of work?'

'Then I suggest you sell your boat.' One of the bouncers came up to McKenzie and whispered in his ear. McKenzie got up and picked up the marker. 'I have to see someone; we'll talk again later. Oh, here's a little coincidence for you. When I was looking for you, I heard about your first wife's new man; interesting character — a cop. After what she's been telling him about you, he's started to investigate your second wife's death. Sounds as if he'd like a chat with you about it sometime.'

'She died in an accident.'

'Of course she did, I believe you, but we're both men of the world, we know how these convenient little accidents can happen.' McKenzie gave Eric a straight look. 'don't we?'

As soon as McKenzie left the room, Anita came back to the table. 'What was all that about, Andy seems to know you?'

'I owe a fellow eight grand; a gambling debt, McKenzie bought my marker and he's demanding payment.' Anita lent towards Eric and dropped her voice.

'Be careful; word is his new muscle's a psychopath.'

'I've dealt with his type before, they're not usually too much of a problem.' He swirled the ice around his glass. 'So, is McKenzie a source of grief?'

She glanced around carefully then spoke quietly. 'Listen, I don't know why, but I feel I can talk to you. He always was Jack the Lad, after the big buck; a bit of a bad boy; guess it was part of the attraction. He's never satisfied; doesn't matter how much we've got; he wants more. People are petrified of him but the only people who frighten him are medics. He's got the white coat syndrome — terrified of doctors even though his health is awful. He's addicted to Codeine — think he's addicted to danger as well.' She pointed around the club. Look at this place; he didn't need to open it, he says the police'll never find it but it's already full of low life selling everything you shouldn't buy. How long will they keep quiet; they'd shop anyone if it suited them. Andy was always a risk taker but he's turned into a monster; he corrupts everything he touches and these days he makes the Krays look like spring lambs.'

'If that wino in the alley dies, this place'll be swarming with flies and cops whatever he does.'

Anita lent back and beckoned the heavy to the table. 'I'll get him moved.'

Miller glanced behind him. 'I've been married enough times to know the look in a woman's eyes that says the fire's gone out.'

She ignored the comment, but asked, 'You married?'

'Twice; one walked, one died.'

'Eric, take Andy seriously, he's pulling in everything he's owed to finance something big. He won't talk about it and there's a lot of new faces around; think it's going to happen in three weeks' time. I'm used to his iffy mates, but this lot are serious players, gives me the creeps just having them here. Take my advice, if you don't pay, he'll set his apes on you and he doesn't make idle threats. He says this is his last job, well, project is what he calls them, then he'll retire. I've never seen him so edgy. Promise me you won't breathe a word, if he finds out, he'll kill me.'

'Do you want to retire?'

'No, singing's what I live for.'

'You're good at it; why don't you get a recording contract?'

'A couple of agents are interested but he won't let me. He doesn't like me having my own money.'

'But you've got a fabulous voice and great stage presence.'

'So, I've been told.'

'With talent like yours, any husband should help you to take it as far as you can, I would.'

'Would you — really?'

'Too true.'

'You're good with compliments, are you trying to pick me up?' Eric smiled.

'Well, I wasn't, but it's a very good idea.'

Anita sat looking at Eric. The house lights swirled, changed to gold and as Eric watched her, he saw desperation in her eyes and to his surprise, felt overwhelming concern for her. She was deep in thought then eventually spoke again.

'Do you have a bucket list for your retirement?'

'I'm not retiring, just getting out of security and clearing my head.' The ice in his glass had melted; he drank the last drops. 'There's only one thing on my list at the moment, take my new boat to the Caribbean, catch fish, go for the simple life; eat fruit, live on white wine and olives and drink cocktails at sunset till I've forgotten why I went there.'

Anita gave him a searching look, then eventually just asked:

'Alone?' Eric took care to get the tone of his reply right.

'Well, who knows? You got a list?' Anita checked around carefully then replied very quietly.

'Yes; get out before the sky drops in on Andy then sing for my supper.'

'Alone?' She smiled. 'Who knows?' She thought for a moment. 'I've fond memories of the Caribbean — the simple life sounds a dream.'

Eric stared into her eyes and tried to see past her sadness. 'You like boats?'

'Yes, love them. We had one once, I used to crew it but Andy got rid of it — it was hot and questions were being asked.'

Eric glanced around, then lent closer and gave her arm a gentle pat. 'Sometimes, dreams come true, especially if you want them badly enough.' The sadness in her eyes changed and for a second, he saw excitement, but it didn't last long.

'Why Andy keeps going, I don't know, he'll either destroy himself or someone else will, or his health'll pack up. He can't see it, but if he goes inside, odds are, he won't come out alive.'

Eric didn't speak for a while, then stood up and as he pushed his chair to the table, he muttered: 'Interesting ...'

'Where are you going?'

'To get some sleep, I've got an early start tomorrow.'

'Doing anything interesting?'

'Tell McKenzie I'll pass on his job offer. Tomorrow I'm going to Weymouth to see a man about a boat.'

'But your ...'

Eric smiled. 'I need to talk to my old mate Lew, he's the Harbour Master.' He looked straight at her. 'You'd like him; known each other for years, he says some very interesting things.'

'So, does a girl get the drink you offered?'

Miller beckoned the waitress over and put a note on her tray. 'Give Mrs McKenzie whatever she wants then keep the change.' Then he turned. 'You take care now and don't give up on your dreams — just make them come true.' Then he looked into her eyes and said very quietly: 'Till the next time,' and left hoping his look had said enough.

As he went, Anita beckoned the waitress closer and took the note from her tray. 'Champagne cocktail and charge it to Mr McKenzie's account,' then gazed at Eric as he disappeared into the crowd.

The following morning, Miller got off the train at Weymouth and carried a large cargo bag to the harbour. The Harbour Master spotted him as he walked along the quay.

'Hi Eric, when are we going to have that beer together?'

'Not right now Lew. Is she good to go?'

'Sure.' He hesitated and asked a loaded question. 'Would this be a day's fishing … or something longer?'

'Something a lot longer.' Lew nodded.

'Stay in touch and let me know when you arrive.'

'Will do — Lew; do me a favour.' He handed Lew a stamped envelope, a slip of paper and a clam phone. 'Phone Detective Sergeant Horton on that number — use this phone — there's enough credit for one more call. Ask him for his address and tell him to keep an eye out for this letter. Tell him there's a job, big one, going down soon and the letter will give him details.'

'Why don't you?'

'He'll recognise my voice. Don't tell him who you are. Put his address on this envelope. When are you going to see your daughter in Woking?'

'Tuesday.'

'Good, post it there. When you've made the call take the sim card out of the phone and throw them both in the harbour. Eric reached into his bag and took out a bottle of whisky. He handed it to Lew. 'This'll help you forget you've seen me.'

'Any messages for anyone?'

'If any man calls, you haven't seen me but if a woman comes and there's only likely to be one, get her to sing "Cry Me a River" and if it does make you want to cry, tell her I'll be waiting at Jack's Bar on Martinique with cocktails at sunset.'

Ecclesiastes 5v10

A CIRCLE OF SEAGULLS

The postcard from England only bore three words: "Phone me — Lew."

Sue came into the room with the coffee. 'Who's that from?' she asked, putting the jug on the table.

'Lew.'

'Is he still in Weymouth?'

Eric flipped the card over. 'Yes.' Eric poured his coffee then phoned his old friend. "How are things in England, Lew?'

'Great – how's life on Martinique, Eric?'

'It's so relaxed it's almost comatose.'

Lew laughed. 'I might be able to help you there; I've just heard McKenzie's dead — died in Pentonville prison a couple of weeks ago.'

Eric turned to Sue, 'Andy's dead!'

261

She lept to her feet, grabbed Eric's arm and shouted at the phone: 'Lew, that's wonderful, absolutely wonderful!'

'Lew — you've made his wife a very happy widow.'

'And that's not all, I also heard that McKenzie sold United Arcadia shortly after he was arrested. The buyer wants you to do a job for him.'

'What sort of job?'

'Apparently, the same one McKenzie wanted you to do before you left for Martinique. Eric; word on the street is this fellow's as bent as a fiddler's elbow but he pays well.' Lew's voice faded, 'someone's at the door, I'll text you his details in a minute. Speak soon.'

Later, Sue went out and Eric checked his texts and phoned Frank Dexter in England.

'Morning. This is Eric Miller; Lew Clarke gave me your number.'

'Ah, Mr Miller. What a coincidence; I heard a rumour about you this morning.'

'Really?'

'Yes, it said that although Andy McKenzie and Sue had been married for years, you met them; he asked you to do a job and suddenly McKenzie's jailed, you disappear and so does his wife Sue. You're a lucky man. If McKenzie hadn't been so ill, you'd be dead by now.'

'Fascinating, I miss all the gossip out here.'

'Are you still in the security business?'

'If the job's right.'

'Did Clarke tell you what I want?'

'No, he only told me you'd bought United Arcadia from McKenzie.'

'That's right when I bought the company, I kept some of McKenzie's staff. I want you to investigate one of them.'

'Ok.'

'Also, I'm opening a night club, cabaret; upmarket; fine dining, that sort of thing. I want Sue McKenzie to head up the opening cabaret. Are you still her agent?'

'Yes, but Did Lew Clarke tell you we live in the Caribbean? Sue's becoming quite a star here.'

'Move back to the UK and I'll make her a star here as well. I want a yes or no answer by noon tomorrow.

The Arcadia job's urgent. If you want it, you'll have to get back a.s.a.p.'

Sue returned from the beach with a seashell. 'When are you going to call Lew's contact?'

'I called him — Lew's right. Some fellow bought United Arcadia from Andy and he wants a security job done. He's opening a night club. He wants you to head up the cabaret. He's pushy, but we could use the money.'

'What's his name?'

'Frank Dexter.'

'Frank who?' For a second, she looked frightened.

'Dexter.'

'Oh!' She went pale.

'You've heard of him?' Sue seemed reluctant to answer.

'Sue …?'

She spoke quietly. 'Yes.'

'And?'

'We dated for a while.'

'But Lew says he's a crook.' Before she could answer, Eric interrupted, 'it's not you and bad boys again, is it? Sue — your taste in men is abysmal.'

She snatched the chance to get out of the situation. 'When will I ever learn?'

'What happened?'

She took her sun hat off. 'It was a long time ago. I broke it off; he was becoming too possessive. Trouble is, Frank, doesn't accept being dumped. He turns up now and then and tries to start up again.'

'So, what's the night club all about?' Sue ran her hands through her hair.

'Who knows?' Eric sensed the time wasn't right to pursue the conversation, so changed the subject and searched for United Arcadia on the internet.

'Did you know United Arcadia runs amusement arcades, lots of them? They've got to be going out of fashion, is he stupid?'

'No, razor sharp.' The sun blazed through the window. Sue pulled the blind down. 'I guess he wants it for the same reason Frank did, it's a cash business. Frank laundered money from his rackets through it.'

Sue looked for her fan. Eric pointed. 'It's over there.'

'Arcadia's legit except Frank put his henchmen on its payroll. Their phoney job titles made their illegal incomes from his rackets look kosher. I didn't get a penny from it but with luck, I'll inherit the money from its sale. If I don't; it's a win-win, you got Frank jailed or we wouldn't be together. So, what does Dexter want done?'

'Investigate a member of Arcadia's staff.'

'Is that easy?' Eric switched the electric fan on.

'Usually. I'll join the company and sniff around till someone breaks cover. Usually, the one I'm after will be the first to make friends.'

'Make friends — you mean keep away from you, don't you?'

'No, the opposite. They'll make friends to keep an eye on me. Didn't you see "The Godfather?" keep your friends close and your enemies even closer?"

Later, Eric carried the breakfast tray and followed Sue to the kitchen. He brushed her hair out of her eyes.

'Love — going back to England is your call; we'll do what you want. Only think about it, you'll have to go back to sort out Andy's affairs sooner or later anyway.' She put her arms around his waist.

'I know.'

'The recording studios are better in England and you'll be able to finish your new album.'

'True, the album is taking too long here.'

'And it's safe for me to go back now McKenzie's dead.' He took her fan from her hand and fanned her. 'Truth is, we're simply not earning enough here.' Eric patted his brow with his sleeve, 'And I can live without another rainy season and more of this heat.'

To Eric's surprise, Sue wanted to return, but he was disturbed by her enthusiasm for the cabaret job. Shortly after dawn on the day they left, they took their final stroll along the beach. Neither spoke. The sky was empty and the sea was deserted. Palm trees swayed gently in the breeze and a swell ran over the rocks and back again. Sue walked along the top of the sand by the driftwood and purslane bushes. Eric was near the water's edge; he held out his hand. She shook her head and pointed to the sand between them, ironed flat by the waves.

'Seems wrong to make footprints, it's so perfect.' She sounded sad. 'I'd like to come back one day. This place is special — I'll miss it.'

'Know what you mean; feels like we're leaving before the party's over.' They sauntered to their boat and left.

It was a Tuesday when Eric and Sue docked in Weymouth. As arranged, Lew was waiting on the quay. He tied the boat up for them.

'How was your journey?'

'It's easier going than coming back. Good to see you again, Lew.'

'And you.' He turned to Sue. 'Hello again, love. So, which is it this time, Anita, or Sue?' He gave her a peck on her cheek.

'Sue — Anita Tregowan's my stage name.'

Eric looked at his watch. 'C'mon, Lew. I'm starving — buy you lunch and we'll catch up.'

They left the harbour, walked up the steep, narrow, twisty streets to Hope Square and sat outside a bistro under a plane tree. The Italian waiter brought the menu and greeted Lew like a long lost friend. After they'd ordered lunch and two bottles of Malbec, Sue lent forward and patted Lew's hand.

'Lew, thank's for telling me where Eric was and keeping an ear out for Andy.' He raised his glass in acknowledgement, then turned to Eric.

'Was Andy McKenzie leaning on you, Eric?'

'Something like that.'

Lew looked at Eric. 'Why all the secrecy; why didn't you tell Sue you were leaving for Martinique?'

'Sue was still married to McKenzie and he was after me. If she didn't know where I was, she couldn't tell him. But, if she decided to leave him for me, I had to make sure she'd be able to figure out where I was.'

'Devious.'

'And ... we'd only met a few times. I wanted it to be her decision alone to leave Andy.' Eric topped Lew's glass up. 'Now Andy's dead, we're getting married. Fancy being best man Lew?'

He raised his glass. 'You bet — seriously; I'm delighted.'

Did many people try to find me?'

'A couple, I guess they were McKenzie's muscle.' Before their meal was served, Sue went to fix her makeup. As soon as she was out of earshot, Lew lent closer. 'Eric, I heard Frank Dexter's been looking all over for Sue. Only, the last heavies who came here weren't McKenzie's goons, they were Dexter's. It wasn't Sue they were after, it was you.'

'But I've never met Dexter.'

'You might not have, but he and Sue have history, they were engaged at one time. He still carries a torch for her. I've heard Dexter's in a big way now. He's bad news and no pussy cat.'

Sue returned; they had lunch then Lew left. Eric emptied the remains of the second bottle into Sue's glass. 'Why didn't you tell me about Frank Dexter before?'

'There's nothing to tell. Anyway, we've both got pasts, I thought we'd accepted that. I don't ask about your wives; I thought we trusted each other and were starting from scratch.'

'Yea, but a couple of heavies from your past are taking too much interest in me and I want to know why.' He lent over the table, put his hand under her chin and raised her head so she was looking at him. 'C'mon — how over is it?'

She hesitated — just a little. 'Over.'

'So, when we're married, won't Dexter give up?'

She threw some bread crumbs to a pigeon. 'He didn't when I married Andy.'

'That's great,' he said through clenched teeth.

'Eric; Frank's a nasty piece of work; people who get in his way tend to disappear.' Sue thought that piece of news made Eric look drained. Eventually, he replied.

'Don't worry, love, I sorted McKenzie. I can sort Dexter as well; leave him to me.' As then they sat in silence he hoped that sounded more convincing than he felt. Neither looking at the other. She threw more bread crumbs to the pigeons and he stared into the sky over the Brewery Building at a flock of seagulls flying in endless circles, getting nowhere. Without looking at Sue, he muttered: 'I know the feeling.'

As soon as they'd rented an apartment, Eric phoned Frank Dexter again and arranged a meeting. United Arcadia's Head Office was in open country and was approached from a motorway slip road. The isolated, rectangular building was surrounded by a water feature like a wide, sunken moat. Besides reception, the only bridges across it carried narrow, one way roads via security barriers to large shutters in the sides of the building. The perimeter road was edged outside by a chain fence and inside by a row of clipped lavender bushes around small, immaculate lawns. The building and whole compound were swept by security cameras and floodlit at night. Eric parked, pressed the reception intercom but didn't offer his name.

'I have an appointment with Frank Dexter at 11.' Eric was shown into Dexter's office. Dexter was sitting behind a large executive desk; he didn't get up or greet Frank but pointed to a low, black armchair set in front of him. Eric looked at Dexter, his demeanour was ice cold and his flint grey eyes matched the colour of his hair. As he didn't speak, Eric started the conversation.

'Who's the member of staff and why do you want them investigated?' Dexter didn't reply but scrutinised Eric's face; it looked lived in, but not always wisely and try as he might, he couldn't read Eric's thoughts which was what Eric intended. 'Why not fire them?' still Dexter didn't reply. Eventually, he lent back in his button back chair.

'It's not that simple.' Even his voice was grey. 'In all the years I knew McKenzie, he was paranoid. At one time he thought there was a mole in his organisation spying for a rival concern. That was the person he wanted you to find. When he was arrested, he thought the mole could be a cop as the police knew so much.'

'So, sack the staff and take on new ones.'

Dexter clicked his ballpen, then flicked it aside. 'I got rid of most of the people on Arcadia's payroll, but I can't get rid of the core ones, it would take too long to train their replacements. Besides it's important that Arcadia always runs smoothly.'

'Could the mole be among the ones who went?'

'Possibly.'

'Why can't you stop the business and make a clean sweep?'

Dexter started to become annoyed. 'That's none of your business. Simply find the person and quickly.'

'So, let's get this straight; I'm looking for someone who might or might not exist and who might or might not be in Arcadia?'

'In a nutshell.'

'Then do what?'

'Just find him.'

'How am I supposed to do that? no one can find someone who isn't there.'

'That's your problem.' Dexter's expression changed at the questions and he started to look angry. 'Look, Miller; you're not filling me with confidence. I heard you're past it, convince me you're still up to the job.'

Of all of Eric's many low life clients, this one was in a class of his own and to make matters worse, he was too interested in Sue. Experience had taught him the best way to treat men like Dexter was the same way they treat others, so he didn't answer for a while. Besides, he was fighting the temptation to break Dexter's nose there and then. Eventually, Dexter lent forward and glared at Eric.

'Well, go on then.'

Eric waited a few moments longer. 'I'm not about to convince you. With a job like this, only a fool would talk to someone who wasn't going to get the work. I don't see you as a fool. You've done your research and have already made your decision.' He shifted his gaze from Dexter and looking at the ceiling continued as if he was thinking aloud. 'Of course, you could be seeing where my breaking point is, well, keep needling me and you'll soon find out.'

Still holding Eric in his cold stare, eventually Dexter responded. 'Ok, what's your fee?'

'Three thousand plus expenses.'

'How long will it take?'

'Difficult to say.'

'Three grand's a lot of dough and I'm in a hurry' He pointed at Eric. 'I only pay on results and you've got three weeks, tops. If you don't give me a name by then, you're out without a penny — got it?'

Frank waited, then eventually replied, emphasising each phrase. 'I don't leave jobs unfinished. If I do yours, I need information.' He didn't wait for Dexter's response. 'I need names, job descriptions, addresses, work history of every employee still here and for anyone who left in the last 6 months. I want their photos and a list of your suspects. I need free rein to go where I like; when I like; I need to be able to report to you and you alone. I need a cover, so tell the staff I'm something like a Business Efficiency Consultant, it'll explain my questions and sniffing around.'

Dexter showed no emotion as he made notes. 'Ok, what name will you use?'

'Eric Smith.'

'Not very original.'

'That's the point, Smiths are difficult to trace.' Dexter wrote on a pad, tore it off then held it towards Frank so he had to get up to take it.

'There's the door entry code, memorise it and don't take it out of this room. I'll make it known you have authority to go where you like, except you are not to go into the Accounts Department.'

'How can you be sure the mole isn't there?'

'They're all my own people. I brought them from my old head office. When will you start?'

'Tomorrow morning.'

'Be here at 8.30. The office closes at 5 pm. I don't allow people in the building after then. I'll have the information you need for tomorrow and your I.D. tag. I'll find you an office.' Eric studied the paper, screwed it up and dropped it on Dexter's desk then turned to go. 'And Miller, we'll talk tomorrow about Sue McKenzie's fees for the cabaret. She still uses Anita Tregowan as her stage name?'

'Yes, see you tomorrow, and don't forget, it's not Miller, it's Smith.'

The following day, Eric was given a minute office next to the janitor's cupboard. It was the dump for broken furniture. As he was arranging what he could use of it there was a knock on his door. A girl greeted him. She had streaked hair and eyebrows applied with a paint roller.

"Ello, I'm T'rees, I gotta show you around like. What's your name?'

'Smith.'

'Smith what?'

'Mr Smith.'

'Ooh, get you. Well, Mr Smith, do you wanna go now?'

Eric picked up a note pad. 'Ok, where do we start?'

'Mr Dexter's office, you've gotta collect an envelope off 'im.' As they left the office, T'rees said, 'So, what do you do then?'

'I'm a Business Efficiency Consultant.'

'What's that, time an' motion like?'

'That sort of thing.'

'Bet you're not very popular, then.' Eric winced as they walked along the corridors and T'rees continued to murder the English language. At Dexter's office, he was handed a large envelope. The first document in it was a memo telling all staff that Eric Smith was heading a new efficiency initiative and instructing them to give him their full cooperation. As T'rees insisted on introducing him as "the new time an' motion bloke," he decided to play up to the title and went to the stationery room to collect a clipboard and stopwatch.

Tree's observation was correct, Eric wasn't popular, but within a few days, he'd narrowed his suspects down to four, two of which were Dexter's suggestions. As he couldn't find anything to nail any of them, he started to make it obvious he was targeting them to see if one of them would panic and break cover, but they didn't. Days passed and Frank was beginning to think there wasn't a mole to be found when he received a note from Frank Dexter ordering him to his office. He took a long lunch first, then went. As soon as he entered the room, Dexter demanded:

'How far have you got?' Frank told him the four names. 'I gave you two of those. how much longer are you going to be?'

'You can't tell, these things take time.'

'I'm not paying you to take time. If you can't find him by the end of next week, you're out — savvy? now, get a move on.' As Frank got to the door, Dexter got up from his desk. 'You haven't told me how much Sue McKenzie will charge for the cabaret?' Frank was expecting the question.

'When do you plan to open?' he asked casually.

'End of August.'

'Ah, that's a shame, she's heavily booked in August and September.'

'Well, unbook her then — I want her to headline the cabaret.' As Frank opened the door, he turned to Dexter,

'I'll think about it, Dexter, but right now, I'm rather busy.'

As he was now under pressure, Eric turned the pressure up even more on his suspects and as he'd predicted, one evening as he walked to the car park, one of the four approached him.

'Eric, fancy a drink sometime?'

He turned. 'Garry, isn't it?'

'Right, I think we need to have a chat, don't you — Crocker's Bar, Brunswick Street at 8.30 tonight?'

Eric kept a straight face. 'Crocker's at 8.30 it is, look forward to it.'

Crocker's Bar was down a side street, on a corner. It's one of those places that come alive after dark and was a haven for night people; the dealers, the damaged and depressed, the street walkers and street cleaners, the lonely and insomniacs and those who needed somewhere inconspicuous to meet people they shouldn't know. When Eric arrived, Garry wasn't there. He bought a beer, chose a table where he could see the door; opened his newspaper and pretended to read. The man at the next table sat motionless and inanimate, staring into his glass. The barman collected the empty glasses without speaking and wiped the tables with a grubby cloth. Taxis lit the room as they passed the window. Shortly, Garry arrived. The barman took a bottle from the shelf, marked the label with a felt tip and handed it over with two shot glasses. Garry crossed the room, set a glass in front of Eric, sat, filled the two glasses then raised his in a mock toast.

'So, have you found who you're looking for yet?'

Eric didn't show any emotion. 'What makes you think I'm looking for anyone?'

'Well, you're sure as hell not a Business Efficiency Expert, are you?'

Garry took a sip, all the time looking at Eric. Eric rapidly summed up his options and decided to take a chance. Returning Garry's look, he said: 'Yes.'

'When was that then?'

Eric took his time again. '5.45 this evening.'

'So, who is it?'

Keeping his poker face, Eric replied: 'You.'

Garry smiled and gave Eric a round of mock applause. 'Well done, Mr Smith, or is it Miller, I'm a little confused?'

Eric looked surprised but quickly countered. 'And you've just confirmed what you're doing — you're a cop.'

'Excellent, Sherlock, how did you deduce that?'

'Most people wouldn't have found my real name so quickly but a cop could.'

Garry looked relieved then they both sat in silence waiting for the other to make the next move.

Eventually, Garry spoke. 'Let's put our cards on the table and stop playing silly sods. I'm pretty sure I know what you're doing and I think you know what I'm doing. You're trying to find a mole. Am I right?'

Eric drained his glass, refilled it, and evaded the question. Eventually, he asked: 'Why did you tell me what you're doing?'

Garry looked around to make sure no one was listening. 'I haven't much time and I need you to do me a favour.'

'Which is?'

'Don't find me.'

'Why would I do that? I take it the drinks are on your expenses, would it be good for my fee as well? If I don't give Dexter your name by the end of next week, I'm out on my ear.'

'There's a reason for the urgency. Look, I shouldn't be telling you this, but I went undercover in Arcadia to get evidence against Andy McKenzie. We weren't getting anywhere until we got an anonymous tip off and were able to arrest him. My job was done and I was about to be recalled when Frank Dexter bought Arcadia and as we've been unable to nail him in the past either, I was left in place.'

Garry stopped talking as two men walked past the table.

'And you haven't got anywhere yet?'

Garry shook his head. 'Dexter's devious and ambitious; he's expanding his empire. The reason he's putting pressure on you is he's about to start a joint venture with an outfit in Nigeria. He wants to get into the drugs game. He daren't do that with a mole in place.'

'I didn't know Nigeria's a producer.'

'It's not, it's a transit route. I need to stay in place to stop that deal from happening.'

Eric put his glass down and leant closer to Garry. 'Look, Garry, or whatever your name is, I need the fee and it's a matter of professional pride to complete a job. If I start failing, the work evaporates, it's that simple.'

'I can't do anything about your fee. All I'm asking is to give me as much time as possible. If Frank Dexter gets into drugs, there'll be no stopping him.'

Eric sat back. 'I'll think about it.'

Garry reached for the bottle and topped their glasses up again. He glanced at the two men who were sitting close to them. 'Eric, I didn't want to do this. If I can't persuade you to act for the common good, I can tell you that if I'm pulled from this job, I'll be back at my desk with enough time on my hands to look into all sorts of things. Things like your second wife's death.'

Eric fought to keep a straight face and control his anger. 'You play a very dirty game.'

Garry shrugged his shoulders. 'We both work in a cesspit; we do whatever it takes.' Garry took another swig from his glass. Eric sensed a slight change in his demeanour, maybe a whisky fuelled change. 'You know, Eric, I'd love a job where I could say "I made that" at the end of a day. The best you and I can do in a day's work is to stop some evil bastard from ruining someone else day.' Eric started to warm to Garry, it was as if they each recognised a kindred spirit. 'You know what I do as a hobby? Marquetry, I'm making a panel of the Three Graces at the moment; it satisfies a need, odd, isn't it?'

Eric knew exactly what Garry meant. 'No, not odd.'

Garry lifted his glass in recognition, but this time, the toast wasn't a mocking one.

'Look, I think we can help each other. You probably know Dexter's opening a night club and he wants

McKenzie's widow; what is she ... your fiancé, to work there, don't you?'

'Yes.'

'Well, if I were you, I'd want him well out of the way. I may be able to help you do it.'

'Oh, yes?'

Garry dropped his voice to a near whisper. 'Dexter has a number of rackets. Each one's ring fenced so if one goes down, it won't take the others with it. The only thing that links them is United Arcadia.'

'Think I can see where you're going with this.'

'The point is, Arcadia's a legitimate business, that's why we haven't touched it so far, but it's the only weak link in Dexter's operation. Dexter's income from his rackets is erratic. If he laundered it through Arcadia as it comes, Arcadia would perform differently from other slot arcade businesses and the Inland Revenue would investigate it. To get round that Frank records Arcadia's real takings in a hand written ledger.'

'Bit Dickensian, isn't it?'

'No, it's smart; there's no way we can hack it. He calls it the Blue Book. To Arcadia's true takings in The

Blue Book, Dexter gradually adds proportional illegal profits from his rackets. It's those figures which form Arcadia's computerised accounts — the ones that are audited. He's clever and patient, but if we can find the Blue Book, we've got him and all his rackets.'

'So, where is the Blue Book?'

'That's the problem, we don't know.' Garry waited as Eric finished his beer. 'Have you heard of Frank's twin brother, Alan?'

Eric raised his eyebrows. 'No.'

'The Dexter twins were partners from the time they were stealing kid's pocket money. Frank's the older one by a few minutes. Since birth, they've had a love/hate relationship.'

'Often the way with twins.'

'Although they look alike, Frank's patient, careful and methodical; Alan's impetuous and careless. They were partners until last January when they had a massive row and Frank threw Alan out. Alan has sworn to get even, he hates his brother now. He'd know where the Blue Book is.'

'That's handy.'

'Yea, but for obvious reasons, I can't ask him for it, but you could.'

Eric's head was spinning; realising the situation had changed, he had to figure out his next move; he needed a few minutes to think.

'I need the loo; be back in a second.' He took his time, made a decision then returned. 'Ok, where's Alan now?'

Garry took Eric's newspaper, wrote an address and phone number on it, and pushed it back across the table.

Eric thought for a moment. 'Look, if I help you, I need you to help me. My first wife's new man is a cop. She's been bending his ear and he's muckraking about my second wife's death. My wife died in an accident; I want it left that way, Ok?'

Garry lent closer. 'Eric, you know I can't make promises, but the coroner recorded her death as accidental; I might be able to put that little problem to rest for you.'

Eric nodded by way of thanks and they exchanged mobile numbers.

'Let's only talk out of work hours and don't forget, the name's Smith.'

Garry got up and picked up the bottle. 'Good to work with you, Eric.'

Eric made an appointment to see Alan. His office was on the third floor of a dilapidated "60s" office block. The lift was broken and the stairwell stank like a public toilet. As Eric climbed the graffiti covered stairs, he tried to visualise Alan Dexter. When he entered his office, he wasn't far wrong. It was immediately obvious the Dexters were brothers, except that Alan was overweight and unlike his brother's frigid, focused expression, a boy stared out of his podgy face.

Alan's office was stale and untidy. His battered desk was surrounded by two huge T.V.s, both playing racing channels. There was a blackboard covered in chalk scribble, a coat stand, binocular case, and a Brown Fedora. His desk had two phones, a laptop, three dirty coffee mugs and whatever else was on it was buried under numerous newspapers opened at their sports pages. Alan greeted Eric without taking the cigarette from his mouth.

'What's of our mutual interest then Mr Smith?' he mumbled. His yellow fingers matched his teeth.

'I've been commissioned by Arcadia to do a special job and I've learned you'd like to take your brother down a peg or two.'

'What special job?'

'That's confidential.'

'I bet. Do I look that stupid? it's to have a go at me.'

'No, it's nothing to do with you.' Alan took numerous short puffs and peered through the cloud of smoke.

'Why would you want to help me?'

'Firstly, the job Frank wants me to do isn't in my interests and he's arranged it so I can't get out of it; secondly, for the fee you'll pay me.'

'What sort of a peg would that be an' what size fee?' he flicked his ash near his ashtray.

'Frank off to jail for a long stretch; five thousand fee and no comebacks for you.'

Alan lit another cigarette from his old one. 'Oh yea, try that an' he'll tear you apart.'

'Maybe, but there's an opportunity which'll only be around for a few days; I'm in a position to exploit it.'

'How do I know I can trust you?'

'You don't, and I don't know if I can trust you either, but for a while, our interests coincide; we'd be stupid to con each other. What's more, my loyalty is to the client who pays me.'

Alan blew smoke into the air. 'If Frank's employed you, he'll pay you; he's your client.'

'Not if you pay me first.' It took a while for the point to sink in.

'Five grand's a lot of bread; the job sounds more like two grand's worth to me.'

Eric stood up and slowly buttoned his coat as if he was about to leave. 'Five grand, cash; I'm taking the risks, not you.'

'Cash? I can't lay my hands on that much change at short notice; I could do three an' a half at a push.'

'Push harder and make it four; the risks to me aren't worth less.'

Alan blew more smoke then seemed to make a snap decision. 'Ok, but if he doesn't go down, the deal's off.'

'Agreed, but two conditions. The four thousand is in kosher readies, I don't want any homemade notes and I need a little help from you.'

'Like what?'

'I need to know where the Blue Book is.'

Alan peered through the smoke. 'It's in a safe behind a painting in the Accounts Department.'

'A painting?'

'Yea, of a racehorse Frank owned.'

'And the safe?'

'Top of the range, six-digit combination wall safe.'

'What's the code?'

'No idea, Frank would've changed it the second I left. It won't be easy to crack, it's a Congrieve H28. When we bought the office, Frank asked some faces which safes were the hardest to crack, they all said Congrieve H28s; so, that's what we got.'

'Set the building on fire; he'd grab the book and run.'

Alan shook his head. 'No, he wouldn't, the safe's fire resistant, he'd leave it where it is and collect it when the fire's out.'

'And there are no copies of the book?'

'Nope.' Alan's ashtray was overflowing, but he stubbed his cigarette out in it then they both sat in silence. After a while, Alan got up and walked to the grimy window. He spoke as if he was thinking to himself. 'Security's tight; if anyone raids the place, by the time they cross the compound, accounts will have destroyed the book. To stand any chance, you'd need someone on the inside to guard the safe. Is that what you were thinking of doing?' Eric tried to look convincing.

'Something like that.' Alan went back to his desk, picked up a cola can and shook it. It was empty; he crushed it and flicked it towards his waste bin. It was Eric's turn to think aloud. 'Is the account's door code different to the rest of the building?'

'Of course.'

'Would Frank have changed it when you left?' Alan's face lit up and he pointed at Eric.

'He might not have.' He picked up a pad, wrote a number and handed it to Eric. 'The accounts crew aren't always in first thing. Worth a try.' Alan's attitude changed when he saw the scars on Eric's knuckles.

'Alarms?'

'On the same system as the rest of the building; no problem there. So, haven't the cops enough evidence to get a search warrant?' Eric wasn't about to walk into that trap.

'No idea, I'm not a cop.' Alan adopted a knowing look. 'They'd get a search warrant if they thought there was a gun there; a very illegal one.'

'Is there?'

'No, but there could be. I happen to know where there's a Berretta 9000; the one that killed that security guard in Brighton a couple of years back. The chaps are thinking it's too hot now an' want it out of circulation; I could get it. Have you got clearance to move about the building?'

'Yes, everywhere except accounts.'

'Ok – how about this for a plan? The parcel post is delivered at 11 am. If you went to the goods inward dock, that's door 3, immediately after the van left an' put another parcel in containing the gun, it might get mixed up.'

'Nah, someone'd open it, I'd stand no chance.' Alan smiled and shook his head.

'No, they wouldn't. I could address the parcel to a fictional department an' a non-existent employee. No one uses their initiative; it's drummed into them to just do their job an' mind their own business about everything else. I've known mail addressed like that to lie around for days before it's opened. If you could deliver the parcel, have the police on standby and get to accounts to guard the safe, it might work.'

'Frank would deny any knowledge of the gun.'

'Course he would, but the cops would have their excuse to search the building an' find the book.' He sat back and looked pleased with himself. As Eric thought it over, he was inclined to think the look was justified.

'Sounds good to me, I'll check the accounts door code first thing tomorrow. Let you know one way or the other. You make sure you can get the gun and the cash. He leant over and picked up a paper from the floor. Call me on this number when you're ready. Any day better than another for the job?' Alan was looking through his desk drawers, presumably for more smokes.

'Friday. Frank usually visits his other interests on Fridays. He sometimes takes the accounts manager with him.' Although the meeting was over, Eric sat in deep thought.

'Problem?' Eric wrinkled his forehead.

'Yea, it won't take Frank long to realise who set him up, he could still get at me from the nick. I'm too exposed.' After a while, he'd made a decision. 'Ok. Wrap the gun in a small package, I need to be able to put it in my pocket and you wrap both packets yourself. I don't want any mistakes; my ass is hanging out on this job. Don't forget; that's two parcels. No dosh and I'm a free agent — comprende?' Alan pointed at Eric.

'I've had a thought as well.' Eric tried not to look surprised. 'Frank'll be able to claim the parcel's been sent in error, the cops won't be able to pin the gun on him.'

Eric pursed his lips as he thought. 'Ok, right, use your printer and make a delivery note. Address it to 'Mr F. Dexter. United Arcadia.' Add Arcadia's address; date it sometime last week, 'To goods as requested.' For heaven's sake, don't put anything else on it, then wrap it in the parcel; that'll sort it.'

Eric got in early the following morning, went to accounts, and tried the keypad with Alan's code. The door opened. He quickly closed it and as he turned, a secretary walked around the corner; she looked formidable; her lipstick matched her scarlet talons.

'What are you doing here, this is a restricted area?' Eric instantly switched on his most beguiling smile, drew himself to his full height, pushed back his shoulders and went on a charm offensive.

'I am so sorry, I'm new here. I'm lost; trying to find stationery; all these corridors look the same; I've wandered all over the place.' It worked, the secretary came towards Eric and smiled back.

'I know,' she said, her voice now saccharine sweet, 'I kept getting lost myself when I came here first. Downstairs, turn left, third door on the right. You are?' Eric held out his I.D. tag as far as the lanyard would permit.

'Eric Smith, Business Efficiency Initiative.' Eric couldn't see her I.D. tag. 'And you are?'

'I'm accounts, we don't have I.D. tags — Gillian Whelan;' she stepped even closer and dropped her voice the best part of an octave, 'any problems, you give me a call Eric, extension 214 ... be very pleased to help.'

'Oh, I will, thank you, Gillian.'

Eric returned to his office and rummaged through the broken furniture. He pulled a large chewed up dictionary from under a desk, held it in one hand but it was too heavy, so threw it back. After more burrowing, he found a box file, opened it, ripped the papers and index out and threw them behind a cabinet. Holding the file by its corners with three fingers, he went to Stationery and got a large marker pen and paper. On returning to his office, he wrapped the file as a parcel and then wrote on it in large letters: 'E. Smith. Business Efficiency Initiative. Office G17' tucked it under his arm and left for the day. That night, Eric phoned Garry to tell him the plan was on. A few minutes later, Alan called Eric to say the gun parcel would be addressed to J. Ainsworth. Maintenance Dept. B. They decided to start their campaign on Friday at 11 am. Garry agreed to handle the police raid and to guard the safe in accounts. As they finished their conversation, Eric asked:

'Know what the weather forecast for Friday is Garry?'

A few moments later, Garry replied: 'Cloud and intermittent showers.'

'Great. Check the parcel carefully for prints, you never know what goodies you'll find.'

'Where will you be after 11.30 on Friday, in case we need to speak?'

'No idea, probably visiting an aged relative who's seriously ill.'

'What relative is that?'

'No idea, I haven't decided yet.'

On Friday morning, Eric, wearing his old raincoat, drove to Alan's office to collect the two packets. As Alan handed them to Eric, he gave him a knowing look and wiped them carefully with an old duster. Eric was impressed; clearly Alan was a seasoned player of this game. Eric put the two small parcels, one thick, one thin in his pocket. On his way to Arcadia, he pulled into a layby, switched the engine off, tore the thin package open, and counted 200, £20 notes. He put that in his jacket pocket and the other in his inside raincoat pocket then turned the radio on and relaxed. At ten o'clock, he drove towards Arcadia and parked in a farm gateway and waited for the parcel delivery van to pass. It was on time. He allowed 15 minutes more, then drove to

Arcadia's entry barrier and pulled alongside a post with a speaker phone. He punched in the passcode on the pad, drove to the Door 3 barrier post, punched in the code again. Nothing happened. He did it again. A few seconds later, a metallic voice addressed him from the speakerphone.

'Are you alone in your car, Mr Smith?'

'Yes.'

'When the barrier rises, drive forward, wait for the door to open, go in and stop on the yellow hatching on the floor and turn your engine off. Open the boot and all your doors then stand away from the car.' The roller shutter closed behind him. He was in a wide, ill lit passageway that crossed from one side of the building to the other. There were metal cabin doors set into the walls along either side. Above each door was a lamp. He was trapped in. Eventually, a green light lit above door number 4 and the voice addressed him from the P.A.

'Door 4 is open. Bring your parcel into the room. Leave your car as it is.'

Eric picked up the box file parcel from the passenger seat and making a show of it being light and holding it with one hand by its corner with the address facing out, slowly walked to Door 4, taking care the surveillance cameras could read the address.

It was important that anyone watching would think he was seeing how long it would take internal mail to deliver it to his office. The small room was cold and bare. The floor, walls and ceiling were concrete; there were no windows. The light was recessed into the ceiling; it was like being in a tomb. Besides a trolley, the only other furniture was a kitchen chair. The electric door closed and locked behind him. The voice addressed him again.

'There is a hatch in the wall facing you, when it opens, place the parcel inside.' The hatch slid up and Eric, standing as close as possible, shielding himself from the camera, flicked the parcel from his raincoat pocket in before placing the box file on top. The voice continued. 'Please return to your car. You may close its doors and start your engine. Wait for the shutters in front of you to open and the red traffic light to turn green.' The electric door lock opened and he left the building. The exit barriers opened automatically. Rather than turning to the staff car park, he left the compound, drove to the bridge over the motorway and waited. To his relief, he saw a number of approaching flashing, blue lights. It was a convoy of police vehicles. He waited until they left the motorway for the slip road, switched his engine on and went home. Sue was loading the washing machine when he arrived. She looked surprised.

'Hello, love, you're back early; everything, all right?'

'Yes, fine, I only went in to wrap up a few details.'

'Really? have you sorted Frank's problem already; he paid you yet?' Eric suppressed a smile and took the money from his pocket.

'Oh, Dexter you mean, yes, problem solved and paid in full; seemed very satisfied with the service.' Then he muttered; 'for now.'

WHO KNOWS?

The company's chairman rose from his desk and straightened up with difficulty; without thinking, Eric Miller looked surprised. The chairman noticed.

'The inner you is timeless, Mr Miller, age cannot weary it but the outer you falls apart at an alarming rate. Take my advice, don't get old, it's not to be recommended.' He smiled and handed Eric a cheque. 'Thank you; I hope we don't meet again — at least not here.'

'You're welcome. Is there a London & Counties Bank near here?'

'Right on the High Street, on the corner.'

Eric left the Art Deco office block and hurried down the High Street. As a Security Consultant, he'd had years of low key relationships with clients. When companies had internal security problems, he was their knight in white armour, when he found the culprit, he was shunned; it was the way of things. He ignored the crossing and dodged through the traffic.

Work was scarce and money tight; he needed to pay the cheque in before he exceeded his overdraft limit.

As Eric approached the bank, he passed a charity shop; a poster in its window caught his attention. It read: "Do you know this man?" The man in question was 40 something and had a haggard face and sad, staring eyes. He looked very dead. The door was open; Eric took a poster from the pile on a shelf; went to the bank, got a bus to the station, and caught the 16.45 train home. The carriage was mostly empty and the journey was familiar. Eric unlocked the tray table in front of him, took the poster from his pocket and propped it against the seatback. The face wasn't that of a down and out wino, it was refined and intelligent and as Eric studied it, he couldn't help muttering aloud the question that was racing around in his mind: "Why did you die alone?" He read on:

Male, age 40 – 45, height 5'11', body badly decomposed, found in a Beechwood on the outskirts of Cottsgrove, Wiltshire. No apparent cause of death, teeth show dental work. All labels removed from clothing. Possessed no I/D. Identifying marks: part tattoo on upper right shoulder, possibly depicting the tip of a bird's wing. The face is based on facial reconstruction.

Clothing:

- Black leather belt
- Black trainers, worn

- Baseball cap, light blue shirt, underwear, trousers grey, navy gilet
- Raincoat, navy blue

Belongings:

- Rucksack
- Wind up torch
- Small Sony radio
- Toothbrush
- Mug & plate, plastic
- Combo set, knife, fork, spoon
- Empty plastic bottles, 3
- Roll of sheet plastic, plastic carrier bags, 3
- Fire sparker
- Sunglasses

'Ok,' he continued, 'there's something professional about you; most rough sleepers hang around town centres; you were in a remote wood; you wore a peaked cap, sunglasses and no I/D; why were you hiding?' When Eric got home, he gave the poster to Sue, his wife.

'What do you make of that, love? there's something about him; something I can't put my finger on.' After dinner, when they were having coffee, Sue read the poster.

'He is strange; seems well prepared though, wonder if he was in the army?' Eric put his coffee mug down.

'You could well be right; then why hasn't he been identified?'

Sue came and sat beside him on the sofa. She put her hand on his arm.

'It's not your phobia of dying alone again, is it?'

'Maybe.' She handed the poster back.

'If it worries you, why don't you call the police; have a chat, their number's on the poster?'

The following day, as Eric didn't have any appointments, he phoned the police and was told they'd made the usual enquiries, advertised, checked the man's DNA, arranged a Post Mortem, checked UK and Interpol's missing persons databases, followed up the 23 names suggested by members of the public, no two of which agreed and as they were satisfied, he died of natural causes, handed the case to the Missing Persons Unit.

'Is that it then?' Eric demanded, a little bruskley. The officer replied in a resigned tone.

'Sir, we have 1,000 unidentified bodies on file and thousands of missing persons a year to deal with. Our resources are limited, we do what we can. Why don't you call the Missing Person's Unit? they're based in the National Crime Agency in London.'

Eric logged onto the Missing Persons online records, but it didn't provide anything new except the case reference number. After endless phone calls to the National Crime Agency, he got to the right department.

'Case reference please? Your name is? Did you know the deceased? What is your interest?... Say again — you're suggesting the deceased was ex-military? Just a moment please.' There was silence. 'I've read the notes; that has been investigated, the result was inconclusive, but probably not. Sorry; we don't allow visitors, not even to look at a tattoo photo; we haven't enough staff. I suppose I could send you a PDF of it — it's in the public domain, so I don't see why not. I'll just confirm that.' There was muttering. 'That'll be alright, Sir, what's your email address? please let us know if you discover anything so we can update our records.' A few hours later, Eric was studying the image. The tattoo didn't seem military, but he called his friend, Andy who was a militaria dealer.

'Greetings, Andy — Eric.'

'Good Heavens, I thought you were dead.'

'I love you too Andy, look, you're ex SAS. I've emailed you a pic of a tattoo, right upper arm, male Caucasian, 40 - 45, found dead, no I/D, maybe ex-military. Could you take a shufty and tell me what you think?' Andy agreed and four hours later he called back.

'Get anywhere, Andy?'

'Maybe. Meet me for a jar and I'll tell you.' Eric met Andy at the White Lion at 9pm.

'I get a similar vibe as you, our man has a military feel. Look at this.' He showed Eric a black and white image of a winged dog tattoo; the top of the right wing feathers were identical.

'Where'd you find that?'

'A reference book of tats.'

'But the MPU said they couldn't make a military connection.'

'They wouldn't without his Service Number, but this tat could still have a military connection.'

'How?'

Andy lent forward. 'SAS pay isn't great unless you're an officer, but there's good money to be made working for private security contractors.'

'What, you mean as a mercenary?'

Andy drank half his pint of Coke. 'Of course. The UK often gets involved in foreign squabbles, usually in ex colonies. Our military is sent in but have their hands tied by what they can do. Bash the wrong heads together and you've got an international incident on your hands with the media screaming blue murder. Used to cost the country a fortune, so these days, the UK sends a token show of force for a while then backs out and offers the host Gov the use of private security companies. They're mostly staffed by ex-special forces. They can do what it takes; I gave it a go for a while. Tell you, being a mercenary's liberating for a soldier. No square bashing, the only rules are look out for your oppo, get the job done and don't get caught. If you do step on someone's toes, the host Gov is usually happy to look the other way. It's great if it doesn't mess with your head.'

'If it doesn't do what?'

'Yea, you train till you're hard as nails, or so you think, then you still get post traumatic stress, a lot of soldiers suffer from it but it's heightened in special forces. You live in an extreme, adrenalin soaked world. One day you're in the jungle having a firefight, the next you're at home walking the dog. Years of constant stress can screw your mind up, it did mine and I wasn't alone. I still get hallucinations and flashbacks. After big opps, we'd get back to base and go on marathon drinking sessions to unwind. Trouble is, after a while, I couldn't stop drinking; messed up my life. Had to join AA.'

'Wondered why you ordered Coke; anyway, what's that got to do with our man?'

'He might have been a mercenary and the black dog tat could be his squad emblem. He might have run into the same problems I did; I wasn't unique by any means; a lot get depression. He might not have been running from someone, he might have been running from himself.'

'Could many have the black dog tat?'

'Probably not, there were usually about 6 in my squad at any one time, some come and go, so probably 10 could have the same emblem.'

'Could he have been a regular?'

'Possible, but doubt it.' Andy finished his Coke and stood to go. 'If you're interested, try an advert in Soldier Mag for any Black Dog oppos from say 1990 to 2010 and see what surfaces?' Eric ran the advert but didn't receive any replies, then phoned Andy.

'Any more ideas?'

'Yea, try a clairvoyant.' Andy could always be counted on to be helpful.

Three days later, Eric was sitting in the office he'd converted from his garage. His desk was covered with maxed out credit card bills and overdrawn bank statements. There was a small sofa with a pile of old Professional Security magazines on a coffee table by the door. He was gazing out of the window when the doorbell rang and a thick set man with a shaven head entered.

'Mr Miller?'

'Yes.'

The man handed Eric his card.

'The name's Browne. I work for Webston Collection Services.' Eric swept the papers into his desk drawer. 'We're retained by a major UK bank.' Eric pointed to the sofa. 'Our client had a customer who absconded owing a large sum. Subsequently, the customer was pronounced missing, presumed dead by the High Court.'

'So?'

'Mr Miller, debt doesn't die when you do and our client suspects their customer's death was fraudulent.'

'Why?'

'There's some evidence he was alive after the High Court pronounced him dead.'

'Why are you telling me, I'm not a Private Investigator?'

'I'm aware of that, but there is a possibility that the man we seek is the one who interests you, but we haven't been able to prove it.'

Eric leant back in his chair. 'Strange world, isn't it? but, Mr Browne, even bailiffs can't extract money from a corpse, so what concern is that of mine?'

'They can from its estate. Lenders take a serious view of fraud. If they accept it lightly, it makes them more vulnerable. My client adopts a robust attitude to such matters. May I ask you, what is your interest in the dead man from Cottsgrove?'

'Curiosity to know why someone could die alone and not be claimed by anyone.' Browne thought for a moment.

'The police nor the MPU have got far. What are your professional fees, Mr Miller?' Eric got up and handed Browne his brochure.

'My fee schedule's on page 3.' Browne speed read.

'May I keep this?' Eric nodded. Browne gave Eric a straight look. 'I think you know more than you're saying. What would you say if I retained you to prove that the Cottsgrove man is James Gareth Denson? If you can provide evidence the High Court will accept, my client can proceed against his estate for fraud and will be happy to pay you £2000. If someone else proves it first, or the evidence is rejected, you get nothing.'

Eric smiled. 'Verbal contract with no witnesses? I do your work then get nothing — I don't think so.'

'In your place, I'd say something similar. If you agree, the office will send you a legal contract; have your solicitor check it out.'

'That's different, let me see it.' Browne got up, nodded to Eric, then left. Before Browne came in, Eric was searching for a needle in a haystack; now he could work backwards and get paid for it. He checked Webston Collection Services on the internet. They were a major provider of debt services to the banking and corporate sectors. Eric poured a large scotch to celebrate. First thing the day after next, he received an emailed contract; the terms were as Browne said. He signed it.

Late the following morning, Eric was making his third coffee when his office doorbell rang. He opened the door to a tall, slim man with ebony black hair. He looked mid European, Italian maybe.

'Mr Miller? Marcus Fabbri.'

'What can I do for you, Mr Fabbri?'

Fabbri fidgeted with his briefcase; it was cheap brown plastic.

'I was hoping to have a word with you on a rather delicate matter, is it convenient?' Eric pointed to the sofa. 'I am informed you have shown interest in a body found in woods near Cottsgrove.'

'Informed by whom?'

'Someone in the MPU.'

Eric leant back in his chair and ran his hands through his hair.

'Which is it then, you've come to warn me off or is it to buy me off?'

'Oh, nothing like that, I assure you. Actually, I've come to ask you a favour.'

Eric groaned. 'Go on,' he said with as much resignation as he could muster.

'I work for a small society called Evanesco.' Eric started to type the name into his search bar. 'Oh ...' Fabbri said, pointing at him, 'you won't find us on the web ... least not that one.' Eric looked at Fabbri with raised eyebrows.

'Where then?'

'Ah ... the dark web.'

'Mr Fabbri, if that's your name?' Fabbri agreed.

'It is.'

'I'm a busy man, please get to the point.'

'I've come to ask you for an indulgence. You see, our society ... by the way, you're not recording this, are you?' Eric shook his head. He was undecided whether to be intrigued or exasperated. 'Is dedicated to helping people disappear ...'

'What — like Murder Incorporated?'

'Oh no, nothing like that; definitely not. You see, some people get their lives into a dreadful mess. They get into unfortunate relationships, marry in haste, gamble, get hopelessly in debt; you know the sort of thing. They're often unable to sort themselves out. Now, although we encourage clients to try to fix their problems and offer help where we can, sometimes, it's just better to start again. Then, we offer a fresh start, provide a blank sheet, we're their reset button... we help make sure their past stays in the past.'

'You mean, you help them run away?'

'Oh, no, we encourage our clients to start again, never to run away, that always ends in disaster.' He smiled at Eric as if he was about to tell him a joke. 'We live on a ball, run for long enough and you'll end where you started.' Eric didn't smile. 'Running away leads to disaster — and unmarked graves.' Fabbri was serious about that. Eric was just going to speak, but Fabbri interrupted him.

'There's no law against disappearing, least not for an adult. Unfortunately, to completely vanish leaving no trace and to fully restart requires a certain amount of ... how shall we say? Legal dexterity.'

'You mean you break the law,' Fabbri replied in a quiet voice.

'Your words, Mr Miller, not mine.' Eric sensed Fabbri was a sharper cookie than he appeared and changed the subject.

'Surely, everyone and their roots are from somewhere else; isn't that running away?'

'Indeed, humanity is migratory, as you say. We're all ultimately from somewhere else, but going somewhere for a purpose is different from running from somewhere aimlessly.'

'What's that got to do with the man from Cottsgrove then?' Fabbri looked to see if the door was closed.

'Well, one can never be 100% about these things, but he might have been one of our early clients.' He quickly went on 'Since then we've made several improvements.'

'What's the problem, walk out and change your name. What else is needed?' Fabbri laughed as though he was indulging a child.

'A lot; it takes special expertise — our expertise and careful planning. You need to get your affairs in order, settle and close all utility accounts, council tax, loans, mobile phone. You need to buy a PAYG burner phone, preferably second hand, pay for it in cash, get rid of your possessions, not on eBay, use car boot sales. Don't use credit cards, close them, use cash. Change your appearance. Quit all social media; delete everything; change your name by deed poll. Cut ties with everyone you know; the lot; family included and when you leave, use public transport. Book into a B&B somewhere busy like London; don't go to the countryside; hide in crowds. Oh, and do it all without anyone noticing.' Eric was surprised.

'Point taken; so, what went wrong when you started?'

'We now know it takes a special type of person to be able to do all this. These days we screen people carefully. We decline the majority of enquiries. We think Cottsgrove man might have left his finances unresolved. Other people might forget you, a creditor never will. Cottsgrove man started running and kept changing his name. Also, we now insist clients always carry their new identity with them. If they haven't changed their name by deed poll, we have specialists who can create something for them.' He smiled at Eric. 'Saves the situation we're in now.'

'But the guy's dead now, what's the problem?'

'His estranged wife wanted to remarry and after the usual 7 years wait, got a High Court Certificate of Presumed Death.' Eric realised the problem.

'If Cottsgrove was her husband, she married bigamously.'

'Possibly, it depends on the timing of events. Shortly before he left, they took out a large mortgage and life assurance policies on each other and bought a big house. If she knew he was still alive and got a Certificate of Presumed Death, she committed fraud, but on the other hand, it might all be above board and legitimate. It's not for me to say. She and her new husband now have a baby girl.'

'So, what is it you want Mr Fabbri?'

'I've come to ask you not to name Cottsgrove man.'

Eric stood, leant over, and rapped on his desk with his finger.

'Have you? It might have escaped your notice, Mr Fabbri, but Cottsgrove's ex wife might be guilty of fraud and bigamy in which case you and I could go to jail for conspiracy.' Fabbri didn't reply. 'And I'll have you know, I've been retained by a debt collector to establish who Cottsgrove man is.'

Fabbri looked down at the floor.

'I'm quite sure she's perfectly innocent.'

'Oh, are you? I don't think you care whether she's guilty or not. You just want to protect your reputation, but if you're that concerned, you must have a name in mind. We can save ourselves a lot of grief if we compare the names we both have.'

Fabbri slowly shook his head.

'No, Mr Miller, that's not going to happen, it would break client confidentiality.'

'So, you want to prevent a bank who lent in good faith from seeking recompense from his estate, stop the Police from investigating a fraud, protect your reputation and what's more, you want us to break the law and me to throw a fee away. Not asking much are you? what can you put in the pot then?'

'Unfortunately, we're not in a position to pay you any compensation, Mr Miller, but I would ask you to consider this. When someone disappears, others are affected as well, often perfectly innocent parties;

it can take them years to recover if they ever do. In this case, I feel a certain responsibility and am inclined to give them the benefit of the doubt. Why destroy their lives? If Cottsgrove man as you call him was our client, he disappeared and changed his name by deed poll, was pronounced dead, started running and unofficially changed his name once, maybe twice more. The old him no longer exists but it will be the old him you'll try to name. You're unlikely to find his subsequent unofficial names — so, what name will you give him if you're able? If things are left as they are, this man will be buried and his ex wife will be able to live her life in peace. If you name him, can you live with the damage you'll do?' Fabbri got up and locked his briefcase. As he turned, he said in parting: 'Mr Miller, please don't name him.'

After Fabbri left, Eric took his thoughts for a walk through the fields by the river and when he returned, phoned the council. He was put on hold then asked to choose between umpteen options, none of which were what he wanted, then was sent around endless departments until eventually, he got through to the Bereavement Services Officer who told him Cottsgrove man's funeral was on Tuesday at 9am in the City's East Cemetery. He told Sue but didn't tell her he'd been retained by Webston Collection.

'You're not still wasting time on him, are you?' Eric didn't reply. 'Have you found his name?'

'I'm getting close.'

'What are you going to do?' Sue asked as she flicked through a magazine.

'His funeral's on Tuesday; he'll probably be buried alone.'

'He died alone; so, what does it matter?'

'Dying alone's bad enough, being buried alone's worse. Think I'll go, give me some sort of closure.' She shrugged her shoulders.

Eric arrived at the Cemetery at 8.40am. There was only one newly dug grave, it had a pile of earth along one side. A Volvo digger was parked nearby. No one else was around. After a few minutes, an old Honda Civic drove up and a man wearing a badly fitting suit got out, looked at his watch and walked over. Eric met him.

'9 o'clock — man from Cottsgrove?' Eric asked.

He nodded. 'Did you know him?'

'No, did you?'

'No, I'm from the Council. When there's no one to attend, somebody from the department comes out of respect.'

'Gruesome job.'

'No, I rather enjoy it — gets me out of the office — only time my phone doesn't ring.'

'Do you get many of these then?'

The man from the Council looked surprised at the question.

'Heavens, yes, Councils handle thousands a year and growing. Blooming expensive too. Costs £1,800 a time — big charge on the Rates — and that's with no extras, no gravestone, no flowers, common grave shared with others.' As they were speaking, a lady vicar approached them. The Council man whispered to Eric. 'Does this out of the goodness of her heart, bless her; not paid for it you know.' The Council man greeted her. 'Morning Vicar.'

'Morning John.' She replied and acknowledged Eric. After a few minutes, a hearse arrived and stopped nearby. Another car followed and parked somewhere out of sight. Four pallbearers dressed in identical black overcoats got out, removed a cheap coffin from the hearse, carried it to the grave, stood two on each long side then at a signal from the senior one, gently lowered it into the grave. They bowed; then the vicar stepped forward and read from a small book.

'Almighty God ...' Eric saw a movement by the trees and looked over. A man was watching them.

'We now commit our dearly beloved brother to the ground.' She made the sign of a cross. 'Earth to earth, ashes to ashes, dust to dust ...' The man by the trees looked familiar, but Eric couldn't place where he'd seen him before, he was standing in a shadow. The Vicar closed her book and nodded to the pallbearers who bowed again and left. The man from the council thanked her. She smiled at him.

'Thank you for coming, John.' As she turned to go, a man in a yellow high vis vest started the digger and drove towards them to fill the grave in. The Vicar faced Eric.

'A tragic end of a life. Did you know him?'

'No; I didn't know him, Vicar.'

'Well, at least he's buried amongst people like him.'

'People like him...?' Eric looked confused. The man from the Council intervened.

'Of course; it's a common grave.' He waved his hand over the whole cemetery. 'How many headstones do you think are here?'

Eric shrugged his shoulders.

'No idea, few thousand, maybe.'

'Could be, but there's over 100,000 buried in this cemetery, well over — most don't have grave markers. Does it really matter if he hasn't either?'

The vicar spoke to Eric.

'Why did you come if you didn't know him?'

'I don't like the thought of someone being buried alone.'

The vicar smiled at him.

'That's a lovely thought, I know what you mean. Makes you wonder why some people get their lives into such a mess.' She put the small book in her coat pocket.

'If we'd walked in his shoes, would any of us have acted differently?'

The vicar nodded in agreement. 'Indeed,' she said, 'there but for The Grace of God. Nice to meet you — hope we meet again. Mr?'

'Miller; but hopefully, not here.'

Eric took his keys from his pocket. The man from the shadows joined them. It was Browne.

The vicar did her coat up. 'I wonder who he was,' she said to Eric.

Browne faced Eric as well. 'Yes, who was he, Mr Miller?'

Eric opened his car and turned to the vicar.

'In the end, I doubt if even he knew.' Then answered Browne. 'Who knows? He could be any one of us.'

INHERITANCE

Eric Miller looked troubled as he studied the bank statement yet again. He didn't notice Sue hurtle past him, dusting everything for the second time. She was reaching boiling point and snapped at him.

'Eric! For heaven's sake — he'll be here in a minute.'

He sighed and put the statement in a drawer. 'You're obsessed with this meeting; calm down; chill out, it'll be fine.'

'It's all right for you, you're not meeting a brother you didn't know you had. And I'll tell you this, I've got a bad feeling about him; I can smell a crook a mile off.' Eric placed a large envelope on the coffee table.

'Give the poor guy a chance, he might be very nice.'

At the stroke of 10am, the doorbell rang. Sue greeted a well fed man in his 60s. He had impeccable short brown hair, a tailored blue suit, immaculate shirt and tie, high gloss shoes and a switched on smile showing perfect teeth, American style. In his left hand, he carried an extravagant bunch of flowers and in his right, a rectangular parcel. He carefully put the parcel down and presented the flowers to Sue.

'Hi Susan, I'm Vernon — how you doing?'

Sue was rarely flustered; she was now. 'Hello … Vernon.' She hesitated, blushed, and pulled Eric forward. 'This is my husband, Eric.' Vernon crushed Eric's hand.

'Good to meet you, Eric.' They settled their visitor in the lounge and as Sue put the flowers in water, Eric poured three coffees. Vernon smiled at Sue. 'Well, this is kinda awkward for all of us.' He adjusted his tie; it didn't need it. 'I'm sorry if what I have to say comes as a shock; it did when I first heard it. Susan, I'm your half brother; did you know about me?' Sue shook her head.

'No, the news came out of the blue.'

'Have you received the papers from our lawyers?'

'Grainger & Cook? yes.' She emptied the envelope onto the coffee table.

'Okey dokey.' Vernon took a photo from his pocket. 'Well, my name is Vernon T. Carlson. My dad, that is, our dad was Bernard — Bernie to his friends. Here's his photo.' He handed it to Sue. 'That's him with my mom on their 40th wedding anniversary. It's a copy; had it made for you. Dad was a Tech Sergeant in World War II.' He stopped again and looked straight at Sue. 'You know Susan, you have Dad's eyes.'

She gave him a weak smile. 'It's Sue — call me Sue.'

'Ok, Sue. Well, Dad was a motor engineer.' He looked at Eric. 'I don't think you have Tech Sergeants in the British Army.' Eric didn't reply. 'He was stationed here in England for a while; guess that's where he met your mom.'

There was a strained silence. Sue got up and gave Vernon a photo. 'That's my Mum and Dad in …' She stopped and swallowed hard. Vernon came to the rescue.

'I know, I didn't know anything about this until shortly before Dad died either; he was 94. He started to remember things way back as if they were yesterday. He knew he was dying and told me a lot of things; must have been some kind of confession; shook me up too. Guess we shouldn't make judgements; strange things happen in war. I'm his only child, well, besides you that is.' He smiled, nervously. 'Anyway, towards the end of the war, he was transferred to the US 10th Armoured Division in

Garmisch-Partenkirchen in Bavaria.' He glanced at Eric. 'It's near Austria, and was there until he was demobbed in 1947.'

'Isn't that where they hold the Passion Play?'

Vernon shook his head. 'No Sue, that's Oberammergau. Dad liked Bavaria, said it wasn't all bombed to hell like industrial Germany. As the Allies pushed across Germany, the Nazis moved their stolen artwork ahead of them towards the Austrian border and stored it in disused salt and copper mines. They put their stolen gold anywhere secure; a lot ended up in Garmisch post office. Strangely, Garmisch became a major US R&R location, full of military personnel letting off steam before being shipped stateside. Anyhow, Dad said when the war ended, military discipline and law 'n order went out of the window. The area was awash with gangs of deserters and starving locals. There were drug dealers everywhere."

"Drugs in the 1940's?" Eric sounded sceptical.

"Apparently so, I was surprised too; also, the only place locals could get anything was on the black market. Dad had a pal in the US stores, and like a lot of guys, he made a heap of dough. The whole lot of 'em were working one fiddle or other, Top Brass included; he said every third man was a Third Man." Vernon was the only one to smile at the joke.

Eric tried to ease the situation. 'What was your dad like then?'

'A great guy Eric, lifelong Republican, go getter, golf club president, member of the Moose Lodge; one very sharp cookie. I learned everything from him. He taught me no one owes you a living, you gotta do what it takes, cut corners if have to, take care of number one, 'cause at the end of the day, all that matters is what ya got stashed; know what I mean? you'd have liked him; everyone did.' Eric's expression showed he wouldn't.

Sue got up. 'Would you like some more coffee, Vernon?' she pushed the plate of biscuits towards him.

'Well, that would be nice,' he hesitated — 'Sue. Thank you. As I was saying, Dad was an ace card sharp; could deal off the bottom with the best of them.' Vernon's face lit up in admiration. It was becoming clear his father was a role model. 'Dad met an officer who'd been in Altaussee recovering stolen artwork and won the painting from him in a poker game.'

'Is that the one bequeathed to me in his will?'

Vernon patted the brown paper parcel. 'Correct.'

Sue looked troubled. 'Your Dad won a stolen painting in a poker game?'

Vernon lost some of his bravado and gave a nervous giggle. 'I guess there's nothing to worry about, Sue, the Statute of Limitations ran out in Illinois years ago and who's to know anyway?' he straightened his tie again and pressed on. 'When Dad was demobbed, he brought it back to Springfield...'

'Where's that?'

Vernon turned to face Eric. 'Illinois; where he and Mom grew up; it's where they were engaged when he was conscripted ...'

Sue interrupted. 'He was engaged when he met my mother?'

Vernon nodded and looked embarrassed. 'Guess so, like I say, strange things happen in war.' He quickly regained his composure. 'They got married when he returned and started the car lot. He and Mom ran it together. She could flip a car as fast as any of us. When Dad took sick, she ran the whole show; she overdid it and died a few years back. Now my wife Donna and I run it; we got an eighty car inventory, Chevy specialists.'

Sue moved to the edge of her seat. 'How did your dad know about me and where I live?'

'I guess he knew where your mom lived during the war. She must have made contact to tell him about you. He told me he kept track of your mom for a good while. I've been looking for you since he died; wasn't easy, you've moved about a bit.' He reached into his pocket and took out one of Sue's CDs. 'Bought this in Chicago — told Donna; Anita Tregowan's my sister's stage name — some voice; kinda cute too, huh?'

Eric looked surprised. 'You know Sue's stage name is Anita Tregowan?'

'Amazing what you can find out if you ask the right guys.' Vernon gave Eric a canny smile. Sue didn't comment; it felt creepy having a half brother you'd never met think you were kinda cute. 'Dad told me he couldn't tell anyone he had an English daughter; Mom was the jealous type, it would have wrecked their marriage, but he always made it clear I wasn't going to inherit the painting, it was for someone special.'

Sue seemed agitated. 'So, when your dad won the painting, didn't he ask where it came from?'

Vernon laughed. 'Heavens no. Garmisch wasn't the place you asked questions. Sounds as if nobody saw anything, heard anything, or asked anything, if you did, one day you could wake up dead. They were forever dragging bodies out of the river. Oh, you haven't seen the painting yet, have you?' He unwrapped the parcel to reveal an old, dark, river landscape in an ornate gilt frame.

'It's a Jan van Goyan, oil on board, painted around 1645. A few years back I took it to Sotheby's in Chicago for an appraisal. They said in the right auction it could fetch $40,000 to $60,000 — that was then. You've gotta remember after the war, money in Germany was worthless so everyone was bartering with whatever they could get hold of. Dad said you wouldn't believe what you could get for a few packs of Lucky Strike — it was dog eat dog, besides, our boys put their careers on hold to do their bit and were well out of pocket on army pay; they reckoned a bit of loot was kinda compensation.'

Sue held up one of the lawyer's papers in front of Vernon. 'Is this the receipt I've got to sign?' she sounded rattled.

Vernon lent forward. 'That's the one, but don't give it to me, send it to Grainger & Cook.'

'So, Vernon, your dad's definitely my biological father, there's no doubt?'

'Can't see why he'd say so if it wasn't true. Maybe pick your moment and ask your mom.'

'I can't, she died last year and Dad died years ago.'

Vernon's look of sympathy seemed genuine. 'Maybe it's best to let the past rest in peace. Look you guys, I've got a meeting tomorrow, a collector's got some vintage Chevy's for sale; then I have to get back to the States on the double. Sales at the car lot have been slow lately; we've had to let a lot of staff go and Donna's pretty stretched. Could I take us all to dinner, can you make tonight?'

There was silence as Sue looked at Eric. 'We'd love to, but I'm on tour soon and I'm pretty tied up with packing and things.' She hoped the excuse didn't sound too tame.

'Oh, that's a shame. Ok, maybe another time; we'll keep in touch, Zoom maybe and when things pick up, Donna and I would love to come visit for a vacation. Maybe we could all get together and you could show us around.' They thanked Vernon and said goodbye. As Eric was about to stand the painting on the sideboard, Sue snatched it from him.

'Get that thing out of here, now!' She shouted.

Eric looked amazed. 'It's worth forty to sixty thousand dollars … thank you, Vernon!'

Sue was furious. 'All you can see in this is money. I've just had my roots torn up and traded for a stolen painting, a card sharp and that creep, Vernon.'

Although Sue was near to tears, Eric didn't seem to notice. 'What do roots matter; we're desperate for this sort of cash?'

'Roots matter when you haven't any.'

'Sue — Vernon brought you the painting; he could have sold it in the States and trousered the money and said nothing, and don't forget, for all his faults, you've now got a brother.'

'Eric — the painting's stolen — it's hot. Whatever happened to it since the Nazis stole it doesn't change a thing; when it's hot, it's hot. I don't want it — it's going back to the family it was stolen from.'

Eric raised his hands in exasperation. 'Oh, sure, just like that. Don't forget, you don't know where they lived, you inherited it legally and the owners will be long gone.'

'I'd need to donate my brains to science before I believe it's a legal inheritance. Vernon's father just wanted to save his son being charged with receiving a painting stolen from a holocaust victim; I'm simply a convenient solution.'

'Oh, c'mon Sue; you were engaged to one crook and married to another — why the twitchy conscience now?'

'I'm aware of how I lived in the past, thank you, Eric. My values are different now. Ok, I admit it, crime was exciting, we made money — lots of it, but it was never enough; wealth's addictive, worse than ice; it warps your values and comes in a package with distrust and loneliness — you can't trust anyone, not even your own people; they'd all shop you to save their own necks. I'm through with trying to justify to myself what we were doing and waiting for police raids — that part of my life is closed; it's over; I don't want to know anymore. She thrust the ball of paper into his hands. 'And another thing; every time I try to bury my old life it comes back up like some kind of knotweed but I'll tell you this: I'm sure as hell not going to inherit someone else's iffy past as well and that's an end of it.' She picked up the sugar bowl and dumped it on the tray. 'You and I may not have much but what we have got is peace of mind and I'm not trading that for an old painting —Ok?'

'But $40,000 would set us up nicely…'

Sue stepped closer to him and put the tray down. 'Look, love, will you please stop worrying about money. I've got it covered — it's all in hand. Everything will be ok after the tour, just sit tight for a few days. But first, we do the right thing with the painting; do what you can to return it to its rightful owners, and I don't mean sell it either — ok? Promise me — pinkie promise?' Sue could be very determined. She was now.

Eric reluctantly nodded. 'Pinkie promise.' She dumped the flower vase on the table, spilling some water, then thrust a blue folder into Eric's hands.

'The tour schedule's in there.' The title page was a flyer for the 'EUROPEAN SOLID GOLD 70's SHOW' featuring some of the 70's acts who were still playing and hadn't fried their brains to oblivion with whacky baccy and the like. Anita Tregowan was backed by the Rex Hall big band.

'What's the best time to call you?'

Sue looked a bit edgy. 'Don't call after lunch; mornings would be better. Thinking about it, it's probably better if I call you.' She tied a label to a suitcase. 'Don't panic if you don't hear from me for the odd day or two.' That sounded strange; previously, Sue found tours boring and longed for someone to talk to. Eric made his living hearing what people didn't say; he filed Sue's comment in the back of his mind, said nothing then glanced through the schedule.

'There's still that two day gap; I thought they were going to fill it.'

Sue tied a luggage strap around the case with the damaged lock. "The only bookings they could get for those days meant too much travelling so we're taking a break in Marseille."

As Sue was packing and repacking, Eric looked online for an art repatriation agency and to his surprise found the International Art & Antique Loss Register in Hatton Garden. He measured the painting, took photos front and back and loaded them onto a memory stick.

Early on Monday morning, Sue's tour bus arrived. As the driver loaded her luggage on board, Eric put his arms around her, held her tight and kissed her goodbye. Even though her singing provided most of their income now, he hated her tours, his worst dream was of Sue leaving him but the irony was she was a free spirit, to keep her, he had to let her fly free now and then.

'Wished I was coming with you.'

'You will on the cruise.' She tapped him on the chest with her fingers. She wore vermillion nail polish, a new shade. 'Now, don't forget, no taking on any dodgy work. I don't want to come back to a house full of hacked off heavies trying to tear you apart or smart ass cops fitting you with a ball and chain. No poker games either. Eat properly and trust me; it's going to be all right.'

With a heavy heart, Eric watched and waived as the bus drove down the road and away, then he had a coffee and headed for Hatton Garden. As he walked past the Red House on Clerkenwell Road, an ancient Range Rover screeched to a halt beside him. The driver's window opened and a cigarette butt flicked out in front of him.

'Eric — get in,' Eric spun around. The driver indicated the back seat with his thumb. Eric slowly got in and before he'd closed the door, the driver took off with the wheels spinning.

'You running a taxi service now, Alan?'

'No, been following you, trying to catch you when you were alone — we got a problem; we need to talk.' They hurtled down several side streets then shot into a multi storey car park and squealed around to an upper floor and parked with a jolt in a corner.

'Come up front.' When Eric sat beside him and closed the door, Alan faced him. 'It's better we're not seen together. Eric, my brother Frank's dying; he's going to be released from Albany prison on compassionate grounds any day soon, he's got an aortic embolism, could rupture at any time. He found out it was you and me who got him convicted an' he's vindictive as hell. Word is, he's trying to get contracts out on both of us.'

'How the blazes did you find that out?'

'Don't forget, Frank and I ran one of London's biggest mobs; I learnt to watch my back years ago. I got someone doing time with him feeding me info.' Alan glanced in the mirror. 'Frank lost touch with our old enforcers but he'll soon find more when he gets out — his name still carries weight in the underworld.'

'We got him nicked?'

'Yes — "we." You know very well you wanted him out of your way 'cause he was sweet on Sue and would have wasted you to get her, just as I wanted to take him down a peg or two.'

'You mean, get even because he threw you out of the firm.'

'He done me out of my half. Besides, you guaranteed there'd be no comebacks when we set him up, it's your problem really.'

'Well, we're in it together now — can't we buy the contracts off?'

'Dunno who they'll be with, Frank always handled that side of things.'

'But if he's dying, what's the problem?'

'He'll get contracts in place that'll kick in whether he's dead or alive. If we don't stop him, Eric, we're dead meat.'

Eric looked floored. 'What shall we do?'

Alan ran his hand across his throat.

'What, you mean we take him out? Are you serious?'

'You'd better believe it. Look at it this way, in a few weeks he's gonna die anyway; we're just bringing it forward a little an' for Pete's sake, we're acting in self-defence.' He gave Eric a few moments to absorb the information, then pressed on. 'An' that's not all, my contact says he's been having a visitor lately — your Sue.'

Eric grabbed the front of Alan's jacket. 'You...!'

Alan gently pushed his hand away. 'Eric, on the level, I'm not winding you up.'

'Your contact's talking garbage. Besides, what makes him think it's Sue?'

'He's a Trusty, he has access to visitor's names. Eric, you do know Frank an' Sue were an item once, don't you?'

'Of course.'

'Maybe she's been saying goodbye; who knows? whatever, he still carries a torch for her an' he never got over her dumping him.'

Eric closed his eyes and clamped his hands on his head. His world had just collapsed. Despair quickly turned to anger; he turned and pointed an accusing finger at Alan.

'Alan,' he said through clenched teeth, 'Frank might be your brother but Sue's my wife and if he thinks I'm going to stand by and do nothing, he's making a big mistake.'

Alan understood. 'Absolutely; I'm right there with you, Eric, this is all shades of nightmare for me an' all; Frank's my elder brother, but I'll tell you this, he's unpredictable an' he's got a vicious side. We got a love an' hate relationship — it's a twin thing.' Eric's response was a dismissive shake of the head. Alan pressed on. 'You know, I was given a hamster when I was six; loved it; spent all my pocket money on a cage. He drowned it to see if I'd cry. He boasted about it at school to show how tough he was. His tough guy reputation's all that matters to him; he'll kill both of us without a second thought to save face.'

Eric groaned and went pale. Alan picked up a cigarette pack from the console; it was empty; he opened the door and flicked it out. 'I've been thinking about nothing else since I heard; can't get it out of my head. I grilled my source an' there's no mistake, your Sue visited him about the time he was told he was dying, probably a coincidence, anyway, how's this for a plan to kick off with?'

Eric cooled down a bit. He thought for a while then turned the radio down. 'Ok, let's hear it then.'

'Frank loves flashy motors. Apparently, despite being a physical wreck, as soon as he gets out, he wants to go for a real drive. Did you know before we fitted him up, he bought a Porsche 911? It's in his garage.' Eric raised his eyebrows. Alan understood what he was thinking. 'It's alarmed to the hilt. He's been getting paperwork ready. The second he's out, he's arranged to have it collected, serviced, new battery; that sort of thing an' he's going to pick it up from the garage forecourt. It's near where he lives.'

'The garage is leaving a 911 on the forecourt?'

'Yea, he wants the work done in a day an' he'll collect it after they're closed. Suits us nicely.' He tapped the side of his nose. 'I happen to know a man who knows a man who can do the biz on the steering, you know, just enough so he can drive for a while — then bosh.'

'But he might survive a minor shunt.'

'Eric, Frank only knows two speeds: stop an' flat out, it'll work, trust me. The other thing is, my contact says your Sue told Frank she's going on a tour, but he doesn't know where or when; but he'll find out. With luck, he'll stuff the car up an' his embolism thing will burst an' finish him off. What you reckon?' As Eric thought the plan over, Alan searched for another cigarette. 'You haven't got a snout, have you?'

Eric glanced around, then spoke quietly. 'We'll have to get a mechanic from out of town; hire him through an intermediary; someone reliable. It must look like an accident; better not talk to each other on landlines — don't meet either ...'

'Eric ... Eric! Grandmothers an' sucking eggs! I'm a Dexter twin. I know what I'm doing; I thought of all that.' He handed Eric an old phone and a piece of paper. He held up an equally battered phone. 'The number on that paper is for this phone — memorize it. I know yours. We'll only switch them on an' speak to each other at 6pm then switch them off after. Don't use them near our homes an' not for anything else. Wipe your fingerprints off an' destroy it when we're done, an' when we speak, I'm Mr Smith, Frank's Mr Jones, you're Mr White. If we need to meet; meet here an' call it: the usual place.'

Eric looked concerned. 'What'll all of this cost?'

Alan thought for a few seconds. 'Let's ante up with four grand each; all costs split down the middle, ok?'

Eric looked uncomfortable. 'Four grand's a problem at the moment.'

Alan thought for a while. 'Ok. Living with Frank's taught me to be prepared for anything. I got a war chest tucked away; I'll fund it to start with; gimme your word you'll square up asap?'

Eric held out his hand. 'You've got it. Now, for the last time, are you absolutely sure about him and Sue?'

Alan looked Eric in the eye. 'Fraid so.'

'Are you certain you can get reliable people to do the job?'

'It'll be tight, but I think so.'

'Ok, let's get on with it.' Eric got out and Alan sped off. That Wednesday, Eric went to the mall car park. At 5.59, he switched the phone on and heard Alan's voice.

'Mr Jones has left the hotel an' gone home. His horse is already at the vet's an' the specialists are ready to attend to it.'

Eric just said: 'Ok' and switched the phone off. He wandered around the car park feeling terrified. He went to the nearest pub.

Two days later, at 6pm, Eric got another phone call.

'The operation was sweet; Mr Jones an' his horse have gone.'

Eric kept busy for the next few days, all the time counting the minutes till Sue could phone. He'd decided not to tell her he knew about her visits to Frank but he couldn't get it out of his mind. He cut their hedges, their lawn and pruned everything in sight whether it needed it or not. Although he was tired at night, he couldn't sleep without several stiff Scotches. Sue phoned a few days later but didn't say much other than the tour was going well and the concerts were well attended. She sounded tired. Every day, Eric left home and switched the phone on at 5.59pm. On Monday, it rang.

'Meet me at the usual place, tomorrow at 11 am.' Eric had an appointment at the Loss Register in Hatton Garden at 11.30; they were interested in the painting and thought they might have a lead.

'Not 11, 10am.'

'Ok,'

At 10 the following day, Eric went to the car park. Alan didn't greet him.

'We got trouble. Our boys did the biz an' I thought Frank had collected his Porsche, but he didn't, a couple of toe rags stole the bloody thing. Frank's disappeared.'

'What?'

'Yea, they drove the 911 like lunatics an' were chased by a RPU.'

'A what?'

'Police Rapid Response Unit; bunch of racers. There was a high speed chase. The Porsche was pulling away then veered across the road doing 108 an' ploughed into a low loader hauling Ash trees. Completely wrote the Porsche off. The toe rags are badly smashed up an' all; had to be cut out. The driver of the low loader's ok, bit of whiplash an' shock.'

'Will they live?'

'Touch an' go. My sources say the Porsche driver works for a tasty firm of car thieves. It was a total nause up. The road was closed the whole day. We gotta hope the Porsche is too badly wrecked for anyone to tell the steering was fiddled. Shame about the car; that model fetches 60 grand or more.'

'So, where the hell is Frank?'

'I dunno — vanished an' why he didn't collect the Porsche, goodness knows. Let's drop out. I'll let you know when I find out more.'

Four days later, just after lunch, Eric's office doorbell rang. He opened the door and drew a breath in shock.

'Hello, Eric, can I come in?'

Eric was caught off guard. 'Garry! It's been a long time — how are you?'

'Detective Inspector Morgan now, if you don't mind?'

Garry showed Eric his Police warrant card. 'Why the card, Garry?'

Garry looked uncomfortable. 'It's not a social call, Eric, I have some bad news for you.'

Eric indicated the sofa, then sat at his desk. Garry looked ill at ease.

'Eric, prepare yourself for a shock. I was in the office earlier and overheard some colleagues talking.' He seemed uncertain how to continue. 'Eric, Frank Dexter's dead.'

Eric was half expecting something like this and had rehearsed his response. 'I knew his health was awful; my wife Sue said she didn't think he'd come out of nick alive.'

'He was released on compassionate grounds; he didn't die in prison.'

'So where did he die?'

'He was driving a hired Ferrari in the Combe Laval Canyon in France — it's in the Vercors mountains.' Garry Morgan scrutinised Eric's reaction with professional care; Eric looked as if he didn't understand. 'It's a balcony road, a ledge cut into the side of the mountain, apparently spectacular views and ok at low speed, lethal at the speed he was going. An eyewitness said a van cut in front of him, slammed on its brakes, then drove off. Dexter swerved and went over the edge, dropped best part of 1000 feet. Of course, it could have been road rage, but the French Police have to consider every possibility, you understand?' Eric didn't seem to.

Garry hesitated. 'Eric — he wasn't alone. Your wife Sue was with him...I'm afraid they were both killed outright.' Eric gasped. 'As I know you, I offered to tell you rather than leave it to some wooden top.' Eric sat in a daze. Garry wasn't sure he'd heard. 'Eric, did you hear?' Eric looked as if he'd frozen. He didn't move; when he spoke, his voice seemed detached from his body.

'But it couldn't be Sue, she's on tour with a 70's revival show.'

'This isn't my case, Eric, so I don't know all the details, but it seems Dexter found out about Sue's tour, flew to Lyon, hired the car, and went to the tour hotel. He was heard telling Sue that driving in the Alps was top of his bucket list and asked her to go with him. They were seen leaving together.'

Eric leapt to his feet. 'But, my Sue? Garry! I want to see her; where is she?'

Garry also stood and softened his voice. 'Eric, the car fell 1000 feet and burst into flames. It's in a difficult place to access and the bodies were ... well ... it'll be a while before they can be properly identified, you understand?' it didn't seem as if Eric did so Garry changed the subject. 'Eric, the French police have ... well ... I don't suppose I could see your passport, could I?'

Eric didn't seem to grasp what was behind the question. 'Don't know where it is, I was looking for it, we're going on a cruise soon; Sue's singing in the cabaret.'

Garry pressed the point as gently as he could. 'Could you dig it out for me?'

Eric didn't reply. He sat heavily with his head in his hands and sobbed and just said 'Sue ... Sue ... Sue,' over and over.

Garry waited a while then slowly edged to the door. 'I must go, Eric. Are you going to be alright? anyone who can be with you; family, friends?' Eric didn't reply. 'I'll drop in again later and see how you're doing. So sorry, Eric; my deepest condolences. Give me a bell if I can be of any help.' He opened the door then turned back. 'Oh, I nearly forgot. When our lads were searching Dexter's place, they found his will. You'll never believe it; he left his Porsche to Sue; suppose it'll be yours now.' He left and gently closed the door.

Looking like a zombie, Eric closed the office and went into the house and finished the bottle of whisky and a good deal of another. He spent that and the following nights shuffling from one pub to another on a marathon bender, sleeping in his clothes during the day. He was a dishevelled, pitiful mess. He didn't eat properly, didn't answer the phone or the door until one morning there was such a ferocious banging on it that he dragged himself to open it. He could barely focus on the figure standing there.

'Shove off whoever you are, there's no one in,' but the figure didn't, it pushed into the hall, closed the door, and propelled Eric to the nearest chair then left and found the kitchen returning a few minutes later with a mug of black coffee.

'Get that down your neck and sober up — I've got some good news; well, good news for you.' Eric forced his hungover eyes to focus on the person in front of him. It was Garry, smiling from ear to ear.

'What news?' he slurred.

'Drink that first and I'll tell you.' Eric did as he was told. Garry took the mug and made another.

'What news?'

'Good news, drink that as well.'

Eric screwed his face up. 'You make lousy coffee Garry, it's too sweet. What news?' Garry watched him drink. Eric belched and drank more coffee. 'You know, Garry, all day and all night I've been calling to every power there is for good news and all I hear is my own voice, then you turn up,' he took another gulp, 'then you turn up grinning like a what's it and you won't tell me the bloody news — what news?'

Garry pulled a chair close to Eric and sat. 'Because I know you, my colleagues have now kept me in the loop. Dexter went to the tour hotel and he and your Sue drove to the Old Port in Marseille and had a drink at a café. He wanted Sue to go with him to the Alps, but his driving was so awful, she refused. He lost his rag left her there and picked up one of the girls from the tour who went gaga at the thought of pulling the infamous Frank Dexter and they went to the Alps. It was her with him when they went over the edge. The day before, several members of the tour had things stolen, money, tablets, credit cards. It took a while for Sue to get replacements. She's been trying to call you but you haven't answered your phone; she's worried sick. As the tour was stuck in Marseille for two days, Rex Hall hired a car and took Sue and a couple of mates sightseeing.' Garry handed Eric a slip of paper. 'This is her new number — call her.'

Eric snatched the paper and rather unsteadily, phoned the number. 'Sue — is that you? Are you all right? I was told you'd been killed ... Sue, say something.' Garry went to the window and pretended to look out. Sue spoke for some time, then Eric interrupted her. 'Sue – who the hell's Rex Hall?' Garry could hear Sue laugh from where he was. 'He's the bandleader; we call him Pops. Eric, he's over 70, 16 stone and gay.' Eric became agitated. 'Sue; I'm coming over. Can you wire me some money? Rome? Ok, I'll phone later, I've got someone with me.' Sue asked him something. 'He's... an old friend.' He ended the call and sat in a daze with tears trickling down his face.

Garry watched for a few minutes until Eric handed him the mug. 'Any chance of more of your revolting coffee?'

'You'd better get cleaned up and eat something. Eric, there's a slight glitch. Dexter's 911 was stolen and wrecked, it's a write off. Sue or you'd better contact the Motor Insurance Database to see who insured it. Only thing is the car's being held as evidence by the Vehicle Recovery Unit and a forensic vehicle examiner is checking it out. Last thing we heard was he was faffing about something odd with the steering, but I can't see it being a problem. If all goes well, I should think there's a good chance of a decent pay out, don't you?'

About the Author

Tony Billinghurst was born in Bristol, England and was one of the post WW2 baby boomers; at school, class sizes were large and peer competition fierce; he wasn't competitive. He published his first story in Ireland in the mid-1960s and since then in literary magazines and anthologies in England, Canada, America, Australia and India. He has wide musical tastes and is fascinated by the past and likes museums, old pubs, impressionist art and the theatre. He prefers the countryside to the town and is a night owl and writes in silence, at night when the imagination is heightened. He currently lives in the West of England with his family.